CARTEL PUBLICATIONS
PRESENTS

They never wanted the power,
but they stepped to the throne

# PRETTY KINGS

# T. STYLES

## NATIONAL BEST SELLING AUTHOR OF *RAUNCHY*

PUBLISHER'S NOTE:
This book is a work of fiction. Names, characters, businesses,
Organizations, places, events and incidents are the product of the
Author's imagination or are used fictionally. Any resemblance of
Actual persons, living or dead, events, or locales are entirely coincidental.

Library of Congress Control Number: 2012956540
ISBN 10: 0984993045

ISBN 13: 978-0984993048

Cover Design: Davida Baldwin www.oddballdsgn.com
Editor: Advanced Editorial Services
Graphics: Davida Baldwin
www.thecartelpublications.com
First Edition

Printed in the United States of America

# Check out other titles by
# The Cartel Publications

WWW.THECARTELPUBLICATIONS.COM

# DEDICATION

I dedicate this to all my
Twisted T fans. I love you babies.

# ACKNOWLEDGMENTS

I dreamed this entire book in one night.
And, I acknowledge all of my fans for
inspiring me to create. I do this for you.

Thank You.

T. Styles, President & CEO, The Cartel
Publications

www.thecartelpublications.com
www.facebook.com/authortstyles
www.myspace.com/authortstyles
www.authortstyles.blogspot.com
www.twitter.com/authortstyles

What Up Fam,

I hope and trust that you all had a great and Happy New Year. We at the Cartel Publications had a wonderful holiday season and beginning to 2013. When you have a moment, make sure you slide by our updated website, www.thecartelpublications.com and check out all the new and exciting things we have in place. We hope you enjoy it just as much as we did creating it.

We will be dropping some incredible novels including my very own, first book. Yeah, yeah, I know, I should have been written a novel, but I know that you can only come out once for the first time and I had to make sure it was the *right* time. It drops by mid-year, so be on the lookout for it.

Ok, now that my shameless plug is out the way, ;) Let's get down to brass tacks, "Pretty Kings". Man, I gotta say, this novel is the freshest concept for a book I ever heard of. I still remember exactly what I was doing when T called me and told me the title and premise. My mouth flew open! I loved it and equally important, I hadn't heard of a story like this. I love fresh shit. I know you will too.

However, before you go, keeping in line with Cartel tradition, we would like to honor an author who's literary work we admire and moving forward we decided that we will not only pay homage to authors but go getters in life and business. In this letter, we would like to pay tribute to:

## "Malcolm Gladwell"

This is an author who wrote a book that T swears by. If more people who desire to attain a goal read this book, we believe they will reach their dream with a purpose and plan. The book is called, "Outliers", so make sure you pick it up.

Ok, I'm out, got work to do! Get your read in; I know you'll love it as much as I did!

Much Love, Success and Happiness.

Charisse "C. Wash" Washington
Vice President
The Cartel Publications
www.thecartelpublications.com
www.twitter.com/cartelbooks
www.facebook.com/cartelcafeandbooksstore
www.facebook.com/publishercharissewashington
www.twitter.com/CWashVP
Follow us on Instagram @cartelpublications
Follow me on Instagram @publishercwash

# SATURDAY
# NOVEMBER 3RD
# 4 00 PM

# BAMBI KENNEDY

I fucked my husband 4,777 times in my life. That's everyday for the 17 years we've been together, minus the days I got my period. My husband knows my body, and I know every mole and hair on his. Sex with him is outrageous, and there's nothing I won't do in the bedroom to please him. From sucking his dirty toes, to licking the crack of his ass, for the sake of love I've done it all.

When it comes to sex we can't get enough of each other. It's so bad that the only time he goes out of town on business is when my pussy bleeds and is out of order. He figures if I'm leaking, another nigga won't taste the goods. It doesn't matter that I've never met a nigga who would turn down the juicy, menstruating or not.

I sigh when I roll over on my white Baldacchino Supreme bed, worth over four million dollars. My husband is not next to me, and I feel empty. I've felt empty a lot lately. I rub my hand over the 28 carat gold leaves carved into the bedpost. My outstretched manicured hand, scarred with tiny cuts, makes me think of my violent past.

The stiff pad stuffed between my pussy lips is the reason I'm alone. Kevin is in LA, right now on business. I grab his down pillow, bring it to my face and inhale. It smells like Clive Christian cologne and I melt. Electricity shoots through my body, and I contemplate playing with myself for the third time that day. But I fingered myself so much over the past few days

thinking about my missing husband, that my wrists are throbbing.

First let me tell you this, I'm Bambi Kennedy, wife to Kevin Kennedy, leader of the Kennedy Kings. Kevin has been in the
drug business since I've known him. Prior to Kevin I was a soldier girl, looking for a way out. He saved me by loving me hard
and spoiling me rotten. Once I accepted his love and he introduced me to luxury boat rides on his yacht, fly private parties,
which we threw here at our ten-bedroom mansion, I knew there
was no turning back for me. I'm all about this life.

Luxurious.

Fabulous.

Royal.

Before we go any further, let me set the record straight. My
nigga deals in cocaine. Not crack. Not weed or any of that other
watered down shit. He deals in the purest and only fucks with the
big boys who can afford weight. I call it the Virgin Pussy.

Kevin is great at what he does. His brothers too. He's so
good that he has given me everything I have ever asked for. The
black drop head Phantom coupe outside, I own that. The ten million dollar home in the suburbs, I live in that. St. Paul's Boarding
school? One of the best schools in America? My twin boys do
that. Life is sweet. Real sweet. *Sometimes.*

In the back of my mind, where I keep the rest of my raun-
chy secrets, I feel like I'm out of my league by being here. Like a
fake. I know the truth about our troubled marriage. And, when I
see Kevin's face, I wonder if he regrets the day he chose me to
be his wife. I also think about where my life would be, if we
never met.

# 17 YEARS EARLIER

*Kevin Kennedy glided through the Washington Dulles In-
ternational airport, on the way to the parking lot to ease into his
big-bodied black Benz. His plane landed late, and he was excited
to tell his brothers about a meeting he just had with Mitch*

*McKenzie in Mexico. Not only was the meeting unprecedented, it would put the Kennedy Kings in a position to distribute the purest cocaine in the United States. Mitch would not only give the Kings the white at great wholesale prices, Mitch was using the most underestimated cocaine hubs in the world to grow his product, Peru, thereby reducing some of the risk.*

*While everyone who was on the plane with Kevin hustled to baggage claim, he had intentions on walking right past it. He never took luggage when he went out of town. He would purchase clothing wherever he landed, and leave the designer garbs for the natives when he left the city. He believed in moving light.*

*Kevin pushed his brown and gold Versace eyeglasses to his face with his index finger as he headed for the door...until he saw her face.*

*Bambi Martin seemed upset as she picked up suitcase after suitcase on the conveyor belt looking for her luggage. The green army fatigue pants she wore tried to drown out the thickness of her ass, and the curves of her hips, but the pants failed miserably. The white t-shirt clinging to her breasts was raised enough to see her cute belly button. Was she a soldier, is what Kevin wanted to know? Bambi's long brown hair hung down the middle of her back, and it swayed from left to right as she searched for her luggage.*

*When Bambi finally grabbed her green army duffle bag, and strutted past Kevin without so much as eye contact, he knew immediately that she was the one. Females threw themselves at Kevin on a regular basis, so it wasn't like he couldn't get pussy. He couldn't even sit in traffic without some chick flashing their breasts to get his attention, or making fools of themselves to get his number. Every now and again he would choose one, take her to a hotel, and fuck her brains out to make sure his fuck game was still on par. But he never, ever, until that moment saw some random chick, and said she was the one.*

*Keeping his eyes on Bambi, Kevin removed the gray bulky Motorola 8900 cell phone from his jean pocket. He followed her out of the airport, and into the parking lot. The sun's rays were strong and caused Bambi's brown skin to sparkle. Kevin was in awe of her beauty. She seemed like she was waiting on someone because she stood on the curb and kept looking at her watch.*

*"I gotta have that bitch," he said to himself. Kevin hit the speed dial on his cell phone to reach his brother Ramirez Kennedy.*

*When he answered Kevin said, "Ram, I'm not gonna be able to get up with ya'll tonight." He slid into a yellow cab. "I'll get up with you later and explain. But, on everything I love, I think I just found my wife."*

*"I guess I'll hear all about it later, because to tell you the truth, I can't imagine Kinky Kevin settling down for nobody," Ramirez told him.*

*"Fuck you, nigga," Kevin chuckled. "I'm out," he ended the call and stuffed the cell phone into his pocket.*

*With his attention on the African cab driver he said, "Wherever she goes, follow." He pointed at Bambi. "But, hang back so she don't see you." He tossed him a crisp one hundred dollar bill to start the tab off right. Kevin decided to leave his brand new black 1995 Mercedes Benz E-Class in the parking lot, to trail the girl he wanted. This was not his plan but he loved it.*

*When Bambi slid into the passenger seat of a black Honda Accord, and Kevin saw the long hair of the female driver, he rested a little easier. It would make his job to bag her a little smoother if another nigga wasn't scooping her up. The cab driver did a good job of tailing Bambi. She seemed unwise that she was being watched from behind.*

*Thirty minutes later they arrived in a suburb of Maryland. "Park a few cars behind them," Kevin told the cab driver. The driver obeyed and Kevin waited for Bambi to get out of the car. When she finally eased out, she grabbed her duffle, and pulled her long hair over her right shoulder. Waving goodbye to her ride, she strutted away from the car.*

*When Bambi walked in the direction of the cab, Kevin eased down in his seat so that she couldn't spot him. He was worth more money than at least five of the houses on the block put together, yet he was cowering down like a bitch. He felt ri-*

*diculous but something about the soldier girl had him intrigued. Had him humbling himself.*

*When he waited long enough, Kevin sat up straight, and looked back to see which house Bambi walked into. He didn't see her anywhere. It was as if she vanished into thin air. He exhaled in anger. Why didn't he approach her? When he faced the front of the cab, and looked to his right again, he was now staring into the barrel of Bambi's gun.*

*Kevin saw his life flash in front of him as he looked into the eyehole of the weapon. Both he and the cab driver threw their hands up in the air to show they weren't armed.*

*Bambi grinned, and tapped the back passenger window.*

*Kevin pointed to the automatic window button, "Can I roll it down?"*

*She nodded. When the window was down she asked, "Who are you and why are you following me?"*

*Kevin didn't know whether to be frightened or turned on by Bambi. She held onto the handle of the gray .45 in her hands with authority. It was evident that she knew guns...well. "How did you know I was following you?"*

*"I saw you in the airport," she explained with her finger still firmly on the trigger. "When you pushed your glasses to your face, and watched me in baggage claim," she paused. "Now answer my question, why are you following me?"*

*"Because you gonna be my wife." he told her plainly. In his mind, Bambi would be the perfect addition to the Kennedy family. She was beautiful, could handle a weapon and had the eye of a killer.*

*"What makes you think that I'd want anything to do with you?" Bambi asked no longer holding the gun as firmly. Besides, she wasn't as scared of him as she was the first time she saw him follow her. Kevin was dangerously attractive with his large brown eyes and model looks and for some reason she wanted him, and badly.*

*"I know you want it because you haven't killed me yet. And, I can look in your eyes, and tell that you've killed before. The way your lower jaw is trembling, you've probably killed*

*many." When he saw her expression soften he continued. "You also not gonna pull the trigger, because you tired of moving around like a man in life. You need a real nigga to take care of you, and hold you down. That's where I step in. You not gonna kill me, because if you do, you'll risk the only opportunity at real love. Now what you wanna do, ma?"*

*He read her from the hair on her head to the soles of her feet. She was done. For five months Kevin courted her, showed her the finer things in life while never sliding into her pussy once, no matter how bad Bambi begged him too. And, when he was ready to make his move, he stepped to her father first.*

*Brian Martin, Bambi's father, immediately liked Kevin, but not for the reasons a father should. He never wanted his daughter to be a soldier in the army, and hoped Kevin could show her what she's been missing. No he didn't like Kevin's drug dealing lifestyle, but he hated the war for Bambi even more. Besides, there was something regal about Kevin that Brian respected. Kevin's age said he was young, but his mannerisms said he was raised properly.*

*Karen Martin, Bambi's mother, on the other hand, didn't like Kevin. Not because he was rude, or didn't love Bambi, but because he sold poison to their people. She saw her daughter's life turning for the worst if she shacked up with Kevin for the love of money. Karen's own marriage was falling apart as she came to the realization that she was in love with another woman. She didn't want her daughter to suffer the same fate, by realizing that she wasn't in love with Kevin the man, but Kevin the hustler.*

*Kevin respected Karen's opinion of him, but knew there was no getting through to her. Instead, he focused on Brian. The only other man on earth besides him that Bambi idolized.*

*When Kevin was ready he presented Brian with a seventeen year family and business plan. In the plan he depicted how he would care financially for Bambi. He listed how he would invest in their futures with stocks and bonds. He even drew out an area showing how much money would be allotted for their children if Bambi bared him any.*

*Although Brian was impressed, the best part of the plan was the end. Because after 17 years, Kevin said he would get out of the drug business, and remain successful due to his plans to be a real estate mogul. Brian gave Kevin his approval to be with his daughter. When Brian did, Kevin proposed to nineteen-year-old Bambi, and the rest was their history.*

I'm at my 28-kt gold dresser combing through my long expensive weave. It's wavy now, but when it's wet, the curls tighten up just the way Kevin likes it. When my iPad dings on my bed, indicating I have a video call, I rush over to my bed and hop on top of it. When I pick up my iPad, and I see Kevin is trying to reach me, I tingle all over my body.

After all this time he still gets me wet. And, not just wet between the legs. That type of thing is normal in our relationship. Whenever I see him or hear his voice, I sweat. My palms. My feet. My back. Everywhere is wet, because I'm always thinking about how I would react if Kevin decides he doesn't want me anymore...*first*. Leaving the Kennedy family doesn't just mean a divorce, in my mind it means giving up my crown. Giving up my place in life. I can't let another woman have what I have. I won't.

I lie on my back, grab my iPad and hit the button to take his call. Immediately his handsome face comes into view on the screen. He strokes his neatly trimmed goatee, quickly and I smile.

"Do you know how much I miss your fucking ass?" Kevin asks. He flashes his white teeth and I feel like a schoolgirl all over again. "You got me out here in LA, geeking without you, baby girl."

I'm sweating again. Sometimes I hate the physical control Kevin has over my body. He owns me. "Stop playing with me, boy. You know you getting tired of me by now." I look at my reflection on the gold mirror on the ceiling, which is surrounded by diamonds. I look younger than I feel. "I don't look the same way I use to when we first met."

Kevin frowns. "Listen, I done told you about saying dumb shit like that to me. You thirty-six years old yet you over there looking like you twenty-four or something. That's why I don't let you leave the house unless one of the Kennedy family members are with you. I don't want a nigga getting the wrong idea," he pauses. "You belong to me. So stop with all that dumb shit. We been together too long, Bambi."

I feel guilty. "I'm serious, Kevin," I tell him trying not to pout. I hold the iPad firmly in my hand so I can focus on his face. "I feel different now than when I did when we first met."

"When you talk like that you make me feel like I'm not doing my job as a man. Like I don't do everything possible to show you how much I love you."

My mouth trembles and I bite down into the flesh of my bottom lip. It's a habit that my son Noah picked up from me. "You do—"

"Then stop fucking with me," he yells interrupting me. "We been through our shit, Bambi. And, I can never stop apologizing for my part in our problems, but you my bitch. You my queen. And, I need you to hold your head up, and recognize that shit. It's really time to start doing that."

Kevin always knows what to say. He's a master at words...a regular Martin Luther King Jr. Sometimes I think I come down on myself every now, and again just to get one of his pep talks. His speeches are legendary. He's good for talking a lot of smooth shit.

"I got you, baby," I say. I grab the iPad and walk toward the living room. "Where are you now?" I ask looking at the background. "It looks like you in a casino or something."

"I am," he chuckles.

"I thought we weren't supposed to be gambling anymore."

"I know, baby. But, you know how my brothers are. We just—," before he could finish his statement Ramirez, Camp and Bradley come into view. They are members of the Kennedy Kings.

Bradley is holding a chocolate cupcake with a yellow candle stuffed in the center. Camp's black eye is as dark as it was when they left home five days ago, but he still looks great. Boxing every week for a hobby will do that kind of shit to your face, but Camp never seems to care.

I'm looking at the richest niggas in America on my iPad right now. Although we have a few cars and this house, being a Kennedy family member actually means leading a low-key lifestyle to the outside world. We stay off the radar. To prove my point, we all live in this house despite having enough money to buy several of our own homes. Maybe we are all addicted to one another. A Kennedy Cult. I love every one of them, and my stomach flutters.

I'm smiling at all of them until they sing, "Happy birthday to you. Happy birthday to you, happy birthday, dear Bambi, happy birthday to you."

Tears pour out of my eyes. I feel guilty. And, since they all can sing, I can't help but feel like the luckiest bitch in the world. Each one of these niggas is fine. The type of dudes you have to look at three times when they walk down the street. Add money to the equation and it makes them addictive. Of course Kevin is the loudest, and most excited out of all of them.

When they are done Ramirez says, "We love you, sis. And we're so proud of you for everything you've gone through and accomplished. We know it hasn't been easy."

No it's not my birthday. Today is much deeper, and although I try to forget each year, for the past five years, Kevin always remembers. I am a drunk. Well, I *was* a drunk. But, I've been sober for five of the seventeen years we've been together, and it's been a rough road. Real rough. Kevin says it's my birthday each year at this time because in his mind I am born again. My alcohol problem is so bad, that Kevin won't allow anybody to bring anything with alcohol in the house. No mouthwash. No cough syrup. No nothing.

Although I'm sober, don't think I don't desire alcohol. There are five things I love in the world. My husband, our sons, my sisters-in-law and my parents, but alcohol is first. If people saw the things I did when I was in the military, they'd understand why I turned to the bottle for emotional support.

"I swear I got the best family ever!" I proclaim looking at their faces. "Ain't nobody fucking with my clique."

"You know what it is, mama," Bradley says. "The Kennedy family or death."

When the front door open, my three beautiful sisters-in-law pour inside. Scarlett's red hair bounces as she walks in arm and arm with Denim. Scarlett's white skin seems flushed, probably because of the frigid temperatures outside. The winter hasn't been a joke this year. In the back of Scarlett and Denim is Race followed by Kevin's cousin Cloud. Cloud is the only male of the Kennedy family not involved in the drug business. The four of them smell like they've been outside, and I smile because I've always loved that scent on Kevin's coat when he comes home.

"Please tell me you talking to the boys," Denim yells running to the couch to look into my iPad. Her naturally short curly hair seems extra ruby red today. She's beautiful.

"Yes, I am. But, I have a feeling it won't be for long," I say.

When Denim sees her husband Bradley's face on my iPad, she plops down and screams, "Oh, my God! I miss the shit out of my dick! When you coming back," she snatches the iPad out of my hand. "I miss you so much, daddy. Jasmine misses her father too! You gotta come back soon."

"Damn, bitch," I say moving toward the arm on the couch when her butt bone slams into my thigh. "You almost broke my leg trying to get at him." I keep telling my sisters to get the video service on their iPhones and iPads, but they never see the value in it until the Kings are out of town.

As I look at Denim's light skin cheeks turn maroon, I laugh. She's so pretty, then again, all my sisters are. Her custom made brown leather jacket squeaks as she gets into position on the sofa. And, the tattoos on her neck peak out from the collar. Every place on her body is tatted up. Denim's body was in tip-top shape, but Bradley made it clear that her perfectly round ass is what had him going.

"Don't be totally selfish," Race says in her squeaky voice as she flops down on the floor. She combs her shoulder length brown hair back with her fingers, and her hair gets tangled in the 20-carat wedding ring. When she gets situated, she leans on Denim's knee and looks at the iPad. "I want to talk to my husband too," she continues referring to Ramirez.

I move out of their way, but it won't be for long. I have to see Kevin's face again before he gets off of the video call. While Denim and Race talk to their husbands, I realize someone is missing. Scarlett. When I look back to see where she is, I notice she's gone. And when I peek at my iPad, Camp, who is her husband, is also gone. Something is up with them, but what?

While I wonder how Scarlett is doing, Cloud walks up to me on the sofa and looks down at me. He's 6'4 inches tall, and his skin is the color of melted Hershey Kisses. His height is how he got the nickname Cloud. They say he's so tall his head touches the sky. Although he's not in the dope game, he owns a popular auto body shop in Washington, D.C, and has that dope boy steez. But, as handsome as he is, Cloud did me wrong, and I will never forgive him. I can hold a grudge longer than the meanest bitch you can imagine, and everybody who loved me knew it.

"How you doing, sexy?" Cloud says to me.

I ignore him, and turn my head.

He plants a soft kiss on my lips, and I wipe it away. Any other time I wouldn't mind his affections, but I don't like him right now. I haven't liked him for some weeks now.

"You gonna stay mad at me forever, Bambi?" He asks looking down at me again.

Silence.

"Bambi, you gotta talk to me at some point," Cloud continues as if we are alone. As if my husband is not on my iPad and my sisters are not next to me on the couch.

"What I tell you about kissing my wife?" Kevin jokes from the iPad. I guess he saw him.

Cloud clears his throat and says, "I been told you I'm gonna steal Bambi from you. I'm just waiting on her to realize she belongs to me," Cloud says jokingly.

"Is that gonna be before or after they find your body in a ditch?" Kevin responds. They always play back and forth about who loved me the most but this time both of them sounded serious.

Eventually Cloud joins the call with my sisters and when they are all done, it's just Kevin and me alone on the iPad.

"Finally," I say to him when I look down at his face. "Now I get to talk to you in peace."

"Go to the bathroom," he says in a sexy voice. "I want to see that juicy pussy before I go handle business."

When Kevin asks me to do something, he only has to ask once. I hustle to the bathroom, sit on the toilet and remove my pink panties. Before showing him my box, I flip the iPad over and toss the menstruation pad in the trashcan. I was on the last day of my cycle and should be good. But, even if I were bleeding, Kevin would still want to see my box. He's even eaten me out before while on my cycle.

When I was done prepping, I grab my iPad, sit on the toilet, open my legs and gave him a close up of my wet pussy.

"You been playing with yourself again haven't you?" he says licking his lips.

I never understood how he knew it, but he could always tell when I took care of myself. "I did a little something, earlier today."

"What you thought about when you were flipping that pussy this time?" He asks in the seductive voice he uses right before he pushes into my body. "If it's another nigga I'll kill you."

"How you licked my pussy for an hour while I was sucking your toes," I moan. "You know the nastiest shit always turns me on, Kevin. That's probably why you chose me."

He chuckles. "That's one of the reasons I chose you, and that's also one of the reasons I made you my wife." He strokes his goatee. "On some serious shit, I don't want Cloud kissing you in the mouth anymore. The look he gives when he kisses you, tells me he feels like he's home in your eyes. I don't want to bury somebody with my bloodline."

"I don't fuck with—"

"Bitch, did you hear what the fuck I said to you?" He yells at me. "Put that nigga in his place, before I get home, Bambi. Blood or not, I don't play when it comes to my wife."

"It's done," I tell him.

"That's my wife," he winks.

"But can you believe it?" he continues as he looks at my pussy lips again. "In seven days it'll all be over. And the promise I made to you and your father will be solid. I'll finally be out of the business, Bambi. Can you deal with a square nigga for the rest of your life?"

"I don't care what you are doing, you will never be square, Kevin," I sigh. "I just wish you didn't have to do all of this. You know, meeting with the Russians and stuff."

"Bambi, the Russians are on me. You can't keep blaming yourself for a decision a man has made."

"I have to blame myself, Kevin. Had I not traded one addiction in for another, by starting to gamble, I would not have lost our life's savings. And, you would not have to go to such a risky meeting with the Russians. Because of me we lost everything, and almost couldn't afford the twins' tuition at school."

"Bambi, nobody but you knows what you went through in Saudi Arabia. As much shit as I've seen on the streets, it probably can't touch what you seen. You know how many times I've seen a child killed? None."

My heart thumps and the memories of the past seem to suffocate me. I turn the fan on in the bathroom and take a few quick breaths. I need some air, and feel like I'm hyperventilating.

"Calm down, Bambi," he says to me. "That life is over now, and stop coming down on yourself because you got weak and gambled a little. It happens to the best of us. And, after this one hundred million dollar deal with the Russians we will be set for life. I'm gonna be honest, whether you dipped into the stash or not, the meeting with the Russians is a power move. We on top after this deal, Bambi. Trust me."

Just recently Avery Graham, the connect Kevin supplies on the east coast called with a deal changer. He said that one of his biggest buyers, Iakov and Arkadi Lenin, wanted to up their purchase, but only if they met the Kennedy Kings personally. The Russians' stated that the reason they wanted to meet with the Kings was because they didn't trust Avery with that amount of money. They wanted to touch their product directly after the dough exchanged hands.

Although Mitch McKenzie, who supplies Kevin with pure cocaine at wholesale prices, advised the Kings against the meting, Kevin didn't heed the warning. The meeting in seven days would be the first time the Russians would meet the Kennedy Kings. It wasn't because the Russians didn't try. They looked everywhere for the Kennedy Kings but their attempts were all in vain. The Kings only made themselves seen to those whom they wanted to, and operating like that worked for them so far. They were ghosts.

While I continue to look at my husband, Kevin suddenly looks to the left. "Put your clothes back on, Bambi," he tells me. "Ramirez is walking over here and I don't want him getting any bright ideas about my goodies," he winks again.

I quickly get dressed and go back into the living room. I look out of the window and I see Cloud's car is gone. Fuck that nigga. I flop back on the sofa and wait for Kevin's attention to come back on me.

"What's up, man?" Kevin says looking at Ramirez.

Ramirez is saying something, but I can't hear him. My heart stops when I see someone I don't know walk into the casino behind Kevin. His expression is deadly, and he looks like he has been wronged. When he releases two automatic weapons from the black leather coat he's wearing, and I try to scream, my voice is trapped in my throat and it makes it difficult to breathe.

When Kevin finally looks at me, he must've seen the horror in my eyes because he says, "What's wrong, baby? Are you okay?"

Ramirez comes into view too and they both focus on me. The next thing I see is sparks flying behind Kevin and Ramirez as the man fires into the casino. Kevin drops the iPad, and it tumbles to the floor. The only thing I can see now is the green square pattern on an ugly cream carpet. Gunfire rings out, along with screams, and before long I can see blood soak the carpet.

I put both hands on my throat, and squeeze tighter. When I do my voice returns and I scream into the house. As if it were in slow motion, I see my sisters running down the stairwell toward me. In that moment, I know that everything in my life has changed.

It's later that night. I'm in my bed. Naked. Not a stich of clothing covers my body. When I look up I see my nakedness in the gold and diamond mirror on the ceiling. I don't look like myself. My eyes are red, and white dry tearstains run toward my chin. I'm a mess. My head is thumping, and I want the feeling of this nightmare to be over.

My husband is not dead. The man who tamed me when I first left the military is not gone. The man who rubbed my body every night when I couldn't get a good night sleep, because I thought someone was going to come into my home and take my life, is not deceased. By some man I didn't know.

When my personal phone line rings, I roll over and answer it. "Hello." My throat is so dry I can feel the two balls that are supposed to be my tonsils rubbing together.

"Good evening, Bambi," someone says to me on the phone.

Nothing about this evening is good and I hate him for being so pleasant. If I could reach through this phone and take his life, I would. "What do you want?" I ask.

"This is Avery, can I speak to Kevin? It's...I mean... well...it's kind of important."

Hearing my husband's name in his mouth makes my chest thump. "I gotta go, Avery. Now is not a good time."

"Wait," he yells out to me before I end the call, "Please don't hang up." He clears his throat. "Listen, I need to speak to Kevin now. There's a meeting taking place on Saturday. A very important meeting, and I need to make sure that he'll be there."

I remember the meeting. "Why can't you go yourself?" I ask, knowing the Russians were introduced to my husband through him anyway. "You can just give us what is owed when the meeting is done."

"Because, I'm not facilitating this deal and the Kings have to be there. Kevin knows that. That was part of the deal. They want to meet the connect."

I hang up on him. My phone immediately rings again. This time it's my friend Sarge but I don't want to talk to him now either. I can't concentrate. The last thing I feel like dealing with is Avery, the Russians and even my friend.

When I stand up. I'm still naked. The cool air reminds me that I'm alive despite feeling dead inside. I guess I should be grateful that I'm living. I could've killed myself and met Kevin in heaven. I don't feel grateful though.

I walk into my double walk-in closet. The place I go to for refuge. Everything is cream inside and a large comfortable loveseat sits against the wall. I never use it. Instead I drop to my knees, the plush cream carpet protects my knees from harm. I push my clothes to the side.

There are two safes in here but I focus on the pink one I had installed some time back. Originally it was to keep my jewelry protected, but I've since sold it all off to gamble, I don't have anything nice outside of my wedding ring left.

I open the pink safe anyway, and inside are two bottles of Russian vodka. How ironic. They're the only things inside the safe. Suddenly I feel hot, and I want to take my clothes off, but I'm not wearing any. Kevin was so proud of me, when I stopped drinking. If I drink now, all the love he poured on me, to keep me alive would be in vain. I feel guilty. I slam the safe close. I won't make such a weak move.

Instead I move to the black safe...the one belonging to Kevin. I enter the combination and it pops open. Inside is a stack of money, about fifty thousand dollars. It's all I have left in the world. I think about something serious at that moment. I realize without Kevin I have nothing. No money. No assets. Nothing. Even this house didn't belong to us.

It was a gift from Kevin to his aunt Bunny, the most evil woman in the world. When he first gave it to her, she said it was too big for a woman to live alone, and begged him to stay in it and buy her a smaller one. He quickly fulfilled her wish like he always did. I think wanting us to stay here was a way to control our marriage. Although she never said it, I know she loved the idea of us staying in her house. Control. It's all about control. Since Kevin is dead, the house goes back to Bunny. So I'm technically broke.

I kept telling him we needed to leave and buy our own house and he promised that after the deal with the Russians, he'd buy me the home of my dreams. Now, he's gone. My world is crushed and changed. What's to become of my kids? I can't afford their school with fifty thousand dollars.

When I feel my stomach swirl, I stand up, grab the small wastebasket and release the bitter liquid from my belly. It's yellow. It's strong, and it doesn't make me feel any better. Back on my knees, I wipe my mouth with my hands. I remove a white envelope from Kevin's safe. In it is a sheet of paper. On it is a number and the word Fruit Delivery written in red ink. I knew all about this. I know a lot about Kevin's business.

On Saturday, Kevin was to call the number and say one of two things. *Same*, which meant a delivery truck would be parked outside of the house. Inside of the truck would be the keys and the cocaine. The coke would be taken to the Russians in exchange for the money. The other thing that could be said on the phone was *Different*, which required a new address.

As I hold the sheet of paper in my hand I realize this is my only option to survive. If I want to take care of my family, I need to see to it that the meeting goes down without a hitch. My only question is how?

# SUNDAY NOVEMBER 4^{TH} 9 00 AM

# SCARLETT KENNEDY

The last thing my husband said to me before he was murdered was I want a divorce. As I lie face up on the black carpet on my bedroom floor, I can feel the tears well up in my eyes and roll back toward my ears. From my position, I can smell Camp's red dirty boxing gloves. They lay a few feet up from my head next to a red Everlast freestanding heavy bag. I crawl toward them, on hands and knees, and place them against my nose and inhale. When I smell the sour scent of the dry sweat gloves I cry. Hard. My stomach churns. I feel sick.

It doesn't matter that Camp didn't want me anymore before he died. It doesn't matter that he filed for a divorce not even a month earlier. It doesn't even matter that I couldn't tell my sisters-in-law that our marriage was coming to a complete end. All that matters is that I will never get a chance to change his mind.

I drop the gloves, and roll into a ball on the floor. I think about the woman I am. The woman I've always been. I'm abusive, and angry at times. It's not like I've changed since we first got married, it's the way I've always been. I guess Camp couldn't deal with it anymore. Maybe it was becoming harder to lie for my abuse. Because of me, Camp had a black eye almost every other day. If I wasn't punching him, I was scratching his beautiful brown face. I can't count the times his boxing hobby took the rap for my violence. In the past he enjoyed sex with me when I hit him, choked him and spit in his face. I guess those days are over.

I get up off the floor, and walk to my personal bathroom to brush my teeth. That's one thing I love about this house, each room has it's own bathroom...it's own personality. And most of all, privacy. When I walk inside, I hear the water dripping in my black tub. I remember now, I was going to take a bath before I heard Bambi's scream last night. They were murdered, she told us. Our husbands are dead. I shiver.

After I brush my teeth, I throw on some jeans and a baby blue and gold, Juicy Couture t-shirt. I leave to check on my sisters. Although, we don't have the same blood, or even the same ethnicity, I love them more than I love my own family.

When I knock on Bambi's door, it opens. I look inside and she's not there. I move to Denim's door, and can hear her four-year-old daughter Jasmine talking to herself. Since her kid is up, I figure Denim is up too so I don't bother her. I don't want Jasmine coming near me. Kids make me nervous.

I move to Race's room and knock on the door. From where I stand I hear her crying loudly. When I turn her 18-kt gold door-knob, and push it open, the smell of feces immediately smacks me in the face. I see Race on the bed, rubbing her eyes with her fists. But, what is that smell?

"Race, what's going on?" I ask entering her room. "Are you okay?"

The moment I take another step inside she yells, "Get out, bitch! Now!" She throws something at me and I duck before it hits me in the face. "Get out of my room!"

I run away and slam the door behind me. She's taking the news of their deaths just like I knew she would, and I can't blame her. The only reason I'm not having a nervous breakdown, is because I knew in advance that Camp was through with me before his death. I guess I've been grieving for our relationship ending for some time now. It's like I had a head start.

When I hit the elevator button to go downstairs, I can smell food cooking. I step inside the mahogany and gold elevator and the doors close. I look at myself in the reflection on the mirror. I'm taller than the average girl, standing about 5'10 with no heels. My boobs are big and luckily for me, so is my natural ass. I wonder will I be able to find another man now that I'm alone?

When the elevator stops, and dings, I step out. My feet cuddle the expensive cream Italian carpeting on our living room floor. I walk toward the front of the house, and see Bambi in the kitchen cooking. She's wearing her green army fatigue pants and a red bra...no top. I shiver. The only time Bambi wears her fatigues is if she's mad or up to no good. But, even in her fatigues she is so beautiful. Her long brown hair hangs down her back, and her brown skin is flawless. I guess despite the horror stories I heard about regarding her past...war becomes her.

I walk behind her and can finally smell the bacon. "What's going on, Bambi?" I ask looking at her pants. "Are you okay?"

She doesn't look at me, and flips the bacon over in the large black cast iron pan. "You mean besides, the fact that our husbands are dead?" She looks at me and I can see the tear stains on her face. "If you take that out of the equation, I think life for us is great. Don't you?"

She's being sarcastic and I wonder if she's mad at me for something. I don't say anything to her. Instead, I wash my hands. Five more minutes of silence pass between us, and the house phone rings.

"Hello...oh hold on," I hold out the phone. "Bambi, it's Sarge, he says he has to talk to you."

"Not now," she says to me.

"Sarge, can you call back later? Bambi doesn't want to talk right now." I hang up on him and focus back on Bambi. I can tell she's irritated but I want to speak to her. Finally I say, "I didn't mean it that way, Bambi. When I asked are you okay. I know you're hurting, I am too." I take the eggs and cheese out of the refrigerator. Then I remove a glass bowl from the cabinet, and crack the eggs on the rim.

"I know you didn't," she says in a breathy tone. "My mind is cloudy today. Stuffed with so much pain."

"I don't know what to feel anymore, Bambi." I admit. "What are we going to do without them? It's like I feel lost already."

She removes the bacon from the pan and place it on a plate covered in paper towels. "We may have to do some things we not prepared for." Bambi turns around to face me. "We are all we got, Scarlett. You guys are my sisters, and we must stick together if we are going to survive now." She exhales. "I saw the news today. Apparently the man who came into the casino was a disgruntled employee. He killed twenty-six people but they aren't releasing the names until they notify the families." She looks at the phone. "We haven't received a call yet. I don't even want it to tell you the truth."

I step closer to Bambi. "You know Kevin and them travel under false names. Maybe, they don't know who to call yet." I rub her arms. "No matter what I have your back, Bambi. This family is all I have."

It's true. Before marrying Camp my life was ugly. So ugly it's amazing that I'm even here right now. I don't deserve this life. I don't deserve to live.

# 6 YEARS EARLIER

*Twenty-three year old Scarlett Kirk stood in the busy crowd, away from her ex-husband Mark, her mother Courtney and father Joseph. Although they didn't see her, from her viewpoint Scarlett saw them clearly. There was a trial taking place in the District Court of Maryland due to the abuse Scarlett inflicted on her four-year-old daughter Samantha. To Scarlett, court that day felt like the end of her life.*

*Scarlett was a monster, but it was learned behavior. Because she never told anyone that her aunt Reba treated her so violently when she was in her care, they didn't know her mindset.*

31

*She was a child abuser and those types of people deserve to be punished. At the end of the day Scarlett sprayed drain cleaner in her daughter's eyes, because she was crying after being disciplined for using her makeup. And, now she had to answer to the charges.*

*Scarlett's red hair was died dark brown, and pulled back into a tight ponytail. Tears fell from her eyes, and onto her navy blue dress suit, and she tried to figure out why she was so evil. Her abuse didn't stop at her daughter. She struck her husband Mark for everything from not liking the way he looked at times, to not loving her hard enough.*

*Earlier that day, before court, Scarlett gave up all her worldly possessions. Most she gave to her brother Matt and the other things she gave to thrift stores. She was just about to turn over her life to the court system when someone grabbed her softly by the hand. She snatched away, and looked at who was vying for her attention.*

*"No disrespect, I just thought you were my wife," Camp Kennedy said. "Truth be told you're the prettiest thing I've ever seen."*

*Prior to that moment Scarlett never dated a black man. She didn't have any love or hate for them, she just didn't know them. Still, as she stood in front of Camp, she couldn't help but feel a connection. Camp's wide smile, low curly hair and chocolate brown skin made her warm inside. She wondered what life would be like if he was in her world. She could tell either he had money, or that he had a position of authority because he carried himself with extreme confidence. He was a dope boy, but she didn't know. This was a plus since her ex-husband was so weak, and mild mannered.*

*Realizing she had no time for play because she was due in court she said, "I'm kind of busy right now. You better go find your wife."*

*Scarlett turned to walk toward the courtroom, until he grabbed her hand again. "How about we get out of here together," he smiled at her. "I got time if you do."*

*How does he do that? She thought. Make me feel so weak?*

*"What is your wife gonna say?"*

*"I don't know, I haven't found her yet," he explained. "It could be you." She tried not to grin but couldn't help herself. "Maybe we can get some breakfast or something like that," he rubbed his belly. "I don't know about you but I can eat." Suddenly his face turned serious. "That is, unless you have something major to take care of today that's more important than being with me."*

*Scarlett thought about how she was facing time for the abuse. Maybe he was her way out. Her escape goat. One door leads to an incarceration and the other led to excitement. "What are you in the court house for?" Scarlett asked him.*

*"I docked my boat in the wrong place. Had to pay some fines," he advised her. "What about you?"*

*She swallowed. Something told her he could take her away from it all But, if she wanted to start over, she couldn't be fully honest with him. "I...um...have some traffic tickets to pay."*

*"That ain't about nothing." Camp reached in his pocket and pulled out a stack of cash. "Let's take care of that, and then grab something to eat. You coming with me." He walked toward the counter.*

*She grabbed his hand, "No, I'll take care of that later. I kind of want to go with you right now. If it's okay with you."*

*From that point on, Scarlett never left Camp's side. A year later she became his wife and her jealousy, and fear of losing him, caused her to react abusively toward him. In the beginning Camp loved being able to toss her around, and throw her across the room before sticking his dick into her wet pink-pussy. That is until things got out of hand one day. After she found out he was cheating, fought him and called the police. She didn't even think about the warrants out for her arrest and nor did she care.*

*When the police came to the mansion and saw her white bruised skin and the African-American man standing behind her with clenched fists, things got serious. The cops pulled Camp out of the house, beat him and arrested him. They treated Camp so violently that she finally understood that although she was his wife, the world was still a racist place.*

*Luckily Bambi and the Kennedy Kings were not home otherwise they would've hated her for the drama she caused. They didn't fuck with the police, then again, who did? Scarlett was able to get Camp out of jail and Bambi and Kevin were never aware of that fight. Both Camp and Scarlett kept things on a low about their relationship.*

*Life for Camp and Scarlett was up and down during the years they'd been together, yet Scarlett never thought she'd really lose him, until now.*

"We're out of biscuits," I tell Bambi when the breakfast I helped her make was prepared. We made eggs, bacon, pancakes and freshly squeezed orange juice. "I know you like them instead of pancakes. What you want instead? Some toast?"

"I wish you could go to the store and get some for me," Bambi says to me. "It's been years, Scarlett, and I still don't see how you move around without a driver's license. I need to be mobile."

Nobody knew about my warrants. Not even my husband Camp. Because, I never went to court to answer to the abuse charges of my daughter, I could never lead a full life, and that included getting a driver's license. I was even afraid that the police or my family would find me when Camp and I got married. Our entire wedding day was stressful for me, and I had to stay drunk just to relax. In the end I was fine.

"You know I don't like to drive," I tell Bambi as I help her place the expensive Mikasa Chinaware on the table for my sisters. "I wouldn't even know how to act if I had to drive a car right now."

"You do know that slavery is over right?" Bambi asks me. "Us black people are free now and don't have to work for the white man no more."

My heart drops into the pit of my stomach. There's a downside to being a white woman marrying a black man. Don't get me wrong, I love my family, but in the background was always the difference between them and me. My hair is stringy and my skin is cream. Their hair is thick, and their skin is brown. We never called each other out of our names, and we sincerely loved one another, but me being white was always the pink elephant in the room. At least that's how I felt anyway. In my mind I always had to prove myself to them and do more to be accepted in the family. To the point where I was secretly denouncing my own race.

Things were worse out in the world, a black man was involved in a major trial against a white one. During those times if I walked hand and hand with Camp in the street, the world would react violently toward us. I've been called everything from a bitch to my face by black women, to a nigger-lover by my own people. An interracial relationship is not for the weak at heart, and despite people thinking the world has changed, Camp and I knew differently.

"I hate when you say stuff like that, Bambi. You know, about slaves and all," I tell her sitting down at the dining room table. "It makes me feel like you think I think about you in that way."

Bambi stops what she is doing and sits next to me at the dining room table. She grabs both of my hands, and looks into my eyes. I look down at our fingers. My cream hands interlocked in her brown ones look beautiful to me. Like how Camp's and my body look when we make love.

"Scarlett, I'm so sorry," she cries. "You know I don't feel that way about you. My mind is all over the place right now. It's moving a mile a minute," she snaps her fingers four times by her ear. "I'm trying hard to save face, but I don't know what to do right now. Part of me wants to just stay in bed and cry, but the soldier in me wants to stand up and defend us. I still have you all to worry about, and my sons. I'm older than all of you, so I feel some sense of responsibility. And to tell you the truth, I don't know if I'm strong enough."

"Bambi, you don't have to take all of this on your own. If there's something I can do, just let me know." Suddenly my jaw feels warm and my stomach hot. I want to go to the bathroom, but I don't want her to think what she is saying is unimportant to me.

"I'm glad to hear you say that, because I have a plan, but I'm still trying to work some things out in my head first," Bambi tells me.

And, then it happens. I throw up. Everything in my stomach splashes out onto our hands and then the floor. I finally remember what's going on. When Camp decided to divorce me, I stopped taking my birth control pills so that we could have a baby. In the beginning he wanted a child, but because I couldn't trust myself around kids, I denied him that right. When he wanted to leave me, things changed. I figured if I were pregnant he would keep me as his wife.

As Bambi rushes into the kitchen and spins the paper towel rack to clean up my vomit, I realize my move was all for nothing now. Right?

# RACE KENNEDY

The first thing my husband did for me was kill a man. I can't say it was my idea of romance, but I do know I loved him harder for it.

Warm water from my shower runs down my body. Now I can smell the fragrance of the banana candles I lit all over my room, instead of my own body waste. When I learned Ramirez was killed, I lost control of my bowels in my bed.

What am I going to do? Who is going to hold me when another hurricane comes through Maryland, and brings down the trees in my yard? Who is going to speak up for me when my voice feels weak and I can't say what's on my mind? And, who is going to love me? Who is going to protect me?

I step out of the shower after rinsing the feces off my body. The soiled sheets lay next to my bathroom door for me to burn outside later. After my shower, I slip into the tub of warm water waiting on me, so that I can get my mind right. If I try hard enough, I wonder if I can drown myself.

I want to test the theory so I slip deeper into the water. First my shoulders are covered, followed by my neck and shoulder length hair. Under water, I open my eyes and can see the cream and gold celling in my bathroom. My eyes burn a little but I don't care.

Ramirez wherever you are, I'm coming with you.

## 5 YEARS EARLIER

*While most twenty year old girls shopped at high fashion shoe stores, Race Anthony's favorite place to shop was Mostly Monster, a special effects store in Washington DC. Race designed special effect prosthetics for several independent moviemakers. She was so good, that several large movie production companies in Hollywood approached her about relocating. But her Harvard graduate parents, Cindy and Bill Anthony, prevented her from pursuing her dreams in the hopes that she would return to Harvard, for a degree in law. To spite them, Race dropped out of college all together and never went back.*

*Race was walking out of the store with two large buckets of liquid silicone, dangling from her hands. Race hustled toward her black pickup truck so that she could lift the heavy buckets up and put them inside. Standing 5'5 without heels, her plan was starting to feel easier said than done. She was doing a mold, for a rock band of a large, vagina, and it was due tomorrow morning.*

*The buckets of liquid silicone were heavier than she imagined and she dropped one of them down. Luckily it didn't tilt over. The top fell off, and she placed it back on haphazardly. Moving to her truck again, she saw a black Range Rover pull up in front of her pick up truck. The driver parked, hopped out, and smiled at Race who was walking in his direction.*

*Although a shorty, Race was extremely beautiful. It didn't matter that she dumbed down her sex appeal to prevent anyone from taking interest in her. Mainly because she felt like nerds didn't deserve love. Besides, she had loved once and it was the scariest moment of her life.*

*"Damn, cutie," Mr. Range Rover said leaning on his car, and activating his alarm. "You need help?"*

*"I'm fine," she replied although the top had fallen off of the silicone again. She decided to get the buckets into her truck, and walk back to grab the top and place it on later. "Thank you anyway."*

*But, the moment Race stepped to her truck; the bucket without the top toppled out of her hand. The white silicone tilted* to the side, and splashed onto the new shiny Range Rover. The driver's expression turned from lust to anger in less than a second when he observed the condition of his leased ride.

What neither the driver or Race knew was that a few cars up the block sat Ramirez in his black BMW. He was waiting for his girlfriend Diamond to come out of the hair salon. The moment he saw Race leave the shop his heart skipped a beat.

Ramirez Kennedy remembered Race clearly, because they went to high school together, and he was always attracted to her. But, because Race was considered awkward, and he was dealing with Diamond, the chick in the salon, he could never tell her about his feelings. Unlike meek Race, Diamond was loud, tough and a gold digger. Race on the other hand was quiet, and chose to wear plain clothing, despite her mother and father being financially able to buy her any designer label she chose.

In high school Race use to get picked on and laughed at because of her large blue glasses and above-average intelligence. Ironically the main reason for Race's dismay in high school was Ramirez's girlfriend.

One day Diamond took to making fun of Race in front of Ramirez, and he was turned off. It happened when Race was coming out of the school's office after learning she was valedictorian. Diamond was so overcome with hate that she slapped the books out of Race's hand with Ramirez standing right next to her. When Race bent down to pick up her books, Diamond kicked her in the stomach repeatedly. From the floor Race looked to Ramirez for help but he didn't do anything. He never forgave himself for not taking up for Race and denying what he felt in his heart. Fuck Diamond, he wanted Race, but it never happened.

"Bitch, why the fuck didn't you watch where you were going?" Mr. Range Rover yelled at Race. "What you need stronger glasses or something?"

Race examined the splatter which was hardening, all on the side of his truck. "I'm so sorry. I'll pay for it. I promise."

"That ain't gonna be enough, bitch." He stepped to her and grabbed a wad of her hair. "Because, you fucked up my *ride, it means I'll be out of commission while it's repaired for at least a week. Who gonna pay for my time, and inconvenience?"*

*Race was so scared that she felt faint. When she felt it couldn't get any worse, Mr. Range Rover crashed into her face with his fist, knocking her out cold.*

*Two days later Race was in the hospital with her jaw wired. When she looked around her room, there wasn't an available space on the table. Red rose arrangements were everywhere and she wondered where they came from. She didn't have a boyfriend and her parents believed that spending money on flowers was wasteful spending.*

*When Race turned the TV on, the first thing she saw took her breath away. The man, who hit her in the jaw, causing her mouth to be wired, was murdered. His body was found in a dumpster behind a gay bar in DC with the word punk written on his forehead. Instead of being frightened Race was relieved. Mainly, because she didn't know if Mr. Range Rover would come for her after she got out of the hospital. Besides, if Mr. Range Rover was alive, she didn't have anybody to protect her out in the world. She was frightened all of the time, and all alone. His death gave her peace.*

*As Race wondered who could've killed him, her question was answered when Ramirez walked inside of the doorway to her hospital room. "How you feeling?" He asked with sad eyes. "In much pain?"*

*Because, she couldn't speak she nodded instead. Her heart rate sped up because he was one of her secret crushes all throughout high school. Race knew she didn't have a chance because of his beautiful girlfriend Diamond. Not only that, Ramirez never spoke to her prior to this moment. So what was he doing there?*

*"I saw what happened a few days ago," he cleared his throat. "And I'm sorry you gotta go through this shit." He looked around the room. "Only a weak as nigga would do a bitch like that." When she tried to speak again he said, "Don't do that. I don't want you to hurt yourself." He paused. "One of my biggest regrets was going with my mind and not my heart. In*

*high school I was a weak ass kid unable to make decisions for myself. But I'm not a kid anymore, Race and from here on out, I vow to always protect you. I promise you now, no matter what, I will always be there for you. And I will always come back to you."*

*The rest was history when a few years later, he made her his wife and moved her into the Kennedy home along with Bambi and Scarlett.*

I realize killing myself at the moment isn't going to work, so I pulled myself from the bathtub, threw on a black and gold Victoria Secret velour pants set, and called my parents. I didn't have the best relationship with them but it wasn't because I didn't want to be closer. The reason we didn't get along was all on them. No matter what I did, I could never convince my mother that not going to Harvard because I wanted to stay here to pursue my dream in special effects makeup was my decision, not Ramirez's. Anything gone wrong in my life was his fault to hear them tell it, and now I was going to have to tell them that he was dead.

I sit on the edge of the bed and make the call. "Hi, Mommy. It's me, Race."

"How are you, sweetheart?" My mother asks. "Is everything okay? You sound terrible."

"I'm fine," I tell her. When I hear my father pick up the other line like he always does when I call, I sigh. Not two damn parents at the same damn time. "Hi, Daddy...how are you?"

"Race, what is your mother talking about?" He yells. "That drug dealer didn't hurt you did he?"

"Daddy, no! Ramirez would never hurt me," I say in a frustrated tone. *Especially now.* I think. *Because he's dead.* "All he ever did was love me, daddy. Why would you even think something like that?"

"Honey, why don't you come home?" My mother continues. "You sound so sad right now and I want to take care of you. Did you lose your bowels again?"

"Ma, no!" I'm so embarrassed right now.

"Your old room is still available and you can have it. I'll put on your favorite movies, make you some fried chicken and your favorite Hot Colonial Rum drink without the rum. I'll do whatever I have to; I just want you to come home. Bill, make her come home," she cries to my father.

"She's right, sweetheart," my father says, "after all you're still an Anthony and Anthony's stick together. If you're going through a tough time we will support you."

The moment he says I'm an Anthony I grow angrier. "No, daddy, I'm not an Anthony. I haven't been one for some time now. My name is Race Kennedy, and the sooner you remember that will be the moment we can have a relationship. I'll call you both later. Bye."

I didn't tell my parents Ramirez was dead because I didn't want to go home. Although I'm an adult now, they have a way of making me feel guilty, and before long, my bags would be packed and I would be in my old room at their house wearing my old Strawberry Shortcake pajamas again. They don't treat me like a woman. They treat me like the mousy girl who can't make decisions on her own. I hate that about them, mainly because in the back of my mind, I think they are right.

But I still need support right now from an outside source. I love my sisters-in-law more than anything in the world, but sometimes they don't understand me either. They think I'm just some weird girl in the basement making horror masks, and that I don't have feelings. That's a lie and it's untrue. They don't get how it really is to love Ramirez the way that I do, but his girlfriend Carey does.

I know it's creepy, and some may not be able to handle this but I was aware of Ramirez's relationship with Carey from the gate. She is a sweet girl who he met with me when Ramirez and I went to a club a couple of summers ago. Carey is a stripper at *Smack Back* strip club in Washington, D.C, and Ramirez and me are her best customers. Carey is the best because we both fuck my husband and we both love him. Me and Carey's bond with Ramirez makes me love her even more.

I'm about to call Carey to tell her Ramirez is dead when Bambi burst through my door and yells, "Don't call anybody yet. We have to talk first."

# DENIM KENNEDY

I loved my husband harder than my sister; I guess that's why I took him from her. And, now he's gone. Is his death my karma?

As I lie in the bed, with my eyes closed, I'm disgusted when I feel the seat of my four-year-old daughter's urine soaked pamper rub against my face. I take it from her, sit up straight and lift her into my arms. Naked from the waist down, she stiffens under my grasp and babbles like she normally does. I hold onto her tighter, rock her back and forth and cry. We lost the best thing that ever happened to us yesterday.

I cry harder now because I won't get to love Bradley more than I already do. I cry because Jasmine will never know the type of wonderful father he could be to her. And I cry because I thought we would be forever.

Although I'm weeping, Jasmine's babbling has gotten louder. She's autistic and it's hard to connect with her. When I talk to her, I feel like I'm talking to a doll.

Jasmine doesn't make eye contact. She doesn't respond when I call her name, and she seems preoccupied with herself at all times. But every now and again, although rare, she'll do something to make me think there is hope for her. Like when she wipes my face with her pamper to let me know she needs to be changed. Or when I'm making her breakfast, and turn around, only to see her staring at me. But whenever I try to teach her something new, she doesn't respond and will break out into a temper tantrum.

I take Jasmine to our bathroom. I run a tub of warm water, undress us both, and we sit inside. She's in front of me and I'm looking into her eyes. She's occupied with the pink soap bar and I want her so badly to focus on me.

"Jasmine," I say softly, "Your daddy is dead. What are we going to do now?"

Jasmine babbles like she usually does and places the bar of soap over her little lips. I take it from her and ask her again. This time she slaps the water repeatedly, and I try hard not to be mad at her. I give her back the soap and she quiets down.

Why do I hate her slightly in this moment? God, please forgive me for this feeling. I want her to grieve like I do, because her father is dead. At least then I would know that she's alive. Why did God give me a baby who can't love me back? All of the medicine and therapy we give her doesn't make her respond. And, I hate her for it. But, I hate myself the most for feeling this way.

After I wash us up, I pick her up and walk to the bedroom. Bradley's blue baseball cap is on the dresser, where he left it right before he went to LA. I pick it up and place it on Jasmine's head. She throws it off and plays with her fingers instead. She doesn't understand what she just did. She doesn't care. Suddenly I'm jealous of her and wish I could feel nothing too.

After getting us both dressed, my phone rings. It's my mother, and I sigh. My mother is 550 pounds and confined to the bed due to her size. She can't do anything for herself. When she needs a sponge bath, I wash her flesh. When she needs groceries, I pack her refrigerator. When she needs medicine, I buy it. When she needs someone to talk to, because the perverted men who love large women keep breaking her heart, I console her. It doesn't matter that my older sister Grainger lives there and doesn't do a thing but take advantage of both of us.

"Ma, I can't talk right now," I say trying to slide Jasmine's red sweater over her head. When Jasmine doesn't release her fingers so I can put it on, I separate them. She screams loudly until I'm done. When her sweater is on she plays with her fingers again. "What's up, mama?"

"What's wrong with my granddaughter?" She asks breathing hard into the phone. She's so big that the weight presses against her lungs making it difficult for her to breathe. Not only that, she also has diabetes and Kidney disease but she still won't eat right. "And how come you don't let me spend time with her? I haven't seen Jasmine in over a week. Every time you and Bradley come to visit, ya'll tell me one of your sisters-in-law has her."

"Ma, the last time I let you keep Jasmine she got into the ammonia under the kitchen sink. Do you remember that? Had I not come back when I did, she could've drunk it and died. I would've murdered everybody over there including you. Now if you can't even get out of the bed, you can't watch her."

"Grainger was here," she says. "She was supposed to help me. You know that."

"Well Grainger doesn't give a fuck about me! She doesn't even like her niece."

My mother starts crying. Something she always does when she doesn't get her way. "You hate me! You hate me just because I can't get out of the bed. If Grainger wasn't here I would probably die."

"To this day you take Grainger's side when she can't even stand you."

"Don't say that, Grainger is just sick and she needs help."

"Grainger is on heroin, ma," I yell at her. "That's not sick. That's selfish."

"Well we aren't talking about Grainger. We talking about you and I'm calling because I need your help," she cries louder.

"Ma, please stop crying," I rub my throbbing temples. I contemplate telling her that Bradley is dead, but for some reason, I decide against it. She would probably cry harder, make his death about her to get attention, and I don't need that right now. "I'll bring Jasmine over later to see you okay? I'm sorry for yelling at you, ma. I'm just going through a tough time. Now stop it."

She blows her nose and the noise is so loud I feel like she's doing it in my ear. "Thank you, Denim. I don't know what I would do without you."

I sigh. "It's fine, Ma. Now what do you need?"

"I asked Grainger to get my medicine for my diabetes and some ice cream, but she don't have no money right now. Can you get it for me?"

All I want to do is stay in my bed, but if I don't help her, Grainger won't. Remembering how much I despise my sister and her conniving ways, also reminds me of Bradley and how we fell in love.

# 5 YEARS EARLIER

*Denim Cotton watched as her sister Grainger pulled her panties out of the drawer and onto the floor on the hunt for her 9-millimeter handgun.*

*Denim stood in the doorway horrified for a few reasons. Number one she didn't want her sister getting locked up, and number two she loved Bradley and didn't want him hurt, despite the fact that Bradley was Grainger's boyfriend, and not hers.*

*When Grainger found the silver handgun, she loaded and cocked the weapon. She made a move for the doorway but Denim blocked her path. Bradley was in the living room unaware that his life was in danger.*

*"Grainger, why are you about to shoot him?" Denim asked. "Bradley loves you and he doesn't deserve this."*

*"Because, I know the nigga is stepping out on me," Grainger explained trying to push Denim out of the way. "He only comes over here once a week, and when he does stop by he doesn't stay long. I can't even remember the last time we fucked."*

*"What are you talking about, Grainger? The man does everything for you that you ask. Not only that, he was the one who bought Ma her new wheelchair when she couldn't walk anymore."*

*Four years ago Sarah Cotton could get around a little with a cane. But when she broke her ankle, she was confined to a wheelchair. It was Bradley Kennedy who came to Sarah's rescue. He paid for a hospital grade king size bed, which could handle her weight, and a new wheelchair. So Denim thought Grainger was being greedy and ridiculous.*

*"I don't give a fuck about what he does for that fat bitch,"* Grainger yelled in Denim's face as if Sarah was not her mother. *"I'm talking about me."* She stabs an index finger into her flat breasts. *"I know he doesn't love me anymore and if I can't have him, nobody will."*

*"Grainger, if you kill him you'll go to jail,"* Denim sobbed uncontrollably. *"Please don't do this. I'm gonna die if you kill him."*

*Grainger stepped back and looked into her sister's eyes. "Why are you so worried about what I do to Bradley?"* She stepped closer to Denim. *"Are you in love with him or something?"*

*Denim was worried that the sound of her heartbeat would give her feelings away. No she hadn't fucked Bradley. Neither knew the other had feelings, but there was love between them all the same. Their unconscious love was evident to everyone but Greedy Grainger.*

*Grainger should've known right away that Bradley and Denim were falling in love. When Denim was diagnosed with Tuberculosis, Bradley packed a bag, paid for all of her treatment, and didn't leave their house until she got better. It was obvious where his heart lied, and it wasn't with Grainger.*

*"I'll kill him before I let you have him, Denim,"* Grainger said pointing the gun at her. *"And, then I'll kill you too."* Grainger pushed her out of the way and ran to the living room. When she got there, Bradley was gone.

*Denim didn't breathe until she knew he was safe...for now anyway.*

*"You know what, I'm done with that nigga,"* Grainger said, mad she couldn't kill him. *"He's not worth going to jail. But he's gonna wish for the day he could taste this pussy again."*

Just the thought of Bradley fucking Grainger made Denim sick. She had to walk outside to catch her breath. The moment the door closed behind her, Denim covered her mouth and cried silently into the night. She couldn't understand how she could be in love with a man whose only crime was being a good friend. When she stepped down the block, she was thrown off when she saw Bradley's silver Maserati. Slowly Denim approached the beautiful silver car.

"Get in," Bradley told her sternly.

Denim looked back at the house to be sure Grainger wasn't coming. When the coast was clear, she eased into the car. "What are you still doing here?" Denim asked although she was excited to see his face. "If Grainger sees you out here, she's going to kill you. She's going to kill us both."

"Listen to me," he said looking out ahead of him. "I don't love your sister," he looked into her eyes. "I never have, and I never will. I stayed around because I knew that was the only way I could see your face. I didn't want to put you in a position where you had to choose between your sister and me. But, I can't live without you anymore, Denim," Bradley grabbed her hand softly. "But I can't come back here and play this game with this bitch either. Now I'm asking you to do the unthinkable, and be with me. Choose me over your family. If you say yes, I will make you the happiest woman on earth, but if you say no, you'll never see me again. What do you want to do?"

Just the idea of never seeing him again forced an answer out of her. She didn't think about what her family would think about her betrayal. She was in love. She needed him to breathe. "I want to go with you," she said softly. "Anywhere."

He smiled, touched her face and put the car in drive.

"Wait... what about my stuff?" She asked him.

"I'll buy you all new clothes to go with your new life. Let your people keep the rest of that shit."

After telling my mother I would pick up her medicine later, I walked downstairs. My sisters were sitting at the table eating breakfast, and I wondered why they looked so normal.

"We knocked on your door earlier," Bambi says to me. "But you didn't answer."

"I was probably giving Jasmine a bath," I respond. *My husband is dead. My husband is dead.*

"We made you and Jasmine a plate," Bambi walks toward me and takes Jasmine out of my arms. She is wearing a white t-shirt, and her army fatigue pants, which makes me nervous. Bambi places Jasmine in her high chair and sits back in her seat, at the head of the table.

"What's going on?" I ask my sisters. I sit next to Scarlett.

"I know it's too early to talk about this since our husbands died, but unfortunately we don't have a lot of time," Bambi says to me. "First I'm going to ask you not to tell anybody that our husbands are dead. I know it's wrong, but it's necessary."

I frown. "Why not?"

"Because, we need to see to it that something happens before we let the family know."

"Bambi, just come out with it," I tell her. "The way I feel right now, the last thing I wanna deal with is bullshit."

"Well, on Saturday there's a meeting going down with the Russians. Kevin and them have already made arrangements for the white to be brought here once the call is placed. Even though they are dead, I think we should arrange to see to it that they get their package...some kind of way."

I give Jasmine a pancake and allow her to eat it like she wants. I'm not hungry. "Bambi, we not talking about no small shit. We talking about the Russians!" I say stabbing my finger on the table. "You know Mitch didn't even want to supply Kevin and them with the weight because he didn't trust the Russians. So why do you want to facilitate the meeting? It's dangerous. The only thing on my mind is that my husband is dead. I don't even know how I'm walking right now."

"I've been crying over Kevin all morning," Bambi says. "We all have cried over our husbands. But, unfortunately we still have a family to take care of. You have Jasmine, I have my twins in high school and we got each other." Bambi walks over to me and kneels down on the floor. "As far as the Russians being dangerous, nobody has met them, not even Kevin and them. So to call the Russians anything other than businessmen is unfair."

"They're Russians for goodness sake," I yell. "They have a reputation of being sneaky."

"We need that money, Denim," Bambi replies. "That's our blood money."

I heard enough. I grab my daughter out of the high chair while she still holds onto her pancake. "I'm not going to be a part of anything that will put us at risk," I place Jasmine's coat on and then mine. "Shame on you for putting us in such a fucked up position too, Bambi. We just lost our husbands, and I can't help but feel that the only thing on your mind is money."

Before going to my mother's house I got another tattoo on my back that read, RIP Bradley. It was my fiftieth tattoo but I doubt it will be my last. Every tattoo on my body means something to me, and getting inked is the only time I can relax. When I'm done I head to my mother's house.

Once I get to there, I open the door with my key. I walk into the kitchen and place her ice cream in the freezer. Then I walk to my mother's room where I can hear the TV blasted. When I bend the corner, a man I don't recognize is rubbing her chunky foot. Why the fuck did she have me bring her medicine and junk food when she has him here?

*My husband is dead. My husband is dead.*

"Hey, baby," she says waving at me with her stocky hand. The blubber under her arm shakes. "Come over here and give me some love. I miss you."

Jasmine ignores her, sits on the floor and plays with my mother's size thirteen shoes, which she couldn't wear, because she can't get out of the bed.

"Ma, who is this?" I ask her looking at the man. "You had me run all the way across town for nothing?"

My mother's smile melts into her wiggly face. "He's my future husband. Isn't he handsome?"

"I sure am," he says taking my mother's ashy toe and stuffing it into his mouth. "I'm gonna make her happy too. Just you wait and see."

My mother is smiling but I'm frowning. That's one thing I can say...for her to be morbidly obese, it doesn't mean she can't get a man. I never realized so many men were attracted to women my mother's size until she got this way. *My husband is dead. My husband is dead.*

For a second I blank out and stare at the picture in the red frame above her bed. The photo is of her, Grainger and me. My mother is a size 6 in the photo and we were so happy back then. She was a model and had a full life when we posed for the photo. I can't believe everything has changed.

Later that year, after the picture was taken, she met her boyfriend who she knew from high school. He was a lawyer for a big law firm and had always been obsessed with my mother. Since he would take her to company events, and people would comment on her beauty, he got her fat on purpose so that nobody else would want her. We went out to eat so much, that green mold grew in the refrigerator and stayed. Nobody was ever home. Before, long my mother was overweight and unhappy. When she was so large she could barely walk around, he left her for another woman.

When I remember my husband was just killed, and wonder why I'm even here, I grab Jasmine off the floor and say, "I gotta go, ma. You can do whatever you want, just leave me out of it."

"Is something wrong?" She calls out to me. I don't stop moving for the front door. "Denim, is something wrong?"

When I bend the corner on the way to the front door, I run into my sister. Grainger's face is ashy gray, and she's using heroin although she thinks I don't know. Although, she is forty she looks about fifty-five. She's carrying four fake Louis Vuitton purses in her hand. "I was just about to call you first, before I hit the streets, Denim." She holds up the fakeness and I want to puke. "I got these new purses. You want them before I sell them to anybody?"

"I'm not buying that ugly shit, Grainger." I move toward the door again.

"You know what, you really think you are better than me don't you?" Grainger's voice is low and filled with hate.

"I don't think I'm better, I know I'm better. I'm not the one pushing shit in my veins, Grainger, you are."

She laughs and I see all of her teeth are yellow. "You know what, I have a feeling you gonna fall from grace real soon. And, when you do I'll be here to give you a needle, to push dope into that tatted-up arm. Call it my welcoming party."

"I don't care where I fall, I'll never come back here," I tell her. "You and ma deserve each other, because both of you are pathetic."

"And you not?" She grins. "The one who stole my boy-friend isn't pathetic? And you know what, to this day you never even apologized to me."

"Wrong, Grainger," I say unlocking the door. "The only thing that's pathetic is the fact that your niece been here the en-tire time and you didn't say anything to her."

Grainger looks down at Jasmine and laughs. "That baby is a product of what you get when you steal what belongs to anoth-er woman. Her name shouldn't be Jasmine, it should be Karma instead."

I know I have my daughter's hand. And, I know it's wrong to fight in front of her. But, this was the first time I was glad that Jasmine had a foggy brain because I beat my sister into another mind state for disrespecting my child. I plan to take everything I'm going through out on her too. She just better hope I don't kill her in the process.

# BAMBI

**M**y sisters did exactly what I thought they would do, get scared. I know it may seem insensitive of me to come at them about the Russian meeting, considering our husbands are gone, but I've seen so much shit in Saudi that I'm good under pressure. And, at the end of the day grieving for our husbands right now will not help us take care of our family. We need to take action and grieve later.

"I still can't believe Denim doesn't understand why this is important," I say to Scarlett and Race as I put the last dish in the dishwasher. "We must move now!"

"Bambi, you have to give her time," Scarlett replies. "The only thing on her mind is Bradley right now. To tell you the truth, I don't know why any of us are walking around. Our world has been changed forever." She's rubbing her stomach and I still wonder what got her so sick earlier. She said a stomach virus and I hope it wasn't too bad.

"I know why we are able to walk around, it's because we have each other," Race says. "But I have a feeling tonight, that it's gonna really dawn on us when we are alone in our beds. I'm gonna be honest, in my mind at some point they are coming back home."

"They are never coming back home," I tell Race. "And if ya'll want to blame me for worrying about our futures go right ahead. When you're done answer me this, how will we take care of ourselves if we don't set this meeting up with the Russians?" I throw my arms up and twirl around. "Let me answer it for you," I put my hand on my hips, "we won't be able to take care of ourselves. We lose it all. This house belongs to Bunny, we all know that."

"I understand what you're saying," Scarlett responds rubbing her stomach again. "But tomorrow may have been a little more tasteful to talk about the situation."

Race sits on the sofa and places her face in her hands. "I can't breathe right now," Race says. "I can't feel right now." She looks at me. "And, I certainly can't deal with the Russians. You gotta be fair, Bambi. You gotta let us get ourselves together first."

"How the fuck am I not being fair?" I yell. I walk up to her. "Please tell me? Just because I won't drop to my knees?" I fall to my knees. "Is this better now? Because, at the end of the day, this is not helping us get paper. We need to see to it that the meeting goes down on Saturday. That's how we take care of ourselves. You can cry after that...hell...we all can cry after that."

"What happened to you in that war?" Race asks looking into my eyes. The expression she gives me is as if she doesn't know me anymore. "You never told us. Why?"

I try not to think about my days as a soldier. Partly because being over there is what sparked my alcoholism. It also made me realize that the worst thing you can be in the army is a woman.

# SAUDI ARABIA
# OCTOBER 9 1994

*Dark skies unleashed heavy rainfall onto 19-year-old Bambi Martin and her platoon mate. They were in a firing-hole aka funk hole, holding position and ready to attack. Although Operation Desert Storm was over, Saddam Hussein's son Quasay, decided to conceal illegal Iraqi weapons from the United Nations inspectors. Because of it, President Clinton deployed*

*US Troops to Kuwait. Under Operation Vigilant Warrior, Bambi and her platoon mate were deployed.*

*"I can't take much more of this shit, Bambi," Tatiana Clark said standing next to her in the hole. Water flooded into the hole turning it into mud. "They say women are not supposed to be fighting in the war, but here we are in Kuwait anyway." She looked up at the dark purple sky. "It's like we are invisible. I mean why are we here?"*

*Bambi fucked with Tatiana...hard. But, she could never understand why she complained so much. They both were First Class Privates out of the Infantry School in Georgia. Although, Bambi qualified as an expert shooter, the highest qualification for handling assault weapons, including the powerful M16A2, Tatiana qualified as a Marksman and had been proven to be able to defend herself as well. Yet Tatiana was constantly worried about being able to protect herself.*

*Bambi and Tatiana were two of the only three women in their platoon. Bambi didn't care for the third chick. Since Bambi had been in the army for a year, she considered Tatiana to be her best friend, and because of it she schooled her whenever necessary.*

*Bambi wiped the rain from her eyes and looked through the scope of her weapon, turning everything in her view green. "You here because you got tired of your daddy beating on you after he killed your mother. You here because fewer men enlist in the army, because they not strong like us. We protecting our country," Bambi focused directly on her. "And, I'm here because I want my daddy to know I can do something valuable with my life, despite not going to college." Bambi looked through her scope again. "Now stop fucking around, bitch and stand strong on position. We at war."*

*Bambi's father Brian Martin was a four star general in the army and stationed in the Pentagon. He wanted the college life for his daughter, not war. Brian knew first hand how soldiers raped women. But, Bambi was defiant and enlisted anyway, breaking his heart in the process.*

*Tatiana positioned her weapon and said, "You know what, that's why I love you. You're the only bitch who keeps it real with me."*

*Bambi was focused on her surroundings, but was still aware of Tatiana's pain. "We both from D.C, Tatiana. That's how it should be. I get your back and you get mine, always."*

*When it stopped raining Desseray Fulton showed up with her weapon in tow. She was the third chick in the platoon that Bambi hated. She looked down at them in the hole and said, "Private Clark, Sergeant Hall wants to see you right away. He says it's important."*

*Tatiana immediately grew nervous. Sergeant Hall was a lustful man who could be violent if he didn't get what he wanted. Tatiana saw how he looked at her body when she was cleaning her weapon or talking to Bambi. And, she hated everything about him. Now she had to be with him alone, in a foreign country, and she was terrified.*

*"Why she gotta go back there?" Bambi inquired. "If you ask me he should be good on pussy since I know you hooked him up earlier today."*

*Although the darkness concealed most of Desseray's twisted expression, Bambi could still feel the heat she was giving. "Easy, Private Martin. Don't forget, I'm an E3 and that I outrank you."*

*Bambi and Tatiana were E2's, which basically meant they were paid less. It didn't mean that they deserved less respect, but Desseray didn't care.*

*"Now go see the sergeant," Desseray told Tatiana again. "Now!"*

*Tatiana hopped out of the hole and obeyed her command. When she was gone Desseray leaped in her position in the muddy hole next to Bambi. Desseray set up her weapon and looked out the scope. "You know what's better than killing Ragheads?" Desseray asked Bambi.*

*"I don't give a fuck, but I know you gonna tell me anyway."*

Desseray laughed and said, "Soldier dick. They so rough and horny that even the ugliest bitch is beautiful when they out here. That's why I love the war. Never a shortage of good dick."

"I guess you right," Bambi responded. "Ugly bitches like you can make a come up out here. Knock yourself out."

"But is this sad?" When Bambi faced her, Desseray stuffed her hands in her fatigues, entered her pussy and smeared the cum she let one of the soldiers push inside of her onto Bambi's nose.

Bambi was about to beat her ass back to the States, until Desseray said, "Careful Private, if you get thrown out of the army for hitting a superior, what will your father say? You don't want him thinking you failed do you?"

Bambi was about to respond when in a distance she heard soft cries. Bambi turned her attention to her scope thinking it was a set up and they were under attack. That is until she heard Tatiana say, "Bambi, help me. Please."

Bambi was about to spring out of the hole until Desseray pulled her back by the wrist. "Get the fuck off of me, slut! I gotta go help my friend."

"You better stay out of it," Desseray responded grabbing her weapon in case Bambi got wild. "Taking soldier-dick always hurts in the beginning. Besides, it's her first time. But, I'm going to tell you like I told the other bitches, you better get with the fact that in the army, men rule. The sooner you learn that, the easier the war will be."

Bambi thought about her father. She wanted to make him proud, even though he didn't want her there. So she remained in place. But she felt disloyal as her friend cried out for her while she did nothing. "I can't take it," Bambi yelled. "She's my friend. I gotta go help her."

"You go back there and you'll ruin your career in the military at the same time. Everything you've done up to this point is out the window, Bambi. It will be in vain." As if Desseray cared she said, "Remember your father."

After five minutes, silence stood in place of Desseray's cries. And suddenly, gunfire from the enemy reigned everywhere.

*Bambi ducked deeper into the firing hole because she couldn't see where the attack was coming from. Desseray dropped inside with her. Now they were at war... but with whom?*

I'm sitting on the sofa. While I was trying to convince my sisters about how important the meeting is with the Russians, Bunny comes through the door with her key. Aunt Bunny is six-foot two, irritating and nosey. And, for some reason Kevin couldn't get enough of her. Anything she wanted, she got and Kevin spared no expense. Still, all the money in the world didn't make her an attractive woman. Not only was her height intimidating to some, she was loud and wore a lot of gawky jewelry. Her favorite piece was a gold chain with a huge red ruby in the pendant that Kevin bought her. The chain itself was worth two hundred thousand dollars.

"Hello, Kennedy wives," Bunny says playfully walking into the living room. She walks up to me. "Bambi, have you heard from Kevin? I spoke to him early yesterday but haven't received my call for the evening yet. He calls me once a day to check on me you know."

I stand up and walk toward her. "He's...uh...he'll probably call you later."

Bunny looks at me without saying a word. And, finally she speaks. "Do you like living in my house, Bambi?" She looks at the walls and the vaulted ceilings. "I always told Kevin I must love him a lot to let him stay here."

"And I told Kevin we should have moved a long time ago," I say sternly. "But, he told me you kept begging us to stay. In my mind we doing you a favor."

"He told me you said that," she grins. "But, then I told him why buy another house when this one is available. It's too big for my grandkids and me. I'm quite fine with the half of million-dollar house in Accokeek that he bought me. Needless to say once I weighed in on the situation, it was a wrap. Kevin does everything I say."

I bite my bottom lip when my jaw trembles. "Bunny, what do you want?"

"A few bucks," she walks toward my room and I follow her. "No need in coming behind me Bambi, I know the code to the safe."

I follow her anyway into my closet. When Bunny pushes my new dresses to the side and enters the code to Kevin's safe, I feel like busting her in the back of the head. I hated that Kevin told her so much about our personal lives. He felt if we ever died, he would want Bunny to be able to take care of our sons. I saw her being so involved in our lives more like a nuisance than anything else. But, when it came to her, I couldn't tell him shit. He was blind.

Bunny pulls a few thousand from the fifty thousand dollar stack and I do all I can to keep a straight face. If I tell her Kevin is dead, and that the fifty thousand is all I have left in the world, she'll throw me and my sisters out with the quickness. I have to let her financially rape me, and convince my sisters that we must see to it that the meeting goes through as planned.

Bunny tucks the money in her dirty white bra. She steps out of the closet and sits on the edge of *my* bed. "I never did understand why you all would spend millions of dollars on furniture," she touches the gold leaves on the bed. "But, I must say, it is beautiful." She looks up at the cream silk canopy drape.

"You have the money, Bunny. Now what else do you want?"

"How are my grandsons? It must be hard on them being seventeen and thrown into boarding school."

"First of all they aren't your grandsons," I correct her. "You're not Kevin's mother, you're his aunt. Second of all they are fine so don't worry about them. You'd do much better focusing on yourself."

I sent the twins away to boarding school because they were seeing too much money being around us. I wanted them to have an education and a chance at a real life. And, since I knew Kevin was getting out of the drug game soon anyway, I decided they would be best there until he was completely out.

Bunny seems angry about my comment but doesn't respond. "I know you're happy about Saturday aren't you?" She looks into my eyes. She wants me to know that she is aware about the Russians.

I frown. I hate her so much it probably shows in the way my limbs move, but I don't have control over how I feel about her. "I don't know what you talking about," I lie.

She stands up and walks toward my dresser. She picks up a picture of my husband. My skin crawls. She holds it to her face and rubs her index finger over Kevin's head. Suddenly she sits it down and gives me an evil look. "I don't know if Kevin told you, but I am very overprotective of him. To the point where if something happens to him, and I not know about it, I can be a problem."

"Bunny, what exactly are you trying to say to me?" I ask preparing to kill her. "Are you trying to say that I did something to my husband?"

"Let me put it this way, Bambi, when you hold back on me it makes me think you're hiding something from me. I don't like people like that."

"Stop beating around the bush, Bunny. Stand taller and tell me what's on your mind."

"Well here it is, you and I both know about this meeting with the Russians on Saturday. All I'm asking is if you're happy or not, because Kevin is leaving the game for you." She looks in the direction of my crouch. "I guess that pussy is golden after all. To make a man leave what he does best."

"Bunny, you better—"

"I better what," Bunny inquires using her size and weight to intimidate me by walking into my space. "You tell me just what the fuck I better do."

"For starters you better get the fuck out of my face, you big ugly bitch, before you won't be able too."

She steps back and smirks. "Something is going on, because if Kevin was around you would never talk to me like that."

"I'm sorry for the disrespect," I say realizing my mistake.

"I know you are, cunt," she tells me. "Now...Kevin takes care of me and my family, and this thing you did to him by making him leave the drug business hurts us all. What kind of woman would want her man to get out of the game that has given her everything? You're disloyal to the business that made you, soldier. And, I'm just letting you know."

As she walks out of my bedroom, I can feel the word bitch roll upward in my stomach, rise into my throat and walk over my tongue. I swallow it back down, because I don't want to give her the satisfaction of having gotten to me.

Instead I walk into my closet, and toward my pink safe. I need a drink now more than ever. Just one taste. I'm about to put the code in when Scarlett and Race come into my room.

Scarlett walks up to me and pulls me to her. Her body is warm and her red hair smells like strawberries. I want to cry on her shoulders, but I feel the need to be strong right now. After what I've seen in the military, I can handle this. Right? Well why am I trembling, and hoping she doesn't let me go?

"Are you okay," Scarlett asks separating from me and rubbing the sides of my face with her cold hands.

I walk away from the attention. It's too much. I sit on the edge of my bed. I don't say anything at first. Instead I allow the silence to speak for me. When I'm ready, I look at them both sternly. Scarlett's pale cheeks redden and Race is shaking so hard, the tentacles of her hair quiver.

"Bunny is one of the reasons that meeting with the Russians must go down," I say. "If we give up the opportunity to secure our financial destinies, we won't have anything. That man-looking bitch will move into this house, and throw us out on the street. We have to do this for each other; otherwise our husbands would have died in vain. What are ya'll going to do?"

# SCARLETT

I told Bambi she had my full support, and I meant it. I don't want to give this lifestyle up. And, since I met my family, and experienced true love with my sisters, I don't want to let them go either.

When I walk into my bedroom, I strut to my red dresser. Everything in my room is black and red, they are Camp's favorite colors. I open my bottom drawer, push my silk underwear to the left and remove a pregnancy test from a pack of two. I go into the bathroom and remove my underwear. My feet nestle into the red carpet in front of the tub and toilet. Before, sitting down I place my hand on my belly. Can I take care of another child if I am pregnant without hurting it too?

I sit on the coal black toilet and remove a pregnancy test from the pack. I look down at the red strip of hair running down my vagina. Camp likes a little hair so I never shaved it all off. I push down hard to pee so that I can use the test, but nothing is coming out. Maybe unconsciously I don't want to take the test. Maybe I don't want to know if I'm pregnant or not.

When the private phone line rings in my bathroom, I raise up to answer the call. I take the red and black cordless handset, and sit back on the toilet. I never get any calls with the exception of Camp, so I wonder who is on the other line. "Hello," I sigh still trying to pee.

"Scarlett, how are you this morning?" Bunny asks me.

I take the phone from my ear and look at it crazily. What the fuck does she want with me? I hated Bunny more than Bambi, after she called me a dumb white bitch when Camp told her he was marrying a white woman. "I'm fine," I remember my husband is dead and that my response is a lie. "I guess."

"I feel so bad about earlier. I came over to get my allowance from Kevin, and I didn't even speak to you. How rude of me."

"Bunny, I'm tired right now so can you please call back later?" I rise up to hang up the phone until I hear what she says next.

"How is your daughter," Bunny asks. "Has her vision come back, or is it still lost forever?"

I sit back down on the toilet. Urine finally releases itself from my body, and I forget to use the test. "I...I don't know what you're talking about. I...don't have any—"

"You were married before you got with Camp," she cuts me off. "Your ex-husband's name is Mark Kirk. He divorced you due to domestic violence. While divorced, your daughter Samantha stayed in your care. You lost your temper, although I'm not sure why, and sprayed something in your child's face resulting in her permanent blindness. Your husband filed to have her removed from your home, and you were due in court to answer to charges of child abuse. Instead of staying and facing the charges, you ran off with a black man and marry him. To this day there are warrants out for your arrest," she pauses. "Now Scarlett Kennedy, are you sure you want to tell me you don't know what I'm talking about?"

Silence.

"What do you want?" I ask as tears roll down my face. I cry harder on this toilet than I did when I first learned my husband was killed. "Why are you doing this to me? I've never bothered you, Bunny!"

"Shut the fuck up, bitch," Bunny tells me. "Now answer my question, did Bambi do anything to Kevin?"

"What?" I yell wiping my tears. "No! Bambi would never do something to Kevin. She loves him too much."

"Well has something happened to him, and the rest of my family members? Because, Kevin hasn't called me today, and it's out of character for him."

"I don't know anything about that, Bunny," I say in a breathy tone. "I'm sure he'll call you later," I lie. "Just give him some time. It's still early." I feel faint. My stomach churns and I sob louder.

"Calm down, Scarlett," she says. "Now I believe you don't know anything, but I'm not sure about that Bambi bitch. So I want you to keep your eyes and ears open, and I'll call you back later when I need you."

Before Bunny hangs up I ask, "What about the things you know about me?"

Bunny laughs. "Scarlett, my dear, I won't tell anything about your past. So rest easy."

I exhale. I'm not a racist person, but the word nigger sits on the edge of my tongue, and I contemplate yelling it out.

"After all," she continues, "I know that if I tell that you're a baby beater, that no one won't want to have anything else to do with you. They'll probably throw you out on your lily-white ass and everything. The last thing I want to see is you out on the streets. I need you," she giggles. "I'll be in contact soon, Scarlett. Enjoy the rest of your evening, but please remember that I own you."

# BAMBI

I open the door when my doorbell rings. When I see Cloud standing outside, I cringe. Does he know about what happened in LA to Kevin? I need the secret of Kevin's murder to keep until Saturday.

"Hello, Cloud," I say not as mean as I normally am to him. "What do you need?"

He walks in and kisses me on the lips again. His lips are cold today, not warm like they usually are. I think about what Kevin said, about him not kissing me, but bite my tongue.

"What's up, kid?" He asks walking into the house. "Kevin hasn't called me to tell me what he wants to do with his truck. You talk to him yet?"

I follow him toward the living room. He's very attractive and I could never understand why he didn't have a girlfriend in his life. He seemed content hanging around the eight of us on the solo tip. I guess he was trying to get at me.

"He called earlier," I lie clearing my throat. "He didn't say anything about his truck though. When he calls back, I'll ask him what he wants you to do with it then."

He looks at my fatigues. "Aw shit. What's going on?" He walks up to me and rubs my shoulders. Why does he touch me so freely when I don't give him permission? It makes me nervous. "You two have a fight again?"

I step out of his embrace. "No, I'm fine. But, I'll tell Kevin you came by."

"Bambi, what's wrong with you? I know I'm not my cousin, but you can talk to me about most anything. I know you know that. But, holding a grudge against me this long is totally ridiculous."

I want to tell him about his cousin. I want someone other then my sisters to know about what happened to Kevin. I can still see the darkness of his blood that came into view on my iPad when he was killed. But, I can't trust anyone right now. I'm still unclear on who the enemy is and who may have a stake in the one hundred million dollars on Saturday.

"Cloud, I really want to get some sleep. I lied to you earlier, Kevin and me did have another argument, and you're right, I'm taking it pretty hard right now. But, its marriage shit and it's nothing for you to worry about. Besides, you made that clear to me before remember? When I came to you about him?"

He seems disappointed.

I walk to the door and open it. "I'll tell Kevin to call you," I say to him. "Okay?"

He walks toward me, kisses me on my lips again and rubs his hand over my face. Without saying anything else, he walks out. I watch him until he enters his car and closes the door. For some reason, I have an idea. Although Kevin and his cousins can't attend the meeting, I know someone who can.

I sit on my bed and call Mitch McKenzie. Mitch is a longtime friend, and supplier of the Kennedy Kings. At first I thought he was a gimpy white man, who was hanging with the Kennedy Kings for some sort of thug clout. Before long I discovered that Mitch was not a thug, he was the Kings best kept secret.

I'm a true hustler's wife. Some bitches call themselves hustler's wives but can't tell you that in 2010, Peru surpassed Columbia in the production of *pure* cocaine. Columbia's coco crops get thinned out on a regular basis by toxins, reducing the quality. However Peru's crops are mostly untouched by toxins, so we talking about that pure shit. The organic. The white gold. Virgin Pussy.

What most so-called hustler wives also can't tell you is that global warming has changed our world. What does this mean? Natural disasters. In my area alone we've had back-to-back hurricanes that caused a lot of damage. This means that more people are needed to help those experiencing disasters. And, this is where Mitch comes in.

Twenty years ago, Mitch McKenzie, a geeky white boy out of Florida State, started *Sweet Rice Charities*. He didn't like what he was seeing due to humans destroying the planet. So he gathered a bunch of his college friends, and they went around the world to help people who were affected by natural disasters. After awhile Mitch discovered that he was using his own money, and it was getting hard to find government funding. Mitch was worried that he wouldn't be able to help others, and take care of his wife and kid since he started a family. He considered giving it all up, after selling his assets. Mitch's charity Sweet Rice had access to planes and vehicles, which came in and out of the country. If he sold them he stood to make a lot of paper.

Before he put his possessions up for sale, he was approached by the Columbian Cartel to smuggle cocaine into the US using one of his authorized planes. The payout was lovely so he accepted the offer. After the job, Mitch immediately received the funding necessary to keep his foundation going. What he also got was an idea. For the right price, he could smuggle cocaine into the US himself, without the Cartel.

To have a reason for being in and out of the country, Mitch expanded Sweet Rice into the United States. During the tornados in 1999 in Oklahoma, Sweet Rice charities was there to help families regain some semblance of a life. For real you could name any recent natural disaster and I'll bet you my Double R parked out front that Mitch's charity was there.

Things were sweet until something happened...9/11. Now airspace was restricted, but fortunately the service that Mitch and Sweet Rice provided for so many countries, allowed him to retain the use of their airspace.

Before long Mitch put officers and government officials on payroll, and flew his planes in and out of the country with impunity. He changed his cocaine crops to Peru, because the quality of Columbia's cocaine was not the same, and he met the Kennedy Kings. That's where our history started.

My husband and his brothers are the distributors of Mitch's cocaine. As a result, the Kennedy Kings are the exclusive suppliers of this product in the US. You talking about pure cocaine for the price it would cost you to get that stepped on bullshit in the streets. This exclusivity in the price and quality of Mitch's cocaine made the Kings product sought after and desired. This is what brought the Russians to us.

Mitch isn't about being greedy. He just wants enough to take care of his family, and support his charity, but the man is still filthy rich. So, he sells the Kings the coke so cheaply, that they have become the best cocaine connects in the industry.

I tell Kevin all the time that Mitch is a hypocrite, even though I like him. He flies cocaine into his own country, but has a charity for helping people in need. Kevin said Mitch has no respect for people who abuse drugs. But, those needing help due to natural disasters deserves help. Since my life is a disaster, I wonder if he'll help me now.

I call Mitch and his phone rings once before he answers. "Hey, beautiful." He tells me. I'm relieved because I know he could not have heard about Kevin's death yet. It gives me more time. "Are you calling me to tell me that you and Kevin are finally coming to visit me again in Mexico?" Mitch owns an island in Mexico, and loves it there so much he has been trying to get us to relocate forever.

I think about my husband not being here anymore, and pull myself together. Mitch is a drug boss and can smell lies. "I was actually calling you for something else," I say.

"Before you do that let me tell you congratulations on having five years clean. Kevin tells me all the time how proud he is of you, and I feel the same way, Bambi."

I feel warm inside. Despite not knowing how much longer I can stay alcohol free, it makes me feel good that he remembers. "Thank you, Mitch. That means a lot to me."

"I sent you the entire Louis Vuitton winter collection as a gift for your accomplishment, it should be arriving there shortly."

"I can't wait to receive it," I tell him. I clear my throat again. "Mitch, I'm calling on a serious matter. I really need your help."

"Almost anything," he says. And, I believe him.

"As you know there is a very important meeting coming up," I say. "Is it possible for you to meet with the Russians on Saturday instead of Kevin? His flight home may be delayed."

Mitch hangs up. What just happened? A second later my phone rings again. Mitch's voice is deeper, and I discover immediately that there's another side to him. The boss side I didn't know before, because I've never talked to him on a business level.

"Bambi, is something wrong with the Kennedy Kings?" I figure he's on a secure line now. He sounds serious. All of the love he had for me is stripped from his voice.

"No...uh..."

"Well let me clear something up for you, sweetheart," he pauses. "I didn't get to where I am in the business by meeting people. I don't deal with anyone but the Kennedy Kings. And, in the event something happens to them, I have secured enough money to be able to take care of myself and my grandchildren's grandchildren for the rest of their lives. When the Kings are out I'm done with this business altogether. I call it early retirement."

The thought of being cut off of his supply scares me, and I don't know why. It's not like I'm planning to stay in the business after this meeting with the Russians.

"Now I'm going to ask you again, is something wrong with the Kings?" He continues. "Because a very special delivery is in route and I need to know now to stop it."

"No," I tell him quickly. "Kevin is okay."

"Good, now don't ever call me in this way again."

He hangs up. I'm stuck. I'm lost. If Mitch won't do it, and the Russians are expecting our husbands, I don't know what else to do. I can't bring random niggas in the picture. For that amount of money they'll kill us.

I walk toward Race's room when I hear her talking to Scarlett. When I enter, I see Race and Scarlett at her dresser's mirror. Race's back is faced me, and she is wearing one of her husband's Washington Redskins sweatshirts. The hood is hiked up over her head, and the shirt swallows up her frame making her look like a boy from behind. Had it not been for her bare legs, I would not have known...

I would not have known...

I would not have known that she was a *woman*.

They say great ideas come in times of extreme desperation. Because, as I look at her I suddenly realize what we must do. Avery can't meet the Russians on Saturday, and now that I think about it, even if he could I wouldn't trust him with our money. Mitch doesn't want to meet with them to keep his privacy. So, it has to be us. And, since the Russians are expecting the Kings who they never met before, we have to give them what they want. The Kennedy Kings. I just need to see to it that Avery isn't there, because he'll recognize us.

I walk into the room and touch Race on the shoulder. She jumps at my touch. "What's wrong I ask?"

"I miss Ramirez so much," Race sobs looking into my eyes. She takes her hood off and hugs me. "What are we going to do?"

I sigh. Unable to have my real cry until this meeting with the Russians is over. "I saw the news again earlier today," I tell them both. "For now they are unable to identify the bodies, but I'm sure that will change soon." I sit on the edge of Race's bed. She doesn't have any sheets on it and I wonder why. "Which, means we definitely have to push forward with this meeting with the Russians before its too late and the shipment is stopped. If Mitch finds out they are dead we are cut off."

"I told you to sign me up," Scarlett says, proving more to me that she's more go-hard then the rest.

I look at Race. "I'm scared of the Russians. I'm scared of everybody. And, if you make me do it I'm going to tell Bunny, and the rest of the Kennedy family that they are dead. We should probably be doing that anyway. They have a right to know."

If there is nothing else in life I hate, a snitch-bitch is it. "Race, don't ever say something like that to me again, or else our bond is done. I'll move in this world as if I don't even know you. Do you understand what I'm saying? If I can't love you I'll hate you."

Silence.

"She didn't mean it like that," Scarlett says rubbing Race's shoulders. "She's just afraid that's all. We all are."

"Even if we wanted to tell the rest of the Kennedy's that they are gone, we don't even have their bodies yet. So the information is useless." I pause. "I look dead into their eyes. My lips tighten and tremble again. "There comes a time in your life when you have to stand for something or fall for anything. Now is that time."

# DENIM

When I walk into the house, I take Jasmine up to bed and stomp to the bathroom in my room to wash my hands. My knuckles are bloodied and bruised due to fighting my sister. I hurt her badly too. My mother tried to get out of the bed to stop me from beating the breaks off of Grainger, but when she rolled over to step off of the bed, she fumbled to the floor.

It took me, Grainger, her new boyfriend and the D.C. fire department to put her back in bed. I hated my sister for making me hit her, although part of me was happy that she did. I was able to relieve some of the stress I feel from not having Bradley around anymore. Although it helped, it didn't stop the pain permanently.

My sister would love nothing more than to see me fall from grace. And, for me to have to move back home, and be forced into slavery by my fat ass mother. I can't let her have the satisfaction. I won't let her have it.

I catch the elevator downstairs to Bambi's room. When I reach her bedroom door, I notice it's closed. I turn the knob anyway, and walk inside, closing the door behind me. When I hear her talking to herself, I move toward her closet. She goes there a lot to think.

Suddenly I stop, because from where I stand I can see what she is doing. She isn't facing me. She's on the floor, in full military gear. She's still wearing fatigues, the matching jacket and a green hard hat. Her bare feet, dressed in red toenail polish, are the only thing that is feminine on her. A black machine gun lies at her feet, and I wonder what she's going to do with it. What happened to her in that war? And why won't she talk to us about it?

When I step closer to the closet, I notice the smell of vodka. It's strong. Coming out of her pores. Which, means she's been drinking for a long time. My stomach rumbles. After five years, she's given up sobriety. *Damn, Bambi.*

"I know what you must think of me," Bambi says to me without looking at me. I didn't even know she knew I was there. "You think I'm weak." She laughs to herself and strokes the bottle. "Maybe I am." She removes her hard hat and places it on the floor.

I walk closer. "Why, Bambi? You were doing so good? Yesterday you had five years sobriety and everything."

Bambi gazes at me. Her eyes are red. She's so beautiful and so vulnerable now. I hardly see her like this on a regular. "It was bound to happen after awhile anyway, Denim." She strokes the bottle in her hand like it's a big dick. "Without Kevin, there's no need to stay sober. I need this shit just to be able to concentrate." She raises the bottle. "Who am I without alcohol anyway?"

I walk into the huge walk in closet and sit down next to her. I look up and see both her and Kevin's clothes hanging up. When I look toward the back of the closet, I can see a section of military gear, which wasn't there before. With the exception of a few pants, she kept that kind of stuff in the basement. Topics about the war were taboo in our home.

"What about us, Bambi? The sisters?" I place my hand on her knee. "We need you sober."

She laughs at me. Or she laughs at my comment. I can't be sure. "You guys don't need me. Everybody thinks meeting the Russians isn't necessary, and I don't know what to do anymore."

I remove my hand from her knee. It drops in my lap. I don't know if I want to say what I intended to before coming into her room, and seeing her like this. In the condition that she's in, I'm not sure she's able to lead us now. "I don't think meeting with the Russians is unnecessary," I say softly. "I'm ready to do it." I look at the bottle. "If you are."

She spins her head in my direction and her eyes widen. I just made her day. I can feel it. A smile spreads across her face. "Are you serious, Denim?" She asks.

"Yes," I respond although I'm still not sure. "I am."

She stands up and I stand up too. We hug and my foot rubs against the riffle on the floor. "Can we get out of here?" I look down at it. "I don't feel safe here."

When we walk into her bedroom, there's a knock at the door. I open it and Race and Scarlett come inside. They look at Bambi and I can tell the Russians have been the only topic of discussion today. It's all in their eyes and they seemed drained.

"Race has something to tell you," Scarlett tells Bambi.

Race looks at her hands and then faces Bambi. "I'll do it. I'll go with you to meet the Russians," she cries. "But I'm still scared. We've never been involved in any of their business before. How can we be sure that we can even do this?"

Bambi rushes Scarlett and Race and the three of them combine their hug. I feel left out. "Can somebody bring me up to speed?" I ask.

Bambi separates from them and walks into the middle of her bedroom. "They are agreeing to meet with the Russians," she starts, "the only thing is if we are going to do it, we can't meet them like this. We must look differently."

"Okay, so what's the plan?" I ask her.

Bambi walks up to me. "We have to dress like men," she holds my hands firmly, like she's offering me physical support. "If we are going to attend this meeting, we have to *be* our husbands."

I snatch away from her. "What the fuck are you talking about?" I walk across her room and it seems like it takes me forever to get to the wall because it's so large. "The Russians aren't stupid, Bambi. We can't go in there, wear men's clothing and try to trick them. Why do we even have to lie? We got the work not them."

"Because, Avery said they only want to meet with Kevin and them," Bambi responds.

"But we look like fucking females and to tell you the truth, I'm happy about it," I reply.

She walks closer, but stops before reaching me. "Denim, we can do this shit. I'm telling you. I thought the entire thing out in my mind earlier tonight. When I was in the army I had to, I mean, I developed the ability to dumb down my appeal. I got rid of anything feminine about me, and that included my voice."

"Why?"

She doesn't respond. "Bambi, why did you do that?" I ask again.

"It doesn't matter," she says. "Just know that I did it. And, since Race makes silicone masks all the time, she can make ones for us. This meeting will go of without a problem if we all commit to it."

"They have to be partial masks because the full ones will limit facial features," Race responds letting her nerd come out.

"I don't care what you say, you not going to be able to sound like a man—,"

Bambi drops her voice and says, "Don't tell me what I won't be able to do." Her low throaty words sound so much like a man; I look around the room to see what nigga has slid inside of here. I get chills all over my body. If she would've called me with that voice, I would not have believed it was her.

"I can do this," Bambi says in her regular voice. "I can facilitate this meeting. I just need the three of you there."

"Well what about the rest of us," I say throwing my hands up. "I can't do any of that shit. And, just one look at Race will give us away."

"Thanks for the vote of confidence," Race replies.

"I don't want you to sound like me," Bambi says. "The only thing you have to do is learn to stand like a man, and you gotta do that in five days. I'll do all of the talking and everything." She looks at all of us. "You have to trust me."

"I'm not going to lie, since Bambi has stopped drinking she's been reliable," Scarlett says to us. "If she thinks we can do it, I'm going to follow her."

Bambi wipes her mouth with the back of her hand. I guess to wipe the guilt or vodka from her lips.

"This is dangerous, Bambi," I say. I want to remind her that she just drank a whole bottle of vodka in the closet, but don't want to do it in front of our sisters. "We are talking about Russian drug dealers, Bambi. Are you sure about this?"

"I was in the US military for two years, and I was the best at what I did," she says to me. "Trust me, I can bring us through this meeting alive." She looks at all of us again. "Are you all in or what?"

It takes forever, but one by one we say yes.

Having gotten her way, Bambi smiles and claps her hands together excitedly. She's about to say something until her phone rings. She walks over to it and holds the receiver closely to her ear. Then she says, "Hello." Silence. "Don't worry, Avery," she looks at all of us. "You can tell the Russians that The Kings will be there. That much I promise you."

# THE RUSSIANS

*A*very Graham sits in his dining room chair. Across from him he observes his beautiful wife Tiffany and their nine-year old daughter Crystal. Any other time this would be the perfect picture of family and love, instead its one of the worst days of his life.

The black scarf tied in Tiffany's mouth is so tight that the lower part of her brown face is blue. His daughter Crystal's eyes are covered as well as her mouth. The only thing Avery can see on her is her nose. Both of them are tied in the chair, with their arms behind their backs. They've been like this for days, only being untied once a day to eat and use the bathroom.

"They'll be there," Avery tells The Russians after ending the call with Bambi. He looks at his family. "I'm so sorry." He begins to cry. "Please forgive me," he says to his wife and kid.

"Good work, Avery," Iakov Lenin says rubbing his shoulder. "And don't worry about your family, they're fine." His Russian accent is definite. The clear cup of vodka he never leaves home without is held firmly in his hand. "You did well." He scratches his brown hair with his free hand.

"Yes, I agree," responds Arkadi Lenin, Iakov's brother. He sits on the edge of the table and looks down at Avery. "Before long we will be out of your hair," he palms Avery's head, "and your beautiful family will be back together."

*The Russians have piercing blue eyes and feline like features. Their lips slant downward and clues of their heritage are written all over their faces.*

*The Russians came to America many years ago with the dream of becoming engineers. They migrated to Alaska and pursued their goal with great passion. As they observed modern lifestyle, they noticed that he who had lots of money, made the rules. Making a mere one hundred thousand dollars yearly would not suffice. If they were going to be rich, they needed a foot into the drug trade.*

*The Russians put their money together and moved to Maryland. They could've gone to popular cocaine cities like Los Angeles and Las Vegas, but the markets were oversaturated with drug kingpins already. But in Maryland, they could learn the business and move slowly. They bought a cocaine pack from a small time dealer name Rico, and sold it to a few rock bands on the coast. At first business was good, but before long they lost their clientele because the quality of Rico's product decreased although his prices increased. Their business with Rico wasn't in vain, because the Russians studied him carefully. When he wasn't looking, they learned whom he did business with, and documented the hand-to-hand cats in Rico's territory. When The Russians learned all they needed to know from Rico, they met another connect in Mexico called, Shorty Valdez.*

*With Shorty in their pocket, they murdered Rico, froze his body parts and sent them to the lieutenants in his organization. The message was clear. Get with us or die. Using fear, The Russians claimed Rico's soldiers and territory. Before long, their reach extended to Maryland, D.C., Virginia and parts of New York. But, they wanted to be bigger.*

*After some time they grew even larger but Shorty refused to drop his rates despite the business The Russians were giving him. Before long they learned of the Kennedy Kings, drug connects in the Washington D.C. area that had the purest cocaine the United States had ever seen. Since they couldn't reach the Kennedy Kings directly, no matter how hard they tried, they eventually were introduced to Avery Graham, one of their distributors.*

*Although Avery stepped on his product a few times, the quality was still better than that of Shorty Valdez and Rico's put together. So the Russians dropped their relationship with Shorty and used Avery exclusively.*

*For a year, without conflict, The Russians watched Avery turn from a small time drug lord with a few cars and a medium sized home, to a bigger dealer with several businesses and a larger home. But, when The Russians asked to meet the Kennedy Kings directly, Avery refused to introduce them. Not only would putting them in direct contact with the Kennedy Kings risk his pocket money, the Kennedy Kings didn't meet anyone. It wasn't until they hogtied Avery's wife and daughter, that Avery was willing to talk to Kevin and schedule the meeting.*

*Getting the Kennedy Kings to meet with The Russians was easier said than done. When Avery said that the Russians wanted to meet with them, Kevin was suspicious from the gate and he wasn't interested. But when The Russians asked for one hundred million dollars worth of cocaine, suddenly they became important enough to the Kings.*

*To see to it that the meeting went as scheduled, The Russians moved into Avery's home and took over his family. They allowed him to conduct business as usual on the streets, as long as the wire in his pocket, which allowed them to see and hear everything he did, wasn't removed. One false move on Avery's part would result in his home being missiled with his family inside.*

*"Please don't hurt my family," Avery says as he looks at his family.*

*"Why would we do such a thing?" Arkadi says touching his ear. "After all, who's more honest than the Russians?"*

*"Nobody," Avery says.*

# MONDAY
# NOVEMBER 5$^{TH}$ 2012
# 5 00 PM

# AUNT BUNNY

*B*unny *pushes Jasmine's wooden picnic table through the cold grass. The biceps in her arms buckle as she puts it in place. She looks to the left and right, and when ready steps onto the table part, increasing her height. The table cracks under her weight, but supports her for the time being.*

*It is now Monday, and she still hasn't heard from Kevin. Now Bunny is expecting the worst. This was the first time she could remember that Kevin ever went days without calling her. Something dark was going on in the Kennedy residence, and she believed Bambi with her sick military mind was involved.*

*Slowly she raises her body, until her forehead and eyes are peering into Bambi's bedroom. From where Bunny stands, she can see a vodka bottle in her hands.*

*"I knew that bitch was drinking again," she says to herself. "Once and alcoholic always an alcoholic.*

*When Bambi pops up, and looks around her room, fearing she would be seen, Bunny stoops down and falls off of the table, and into the cold grass. She quickly stands up, dusts herself off and walks to the front of the house. When she see's a large brown box out front, she nosily opens it up. It's the new Louis Vuitton winter collection Mitch bought for Bambi. She walks it to her car, pops the trunk and tosses it inside. After stealing, she waddles back up to Bambi's door.*

*Taking a few quick breaths, Bunny digs into her purse, and removes her keys. When she opens the door to the house, Bambi is waiting for her in the foyer. She is not holding the liquor bottle.*

*"When are you going to get enough of snooping around on me, Bunny?" Bambi asks. "I mean don't you have anything better to do with your time?"*

*Bunny is shocked. She thought she was being sneaky, and was caught red-handed. "If you don't want nobody looking through your window, you should close the curtains."*

*"If I do that, how else would you be able to sneak in on me?" Bambi responds. "You've been doing it for seventeen years, Bunny. Get a fucking life already, and stay out of ours."*

*Bunny's face turns red. "Where is Scarlett? I have to talk to her about something."*

*Bambi steps close to her. "After the way you treated Scarlett years ago, I doubt she has anything to say to you."*

*Bunny smirks. "That bottle of vodka you were drinking in the bedroom looked good. I wonder what your sisters would say if they knew you were drinking again." Bunny loved having dirt on people she chose to control. Without dirt, she was useless. "I bet you wouldn't be so high on the pedestal then, now would you?"*

*The smirk on Bambi's face was wiped off. She looks down at her feet and shakes her head. Then she looks up into Bunny's eyes. "If you gonna tell them, go ahead and do it. I'm not about to kiss ass for nobody, and if I started it definitely wouldn't be yours."*

*Bunny pushes past Bambi and meets Race, Scarlett and Denim in the living room. Although liquor was not allowed in the house when Kevin was alive, they are now drinking wine at the table talking about the current condition of their lives.*

*Bunny interrupts them and says, "I know how close you girls are, and I feel bad about what I'm about to say."*

*Scarlett almost faints when she hears those words coming out of Bunny's mouth. She just knew she was about to put her shady life on Front Street.*

*"But, I don't know if Bambi has told you or not, but she's drinking again." Bunny didn't waste time with chivalries or hel-*

los. She got right down to the cockroach type behavior she was known for. "I'm just letting ya'll know."

"I'm sorry," Bambi says to her sisters. "I got a lot on my mind," she continues, not being able to say that the real reason she is drinking due to Kevin's death. "I hope you all can forgive me."

Scarlett and Race look in awe while Denim walks away even though Denim knows already.

Bambi walks to the front door and Bunny follows her. "Look what you made me do, Bambi? You think I felt good about that shit?"

"It doesn't matter what you felt," Bambi responds. "They were going to find out sooner or later so you just did me a favor. I'll tell you this though; you made yourself look worse in front of them just now. I wonder how that speaks to your credibility. Nobody likes a snitch, Bunny. Or a thief. So enjoy the Louis Vuitton set you just stole and get the fuck out of my house."

Bunny is so embarrassed. "Where is Kevin?" Bunny spits. "I want to know and I want to know now."

"He's not here," Bambi laughs. "Maybe he got tired of you after all. I know you been getting on my nerves for the last seventeen years."

Bunny scratches her head. "You know what, it doesn't even matter. He told me earlier when he called to pick up some more money."

Bambi's eyebrows rise. It's impossible for Kevin to speak to her or anybody else.

Bunny moves toward the bedroom and Kevin's safe. Once in the closet she drops to her knees and enters the code. She pulls the safe's door open and takes another thousand from the already dwindling stack.

"Kevin didn't tell you to get more money," Bambi says to her with clenched fists as she watches Bunny violate her financially...again.

"Sure he did," she responds closing the safe's door.

"That's impossible," Bambi yells.

*"Why is it impossible?" Bunny asks giving her a knowing look. Bunny stands up and looks dead into Bambi's eyes. "Bambi, I asked you a question. Why is it impossible for Kevin to say I could get more money? You and me both know there isn't a thing he won't do for me."*

*When Bambi doesn't respond, Bunny smirks, stuffs the money into her large bra cup and walks around Bambi and out the house. Once in her car Bunny says, "Checkmate."*

# BAMBI

I hate that bitch. I hate Bunny so much I can't even stand rabbits anymore, because of her name. As I cruise down the street in my Rolls Royce, with a little vodka in my cup, I can feel the stares coming from my sisters in the back and passenger seats. I try not to think about it; instead I glance at the starlights on the ceiling of my car. When I look at their faces I see frustration. But, they don't know what I endured in Saudi Arabia. They don't know the things I've seen. I need to drink to clear my mind, and I'm tired of apologizing for it too.

## SAUDI ARABIA
## OCTOBER 10 1994

*Bambi was lying on her stomach in a patch of wet sand. She could still smell the urine from the Iraqi soldier who pissed there not even thirty minutes earlier.*

*Last night while under fire, she and Desseray had been separated from their platoon. They didn't have anyway to communicate with the army about their location, because they were under attack and had to save their own lives, and escape. Up until that moment, they were roaming aimlessly around the desert. Luckily they happened upon a small desert fort, which they wanted to take shelter, until they could be reunited with their platoon. There was one problem, it was already occupied.*

When the coast looked clear, Bambi and Desseray crawled closer to the fort on their stomachs. They stopped when a small wall hid them from view, but from Bambi's position she could see her platoon mate Tatiana inside, bloodied, beaten and tied to a chair.

At some point during the middle of the night, Tatiana was taken from the Platoon by Iraqi soldiers, and held hostage. It was pure luck that brought Bambi there and she was not going to let her down again. Bambi could see one soldier in the front of the fort and, one in the back and one inside.

When Desseray peeped over the wall also, and saw Tatiana in a chair with her arms tied she said, "This doesn't look good, Private. We should go back towards our camp and wait for help. The rest of our platoon should be looking for us now."

"There's nothing left of our camp, Desseray," Bambi told her. "We gotta help Tatiana who as of now is a prisoner of war."

"I can't allow this," Desseray responded. "Trying to save her is too risky. It's two of us and three of them."

"Well I'll take two by myself," Bambi replied. "I can do this. But I have to move now. If those Iraqi soldiers are out in the open like that, it means that their transport is probably in route. If we don't help her now we'll lose her forever." Bambi felt beyond guilty for letting Tatiana down when she was being raped, and had no intentions on doing it again. Bambi knew Desseray wasn't a Good Samaritan so she said, "I saw a phone inside too, Desseray."

Desseray's eyes brightened wanting to reconnect with her platoon. "Where, I didn't see it?"

"It's right by her foot," Bambi continued to lie. "From where I am, I can shoot two of them and we can call for help."

Now Desseray was interested. She cocked her weapon and said, "Do what you gotta do, Private. I'll cover you."

Bambi was just about to take aim at the soldiers when she saw a little boy inside of the fort next to Tatiana and the Iraqi soldier. The child grabbed the soldier's hand and the soldier roughed up his curly black hair. She didn't want the child hurt.

"Fuck," Bambi yelled dropping down to hide behind the wall. "There's a kid inside."

"And?" Desseray said shrugging her shoulders. "You have a mission, and if you gotta kill a kid to make it happen so be it."

Bambi was a lot of things, but a baby killer was not one of them. She analyzed the soldiers again. The one in the front was sitting on the step reading some sort of paper. The one in the back, closer to her, was on guard and ready to attack. Bambi removed her shirt and bra.

"What the fuck are you doing?" Desseray whispered.

Bambi ignored her, and spit into her hand and rubbed sand all over her face and neck. She was going for a certain look and needed more sand so she said, "Desseray, spit in your hands and rub sand onto my body." When she didn't move Bambi said, "Do it."

Desseray helped with her sick scene until Bambi was covered in sand from the breasts up.

"What is the purpose of this?"

"I need to appear harmless," Bambi said, "and like I've been out here all day."

Bambi stuffed a knife in the back of her pants, and took off of her shoes. Taking a deep breath, she crawled toward the soldier in the back and said, "rape," in Arabic. "Help me, please."

The soldier was about to shoot her until he saw she was unarmed. No weapon. No shirt and no shoes. She looked like a good fuck and he wanted to take advantage. He continued to move closer to her, until she dropped to the sand, clipped his foot, sending him falling to the ground. When he was down she got on top of him, covered his mouth with her hand and slit into the flesh of his throat. His blood splashed all over her breasts and face, dampening the sand at her feet.

When he was dead, Bambi crawled into the back of the house and peeked through the window. She saw Tatiana tied to a chair, and alone. Bambi opened the door carefully, looked around and entered. Tatiana nodded to the door and Bambi rushed toward it and stood on the side. Two minutes later, the *door opened and the soldier told his son, "To always be sure to wash his hands when leaving the bathroom," in Arabic.*

*Bambi caught the man off guard, pulled him to her breasts from behind and gashed his throat. His blood sprayed over her face and hair making her virtually unrecognizable. When the little boy screamed, she caught him quickly and pressed her hand against his lips, muffling his cries.*

*Desseray seeing the commotion shot the soldier in the front of the fort in the back of the head when he was going inside to help. He didn't see a thing coming.*

*When all the soldiers were dead Bambi released the boy and told him to sit down, and don't move. Frightened, he quickly obeyed.*

*Then she untied Tatiana, and they hugged tightly. "Thank you so much, Bambi," Tatiana sobbed. "I thought I was dead. I thought I was dead and you saved me."*

*"Where is the phone," Desseray asked throwing Bambi her clothes from outside. She looked around. "I thought you said a phone was in here, next to Tatiana's feet."*

*"I lied," Bambi said placing her clothes on after having gotten what she wanted. Her friend safe and alive.*

*Desseray frowned. "So you lied to me? A superior?"*

*"Desseray, get over your fucking self already. We rescued a prisoner of war. Think about the medals you're going to get for this shit."*

*Desseray hated being lied to. So she rushed toward the little boy, grabbed him, placed the barrel of the gun to the back of the child's curly hair, and blew his brains out. "Now I feel better. There's one less raghead in the world to worry about."*

I wanted my sisters to come to the club dressed as men, to prepare us for the meeting on Saturday. Instead of at least trying, Race keeps crossing her legs although she has on a pair of baggy jeans and Timberland boots. Scarlett has on rouge, although she swears she didn't smooth on any today, and Denim wore tight jeans, which showed her phat ass, even though she said it was her most masculine outfit. If we walked into that meeting with the Russians like this, we would be laughed at and then killed.

"I'm ready to go home," Denim says to me while I'm at the bar getting another drink. "We been out here long and we still look like ourselves. Not only that we are starting to get crazy looks."

My body feels like a wave and all was right in my world. I forgot how good it feels to drink, but now I remember. "We only been here an hour, Denim. Relax will you?"

When I remember the little boy who was shot in front of me, I order another drink. Although that was a terrible thing that happened to me during my tour, it certainly wasn't the last.

"Bambi, what is the purpose of this shit," Denim yells to be heard over the music. "We out here, dressed like dykes, while you get drunk. I want to go home," she grabs me roughly by the arm. "Now let's get out of here before somebody we know sees us."

The way that she holds me brings back bad memories. I snatch away from her and grab her throat. I have a firm grip too and if I want, I can break it. I point at her with my other hand and say, "Don't...touch...me...like...that...ever...again."

Denim's jaw tightens and she spits in my face. "Fuck you, Bambi! If you want to stay in here and act like we not widows, that's on you. We're out of here!" She grabs my sisters, the car keys out of my pocket, and they leave me in the club alone.

I wipe the spit out of my face and rub it on my pants. I feel sick at how I just treated them. What am I going to do if they abandon me? I take the cap I'm wearing off, and my long brown hair falls down my shoulders.

I drop my head on the bar when all of a sudden I hear, "Bambi, is that you?"

I turn around, and look up. I'm staring into Cloud's face. "What's wrong with you?" He looks down at me and I feel dirty dressed like this. "Why are you dressed like a nigga?" He looks around the club. "And, where the fuck is Kevin?"

"Don't worry about all that," I tell him. When I try to walk, I fall, and he catches me in his muscular arms.

"I'm getting you out of here," he says, "Whether you want me to or not."

I've think I've been asleep for about an hour, but I can't be sure because I keep waking up. I'm in Cloud's bed. I know because it smells like him. When he comes into the room, with no shirt on and navy pajama pants, my pussy jumps. I know that it's wrong to think about sex, but I always do when I'm under pressure.

"I brought you this," he hands me a cup of coffee. "There's no sugar or cream in it. It's the way you like it."

I take the cup from him and drink half of it. He sits next to me and rubs my leg. The coffee is bitter so I hand it back. I drop to my knees and look up at him.

"Why are you down there?" He grins at me trying to pull me back up.

I stand my position. I rest my head on his knee. I don't tell him but for what I want to do, I don't want to see his face. "Can you put your hands on me?" I ask. "Please."

His large hands run over my shoulders and neck. I close my eyes tight. So tight not even a little bit of light peaks through. Suddenly Kevin is stroking me, not Cloud. I feel like I did back in the day, when Kevin rubbed me to sleep after I awaken from the nightmares of the war that haunted me.

"Hmmm, that feels nice," I tell him. "Please don't stop."

He rubs me harder, and then I stand on my knees. I snake my hand into the opening of his pajamas and pull out his dick. He's hard and thick and I can feel myself moisten. When I stroke him a few more times, pre-cum slides out of the tip of his dick, and I lap it up like a kitten. He moans. He likes it. I know that he likes it. In Saudi Arabia, I slept with over fifty men, and every last one of them loved it.

I'm damaged. The kind of damage you can't repair with a pill or good pep talk.

Before I know it his dick is in my mouth. It's salty and warm. I like it. I push him deeper inside so that it rests upon my throat. I ease down closer, until I can extend my tongue and lick his balls at the same time.

"Fuck," he says out loud. "Bambi, I've never in my life felt anything like this."

I'm good. I'm the best, they've all told me before. I'm just about to take care of him even better, until I smell Kevin. It's not actually him. I know he's dead. Instead I smell the Clive Christian cologne he wears steaming from his jacket on the floor. What a slut I am. Look at me...with another nigga's dick in my mouth.

I pull him out of my throat and bring Kevin's jacket to my face. I inhale and cry into it. When I open my eyes and look up at Cloud I realize this is wrong. *All wrong.* I feel worse when I glance to my left and see the picture of him and Kevin at the club that was taken seven months ago. I quickly stand up, grab Kevin's jacket and run out of the room. Ashamed, and with a wet pussy.

# TUESDAY
# NOVEMBER 6<sup>TH</sup> 2012
# 12 00 PM

# AUNT BUNNY

*A*unt Bunny is sitting on the sofa with her best friend Therese gossiping about everybody's business but her own. They are dressed in colorful muumuus and are passing a blunt back and forth. "You know I never told Kevin how I felt about his wife," Bunny tells her friend as she lights another blunt. "I always spoke good shit about her around him. Now I feel like it may be my biggest regret."

Don't say that," Therese says eager to pull on the fresh batch of weed Bunny has dangling between her fingers.

"I'm serious," Bunny continues. "I know a lot of people who been in that war and ain't none of them turn out right. They all gone in the head. And if something happened to Kevin because I bit my tongue, I will never forgive myself."

"I'm sure he's fine," Therese says. "He might be out getting a little bit of pussy. You not gonna tell me he don't think about another woman from time to time. The same bitch for seventeen years is enough to make anybody disappear."

"Tell me about it," Bunny laughs. "But, even if he ignored her he would never do that to me. He has never not ringed my phone. I still feel like something is up," Bunny points the lit blunt at her and a few sparks fall on her leg. She doesn't bother to swat them away. "I haven't spoken to Kevin since Saturday. I don't know what to do...I mean should I call the police?"

"Why would you do some shit like that?" Therese frowns scratching her gray wig. In her opinion Bunny was taking too long on the blunt hand off. But, since the smoke was free she just had to wait. "The Kennedy's don't invite the cops into their world. You know that." Bunny sighs hearing the truth and hands the blunt to Therese. Finally, Therese thinks.

"Than what can I do?" Bunny asks.

"You said you have the flavor on that white girl," she inhales and beats her chest. "Press her hard enough until she turns red. I bet you'll find out everything you want to know then."

Bunny uses the moment to think about Therese's comment and reflects on her life. Bunny is conniving. She even murdered Kevin's mother, Meredith Kennedy. Sure the papers said Meredith was an addict who eventually succumbed to a heroin overdose. But, what they didn't know about was the hand that guided the needle into her withered vein.

Gloria "Bunny" Kennedy, had been jealous of her sister they called Merry since they were children. When they were growing up, Merry's father came by and spent time with his daughter while Bunny's father spent quality time with his homies in prison.

As teenagers, Merry was considered more beautiful with her almond colored skin and naturally long hair. While, Bunny scared off men left and right with her height, unreasonable body shape and wild large eyes.

All Bunny wished was that Merry, for once in her life, played the second position. Before long she got her wish. When Merry was an adult, she suffered from Multiple Sclerosis. During that period Bunny had never been happier. It brought joy to her heart that finally Princess Merry was given the bad end of life's stick. And, since she was constantly in pain, Bunny introduced her to a man-made painkiller, heroin. Before long Merry didn't know if she was coming or going nor did she care. Heroin was her nigga. Her lover. Her God. Bunny saw to it that Merry had heroin everyday until the hot shot Bunny bought Merry, which took her life. Bunny's reward for her murder? Merry's son, Kevin Kennedy.

*Kevin was fucked up in the head when his mother died. His father was killed at a Poker game when he was a baby so he never got to know him. It was Bunny who nursed him when he was sick. It was Bunny who had proven her loyalty to him. It was Bunny who had his back before Bambi came into the picture. Some said, and it may be true, that Bunny loved Kevin more than she did her own twenty-year old daughter who was on crack, alone and in the world.*

*Moving on what Therese said, Bunny picked up her home phone. "You right, Therese. Let me put the press on Scarlett. Even if she can't tell me where Kevin is, since she's in that house I'm going to put her in charge of finding out."*

# BAMBI

I just put the silver and white Kate Spade place settings down on our dining room table. To tell you the truth I was beat after making fried chicken, greens and mash potatoes for my family. It was my way of apologizing for my behavior at the club last night, and I made a decision not to fuck with the bottle anymore. *You not gonna be able to do it.* The voice in my head tells me. But I don't listen. I'm stronger than the addiction...*honest*. Besides a lot is riding on the line. My sisters are counting on me to lead us into this meeting with the Russians, and that's exactly what I'm going to do. But, I need to be sober to make it happen.

After dishing their plates I call my sisters down using the intercom system. Denim and Jasmine come down using the elevator. Scarlett comes down using the stairs and Race comes upstairs from her monster lab in the basement. I swear that Race is so creepy sometimes. How someone can create horror masks all day long and be a punk in life is beyond me. Shouldn't she be use to gore?

When everyone washes their hands they sit down. "How is everyone doing?" I ask trying to get my mind off of the dick I had in my mouth yesterday. "I know I haven't asked, because I hate talking about it, but I really want to know now." I look at all of them. "How are you taking their deaths?"

Denim looks at me, and guilt for what happened at the club is written all over her face. This morning she apologized ten times for spitting in my face at the club despite me telling her that I deserved it.

"I'm not doing well at all," Denim says feeding Jasmine a piece of chicken. Jasmine opens her mouth, accepts the food, and continues to play with her fingers while babbling. "But I gotta be strong for my baby," Denim shrugs. "You know. I guess we don't have a choice. My family depends on me for everything, and I'm all Jasmine got."

I feel so bad for Denim, because it must be terrible having a lazy-fat bitch for a mother and mooch for a sister.

"What about you, Race?" I ask looking at her. "How are you taking things?"

"I don't want to talk about it," Race says in a squeaky voice. She forks her mashed potatoes.

"Why do you say that?" I ask.

"Because every time I try and talk, ya'll joke behind my back. Talking about me being the monster girl downstairs," she continues.

"I only called you a monster that one time at Halloween because you—,"

"It doesn't matter," Race yells cutting me off. "It hurts my feelings. I've been picked on and fucked with throughout high school. And, I deserve a little more respect in my home." Race wipes her mouth with the white linen napkin. "So don't ask me what I feel when you really don't want to know. I think about it enough when I'm in my room alone."

"I understand. But, it's untrue, we do want to hear your opinion, and I'm sorry if I hurt your feelings," I say although suddenly I want a drink. Race is so depressing that at times, she brings me down too. I look to my right. "What about you, Scarlett? How have you been doing?"

"I'm holding up," she says eating some mashed potatoes. "I know it's gonna get worse after we meet with these Russians. Because, right now the meeting is keeping our minds occupied."

"The meeting is gonna be fine, and eventually we are going to be fine too. Our husbands would want us to stick together, and we have to honor the Kennedy name, and stand strong." I sigh playing with my fork. *God I want a drink so bad.* "And I wanted to tell ya'll that I'm done with the alcohol. I realize now that I can't think straight with that shit." I look up and can tell they don't believe me. "I'm serious, you guys. Think about it for a second, I was clean for five years, until recently. I haven't so much as used mouthwash in all that time. Trust me when I say that this soldier girl got it." I look at each of them in their eyes. "Your lives in my hands are safe."

"Why did Cloud bring you home last night?" Denim asks me out of nowhere. Sometimes she can be ridiculous. I mean we weren't even talking about that shit.

"I'm not sure, but something tells me he brought me home because you took my Rolls Royce and left me at the club," I say.

"I apologized for that already," Denim responds wiping Jasmine's mouth with a napkin. "What more you want me to do?"

"I'm just playing with you," I tell her. "But I had to give you a comeback that was true. I'm over it already," I continue waving my hand. "On the real there's nothing more important to me than honesty, loyalty and family. *This family,*" I stab the table with my index finger. "And I want you all to know that I value that more than I do my own life."

Scarlett moves uncomfortably in the chair. She holds her stomach. I'm worried. "Are you okay?" I ask her preparing to go to her end of the table to check on her.

"I...I'm sorry. I'm fine. I just gotta...well...I gotta leave," Scarlett gets up and runs upstairs. Her long red hair flies in the wind behind her.

"What is that about?" I ask Race since they are closer friends.

"I don't know," she says looking at the vacant steps.

"Let's go find out," I say. We all get up and walk to her room. When we get in her room, Scarlett is lying on the bed crying her eyes out. "What's going on?" I ask rubbing her back. "Did I say something wrong?"

Scarlett rolls over and looks at me. Denim and Race hang behind me. "I want to tell you something, but I don't think you'll love me the same anymore." She sits up straight in her bed.

"Love you the same?" I repeat. Scarlett sounds crazy to me. Not only do I love her, I appreciate the stance she's taken with the Russians issue. So the last thing I have in my heart for Scarlett is malice. "Scarlett, you can tell me anything. I need you to know that."

"You say that now, but what if I did something so awful it can't be taken back?"

"Like what," Race says. "You're scaring me."

"Everybody scares you, Monster Girl." I focus back on Scarlett.

"See, that's what I'm talking about," Race pouts. "Stop calling me names!" She runs out of the room.

"Listen, if you knew some of the things I been through in my life," I reply ignoring Race, "you couldn't say that and be serious. Now I'm telling you that whatever is going on we got your back."

"Scarlett, Bambi is right," Denim says holding Jasmine's hand while she plays with her own wrist. "Unless you hurting kids who cares what you did in your life? We all have shit with us and that's what makes us unique. You gotta let whatever is holding you down off of your chest. That's what we're here for."

Scarlett looks at us and lies back down on the bed. It seems like when Denim made her comment, she hardened up again. Scarlett wipes the tears off of her face and says, "It's nothing serious. I'm just missing my husband that's all."

Somehow I don't believe her. I got the feeling that what she wanted to tell us ran deeper than the obvious.

# WEDNESDAY
# NOVEMBER 7$^{TH}$ 2012
# 2 00 PM

# SCARLETT

I'm wearing Camps jeans, sweat shirt and coat. His New York Yankees cap dangles in my hand. I examine myself in the mirror. I turn left. I turn right, and then I turn around. If you just look at me, and I don't move maybe you'll think I'm a guy. But, when I look at myself stroll from the bathroom to the mirror, I can't stop my hips from switching. I can't stop my hands from swaying. I can't stop myself from feeling like a woman.

I stuff my red hair in my baseball cap. I slide the cap down on my head. Way down, just above my nose. Now I can past for a white boy...maybe one of them wannabe rappers my brother jokes about all the time. I cry when I realize the chances of me and my sisters pulling this gig off with the Russians is slim to none. The only one who can make a go of it is Bambi.

When my phone rings I know who it is now. Bunny has been calling me everyday since the Kings were killed. I want so badly to tell my sisters that she was on to us. But, I couldn't unless they also knew about my past. I was five seconds from telling them about my life earlier, until Denim said what she thought about baby beaters. I can't do it now.

I pick up the phone and answer. "Hello."

"Let me guess, it's Wednesday and Kevin and the boys are still not home."

"How can I help you, Bunny?" I ask removing the cap and sitting it on my dresser.

"Have you discovered if Bambi knows what's going on with Kevin yet?"

This is so stupid. Not only am I sure Bambi knows what's going on...I do too. I can't tell her that because just like she came into the living room and, told us that Bambi was drinking again, she'd do the same thing to me.

"Bunny, I really don't think Bambi knows anything," I lie. "Why don't you just give it a little more time? Kevin hasn't called Bambi either, but she's not worried."

"Scarlett, maybe I didn't make myself clear when I called you the first time. Either you find some information I can use, or you're useless to me. If you're useless to me, I can disregard you and that's trouble for you...you understand what I'm saying?"

"I feel like a snake," I say softly. "Please don't do this to me, Bunny. I need them in my life. They're the only family I have left."

"If you don't find me some information in the next few days I will come over there, and tell them everything I know. I'm talking about the warrants, you abusing your own flesh and blood, and everything else, Scarlett. You got two days...give or take an hour."

When she hangs up I punch myself in the face. My life is crawling out of control. And, to make matters worst, I'm pregnant. I finally took the test and cried my eyes out a whole hour after the results. I'm an abuser. I have a temper. I'm a white woman giving birth to a black child, and I'm a liar. I'm also all-alone.

I haven't spoken to my mother and father in years. So I decide to call my brother instead, who I keep in touch with every so often. I block my number and dial his.

"This must be, Scar," Matt says to me when he answers. "She's the only one who would call me from a blocked number."

It sounds so good to hear his voice. When we were kids, Matt was my protector. But, even he didn't know what my aunt was doing to me in the privacy of her home. My aunt didn't treat him the same way she did me. For some reason her hate was geared solely toward me, and I never found out why.

"Hi, Matt. I miss you so much," I tell him sitting on the floor in my bedroom.

"You don't know how good it feels to hear your voice," he tells me. "Scar, you gotta stop staying away for so long. I haven't spoken to you in almost a year. Are you still married to that nigger?"

An electric volt feels like it shoots through my body. My mother and father aren't what I consider traditional racists. They work with black people everyday, and my father even has some black friends. But, when my parents aren't around black people some of the things they say are hard to hear. The funny thing is, I heard similar racists comments geared toward white people when I'm here. My sisters often forget that I'm white when I'm in the room, but it doesn't make the pain hurt any less. I guess at the end of the day, people are scared of what they don't know...*who* they don't know.

My brother on the other hand is a whole different story. He hates blacks. All blacks. He can't stand being around them and rarely talks to them. I never said anything to my brother in the past about his comments. When he called Camp a nigger the last time I spoke to him on the phone, it was one of the reasons he didn't hear from me in a year. Now things are different. I feel the need to keep it real with him.

"Matt, I love you. With all my heart," I start. "But, if you ever call my husband a nigger, or use that word in my presence I will never speak to you again. Are we clear?"

He sighs. "Well I guess I got my answer. You must be still married to him."

"I'm sorry, Matt. I love you, I truly do, but this man has taken care of me for five years, and deserves a little more respect. I'm not denouncing my race, I'm just in love." I talk to him as if Camp is still alive and my stomach churns.

"Point taken, Scar. When I'm on the phone with you, I'll mind my tongue. But, it won't change how I feel about them people."

"I can respect that."

"Good. Now I don't know if you are aware, but Samantha is doing well. She has all A's and B's in school and a bunch of new friends. Her hair is as red as yours, and I swear when I see her she reminds me of you."

I feel good that she's doing better, but a part of me hates that her life is going on without me.

"Ma and pop are doing good with her," Matt continues.

"She's living with them now?" I ask.

"No, she's still with Mark. He's remarried now. Some Chinese girl he met at his real estate company."

I knew Mark preferred Asian women but he denied it to its death. When we use to watch porn before we fucked, he couldn't get off unless an Asian woman was involved. Since I'm far from Asian, and part Irish with red hair, Mark made me feel inferior. His attraction was one of the reasons for my insecurity.

"That's good for him," I breathe. "I'm glad he's happy now."

"Oh, and aunt Nancy has been helping with Samantha too," Matt says. "Starting next Monday Samantha will be staying with her during the times ma, pop and Mark are out of the country. You know all three of them signed up to sell insurance with that company. Because they work together they are always out of town."

The phone rolls out of my hand. Aunt Nancy is a monster. A cold-blooded monster that gets off on abusing young girls. I don't want her around my daughter, but what can I do? I'm not allowed to be around her either.

"Scarlett, are you okay?" Matt asks. "You got quiet on me."

"I'm fine," I respond wishing I could send a message to my parents to keep Nancy away from Samantha.

"Scarlett, I don't know what happened when Samantha was in your home. To tell you the truth I really don't care, because you are my sister and I know your heart. But, if what they say is true, you need some help." I hear paper rattling in the background. "I have a number for you that I keep in my wallet in case you call. It's a support group for abusers and the abused. Not sure how it works, but from what I hear its effective. Maybe you should call."

He reads me the number and I write it down. "Thank you, Matt," I say holding the small sheet of paper in my hand. "I love you for this."

"I love you too," he responds. "I gotta go, but don't stay away too long. Besides, I have something soft and pretty in my bed right now."

"Ughh! Gross!" I laugh hanging up on him.

I'm about to call the number he gave me when Denim walks into my room with Jasmine. Jasmine is babbling and playing with her bottom lip. Every time she taps it, it jiggles and I wonder how she does that. "Scarlett, can you watch Jasmine for me? I have to go to my mother's house. She went into insulin shock and she's asking for me."

My heart thumps. I haven't been in the company of a child alone since Samantha, and it was on purpose. Whenever Denim needs a sitter, it was anybody but me. She knows that which is why I'm surprised she's even in my bedroom, asking for help.

"I can't do it, Denim," I say getting up off of the floor. "I'm sorry. I'm not feeling too well."

Her face twists up into a frown. "It's an emergency, Scarlett. I realize for whatever reason you don't like kids, but I need your help. It ain't even like I ask you all the time."

"I never said I didn't like kids," I respond. *How does she know I hate kids?*

"Well that's what the sisters told me," she replies. It makes me feel bad that they are talking behind my back, and I wonder what else they're saying about me.

"Denim, I'm not good with kids, that's why I don't watch them. But I never told anybody I don't like them so get that out of your head. Besides, get one of the other sisters to do it."

"They're not here," she says. "I really need you to come through for me right now."

I look at Jasmine. She's still babbling, and playing with her fingers. I realize I don't like Jasmine. She's annoying, and I know she'll set me off. Please God don't make me do it. I don't want to be my aunt. I don't want to hurt her. "I'm sorry, Denim, I can't."

Denim steps back and look like she wants to hit me. "Are you my sister or not?" She's gripping Jasmine's fingers so tightly as she stands in my doorway, that the tips of her fingers turn red. "Or maybe you only watch the white babies. Maybe the black ones are off limits."

"Denim," I yell.

"I said are you my sister or not?" She's so mad at me that her tattoos look reptile, because of the blood rushing to the surface of her skin. "Because if you aren't my sister, and we aren't real family I need to know now instead of faking it with you," Denim continues as tears pour down her face. "Now my fat ass mother is over there about to die and I need a little support around here! Can I count on you or what?"

Silence.

"But...I...it—"

"Scarlett, the only question is can I count on you or not?"

I look at Jasmine who never gives me eye contact. I can hear a voice in my head tell me not to watch her. The voice sounds soft, and protective like it cares for me. I'm confident in my answer to say no. But instead of going with my head I go with my heart and say, "Okay, call me when you're on your way back. Try not to stay out too long."

An hour later I am in my bedroom with Jasmine...*alone*. This is my worst fear. She is on the floor, my favorite place, playing with her fingers. Her babbling is not as loud, and I feel I can do this. Suddenly it seems foolish for refusing to help Denim when she needed my help in the past. Jasmine is not that bad at all. Her voice goes up one octave, but I've heard worse. I just turn the TV up louder to shield the sound. Her voice is very consistent.

I try to focus on the TV show. I think it's a reality show or something, but I'm not sure which one. But, Jasmine's voice grows louder, and suddenly I can't hear anything. It's like she's trying to be heard over the show. I look down at her, and bite my tongue. I can taste my blood faintly. It's salty, and the pain relaxes me.

I focus back on the TV and Jasmine's voice grows louder. A sheen of sweat develops on my forehead. I wipe it off and another sheen pops up on my upper lip. I wipe the sweat off with the back of my hand, and look down at her again. She's louder. Why is she louder? I hate the pigtails in her hair too. Why didn't Denim put her hair in a single ponytail? Or something like that? When I was with my aunt she pulled my pigtails, and drug me around the house by them. My head would hurt for days after.

I get up and rush to the bathroom. From where I am I turn my head, and see Jasmine on the floor. Her voice is gotten louder. It's like she's on my shoulders, babbling in my ear. I cover my ears, but now she's screaming. I wonder if it's all in my mind. I turn the cold water on, and splash some in my face. A few splatters pop up on the mirror, and suddenly my reflection looks distorted. I look like a monster. An ugly monster.

I rush over to Jasmine. My toes press into my black carpet. I look down at her. My fists are clenched, but I'm not about to hit this little girl. "Jasmine," I say softly, "stop making so much noise okay? I can't hear TV."

She doesn't acknowledge me. She doesn't look up at me. I increase my voice louder. "Jasmine, stop making so much noise. Auntie Scarlett is trying to watch TV. Do you want some juice or something?" My smile is stiff and fake. Like the rubber dick under my bed I play with most nights.

Her babbling is so loud now that I can't hear anything, but her voice. Not the TV. Not the sound of the heater that runs constantly, and more importantly not my own thoughts. So I scream, "SHUT THE FUCK UP YOU RETARDED, BITCH!"

She doesn't look at me. Instead she falls back on the floor and cries. Then she takes both of her hands and slaps them against her head repeatedly. The sound that comes out of her now reminds me of fifty people scratching one chalkboard...at the same time. I want her stopped. Now!

I reach down and grab her. I shake her hard. A smile spreads across my face because the noise is no longer consistent.

108

It's broken. Her head shakes rapidly back and forth and I can feel my adrenaline kick up. Now I'm in control. For the first time ever she looks into my eyes. Does she recognize me? Know my name? Will she tell her mother what I did?

I release her, and she plummets to the floor. She's quiet now. She's laying face up, and staring at the ceiling. The peace feels like an orgasm racing through my body. I sit on the edge of the bed, and enjoy what I've accomplished. I've defeated her. I've won. I peek down at her again. Her eyes are open, and she's not dead. Maybe Denim should've shaken her up a long time ago.

I lie down in my bed, and focus on the TV again. I can hear the voices on the show clearly, although I don't know what's going on. I'm at ease until suddenly she starts babbling again. I hop off of the bed and shake her rapidly. So hard that I can smell the feces leaving her body. I rush her to the bathroom, and throw her on the floor. Her chin bounces on the linoleum.

I can't take this. I can't take this noise. I can't be around kids. I turn the water on. It's hot and steam rushes from the tub. I rip her clothes off like the first layer of lettuce. When she's naked I see chunks of feces in her clothes and on my floor. In the carpet by my tub. I push the carpet down. I get angry, and toss her in the tub. Her head knocks against the wall, and then I hear a snap.

From where I stand I can see her right leg hanging awkwardly outward and to the right. It's broken. I've broken her leg. She's screaming loudly. I don't know if it's because of the hot water or the pain. I'm about to call the ambulance until I remember I don't want them coming here. What if my sisters come back and see what I've done? I pick her up and decide to take her to the hospital. Oh my God! What now?

# BAMBI

Me, Denim and Race rush to the counter in the hospital to see what's going on with Jasmine. I'm so scared I've bitten a tiny chunk out of my bottom lip. I can't understand what's going on. I was on my way to visit my mother when I got a frantic call from Scarlett that something has happened to my niece. I'm confused on why Scarlett even had Jasmine to begin with. She never watched her before.

"Yes, I'm here to see about my daughter," Denim says to the hospital receptionist. She's shaking so hard her teeth rattle. "Her name is Jasmine. Jasmine Kennedy."

An elderly patient with a gray-cotton-ball hairstyle pushes out of Denim's way in a wheelchair, to park in the waiting area.

The older black receptionist looks through the chart on her desk. "Oh yes, give me a second, sweetheart." She stops at a point on the page and says, "I'll page the doctor for you. Have a seat in the waiting area. And, don't worry, everything will be okay."

I rub Denim's back while we walk to the waiting area. We sit next to a dude in black sweatpants, with a pair of crutches leaning on his thigh. Race rubs Denim's leg.

"I'm so sorry, Denim," I say playing with the tiny loose piece of my lip in my mouth. My nerves are all over the place. I want a drink. "I know Jasmine will be okay." I don't know if she will be okay. I'm just good at lying. Just thinking about it makes me miss my twins. "Jasmine is a strong little girl you know that.

Plus if there is a God, I know he won't put this type of pressure on you. Not after taking our husbands."

"I'm so scared right now," Race says offering zero to the conversation.

I look at her and roll my eyes. She's as useless as a dead roach sometimes. "We all are scared, Race." I sigh.

Just when I say that Scarlett walks out of the back of the hospital. She's holding Jasmine's yellow Choo-choo train blanket closely to her chest. Her cheeks are redder than her hair and it's apparent she's been crying all day.

When Denim spots her too she pops up, and pushes Scarlett against the wall. The blanket falls out of her hand and floats to the floor. Denim clutches Scarlett's red shirt in her hands and lifts it up to her neck. "What did you do to my baby you, white bitch?" Denim is gripping the shirt so hard that her blue nail pops off and falls to the floor. Now her finger is bleeding. The veins in her neck pop out and make the characters on her tattoos look reptile. "What the fuck has happened to my baby?"

When Denim calls Scarlett a white bitch my stomach spins. It's one thing for us to fight, but it's a whole 'nother thing to take it this far. "Denim, let her go," I say gripping her clenched fist. When she doesn't release Scarlett's shirt I squeeze tighter forcing her fingers to stiffen and open. Denim lets her go.

I stand as a barrier in front of Scarlett. Looking at Denim I softly say, "I know you mad at Scarlett, but let us not forget that she's family. Give her a chance to tell you what happened before you automatically make her guilty. She deserves that much respect." I turn around and face Scarlett. "What happened to Jasmine? How did she end up here?"

Scarlett wipes the tears off of her face. Denim's blood is rubbed on her neck like a passion mark. "I was giving her a bath. The floor was wet. I tried to pick her up to put her in the water, but slipped on the tub with her. She fell in and my stomach hit the edge." She raises her shirt and a red bruise runs horizontally across her belly...just above her navel. She releases her shirt. "When she fell she broke her leg. I brought her right away here. I'm sorry, Jasmine. Please forgive me."

I turn around to Denim and say, "See, it was an accident. Like she told you."

"I don't believe that, bitch," Denim points in Scarlett's face. "She's a fucking liar, Bambi. I can smell liars a mile away. She didn't even want to watch Jasmine so she probably did something to her on purpose."

What she's saying doesn't make sense to me. "Denim, if what you say is true, and she didn't want to watch the baby, why leave your child in her care?"

Silence.

Denim's face twists up. She clenches her fist, and looks at me as if she wants to hit me. I know the look in her eyes. I've felt that way before so I check her right there. "Denim, I know you're mad right now," I eyeball her hands again. "I'm fucked up by this shit too, because I love Jasmine like we got the same blood. But, if you put your hands on me you won't live long enough to see her grow up to become a respectable young woman. I promise you."

"Fuck you," Denim points at me. "And, fuck you too," she points at Scarlett. Denim storms off. Race picks up Jasmine's blanket and follows her.

I turn around and face, Scarlett. "Are you sure that's the only thing that happened? Because what's done in the dark always comes to the light." I remember my past and sigh. "Trust me, I know."

"I never meant to hurt Jasmine." Scarlett looks into my eyes. "You have to believe me, Bambi."

"I believe you," I respond rubbing her shoulder. "I just wish Denim did too."

All of a sudden my antennas go up. When I look to my left I see two dudes step off of the elevator. One short, one tall. I don't know what makes me focus on them, but something about them seems off. Maybe it is the bloodied white towel wrapped around the taller one's arm.

I look back at Scarlett. "Let's go over to Denim and Race to see what's going on with Jasmine. They should know something by now."

The moment we walk to meet Denim at the receptionist counter, the shorter of the two niggas who stepped off of the elevator yells, "Hey, can I holla at you for a minute."

I'm not sure if he's talking to me since the waiting room is filled with people. I look in his direction anyway. "Yeah, you," he says to me. "Where is Kevin?"

Instead of giving Kevin's current status I say, "He ain't here." I dip off to join Denim and Race who are now looking at the short guy.

"Hold up, bitch," he says to me. "I wasn't trying to be rude, but now I don't give a fuck. The nigga Kevin was paid on a delivery that ain't make its destination. What's up with that?"

I'm confused. I know everyone Kevin does business with and his face has never showed up in the rotation. Kevin had Avery and Judah here on the east coast, a dude on the west and a few more throughout the country. Kevin would certainly not be dealing with some hand-to-hand cat like this nigga appeared to be.

"I think you got the wrong person," I say, hoping he'd leave the matter alone. I turn my back to him.

"I got the right person," he continues. He's now standing directly behind me and his voice vibrates through my body. "I'm talking about Kevin Kennedy. Now give a nigga some respect and act like you know."

I turn around. I'm angry I'm not packing heat because I'd probably blow his face back to the elevator. When I look at him I can tell he's a killer. I knew enough of them in my lifetime to validate him. But, I'm never scared. "Look, I don't know who you are, but it's obvious you got the wrong person. My husband would never deal with a nigga like you. Now step the fuck off."

He frowns and tilts his head. Like he's been watching the movie *Boyz N The Hood* one time too many. "What the fuck is that supposed to mean," he asks.

"For starters you in the hospital yelling about shit that should be discussed on the streets. My husband doesn't conduct business like that. That means you non-essential, and non-essential niggas ain't even bringing in enough paper to take care of my thousand dollar hair appointments each month. Now get the fuck out of my face before I embarrass you."

"Bambi," Scarlett says with a worried expression. I can tell she is scared, but I could care less. I'm a Kennedy and I demand respect. "Don't talk to him like that."

"Fuck this nigga," I respond giving him my back again. "Let's go see about our niece. I give none to the rest."

His footsteps grow further away. But, the soldier in me can feel something was off. By the time I turn around to face him, he has a weapon aimed in my direction.

The first shot he lets off ends in the cheek of the lady in the wheelchair. Although Denim and Race drop to go for cover, Scarlett hangs in the middle of the floor in shock. I knock her to the floor with a forearm to the throat right before the next shot pierces the black receptionist's chest. Now she's safe too. That bullet had Scarlett's name on it.

My adrenaline is up again. But I feel a stinging sensation in my body. When I look down, I see my blood everywhere. I've been shot. I'm immediately taken to another time when I was covered in this much blood.

# SAUDI ARABIA
# OCTOBER 10 1994

*Bambi, Tatiana and Desseray were sitting around a camp-fire in the desert at night. Starting a fire could be deadly as the enemy could detect them, but with no water, food or shelter, they'd rather have the convenience of the fire than nothing at all. After saving Tatiana from the Iraqi soldiers they were able to get away undetected. But, they had yet to be reunited with their platoon.*

*Bambi couldn't keep her eyes off of Desseray. She couldn't believe she'd murdered a child for no reason. Many things had already haunted Bambi, but thanks to Desseray, the child's mur-*

der would stay etched in her mind forever. In Bambi's opinion Desseray was the devil reincarnated.

"If you want to kill me just do it," Desseray told Bambi as the glow from the fire made Bambi's murderous glare glow. "Nobody would ever know." She looked at Tatiana. "And I'm sure your best friend over here wouldn't say a word. Seeing as how you saved her life and all. You'll both probably take the secret to your graves."

Bambi thought about the concept of killing Desseray and was in love with the idea. But, when she looked at Tatiana she could tell she wasn't game.

Tatiana cleared her throat and said, "Nobody is going to kill anybody tonight." She was so thankful that she was alive that all she wanted to do was celebrate. And if a little Iraqi child was taken off of the earth for her freedom, so be it. "I'm grateful to you," she looked at Bambi. Thank you for saving my life. I owe you."

Bambi didn't say anything. Every time she wanted to talk to her friend, she would smell the blood and gunfire steaming off of the dead child's body. Oh how she hated Desseray.

Tatiana grabbed a dry branch with some small shrubs, and threw it into the fire. It brightened the fire and she stood up. "I gotta go to the bathroom," Tatiana told them. "I'll be right back."

She was about to go left but Desseray said, "I saw some snakes over there when I pissed earlier. Bang a right."

"No," Bambi told Tatiana not trusting Desseray's direction, "go to the left instead. I don't trust this bitch."

Tatiana shrugged and listened to her friend. The moment Tatiana took six steps out behind Bambi, something ticked. Bambi felt her heart stop. She knew exactly what was going on. The explosion ignited. Desseray's face brightened as she maintained eye contact with Bambi the entire time. The next thing Bambi felt was a powerful force that pushed her forward from behind. When Bambi rolled over, face up; she was sprayed with warm liquid. Looking at her hands she was covered in blood. Tatiana's *blood. Desseray had set Tatiana up by leading her into a landmine.*

*Desseray knew Bambi would tell her friend to go the opposite way if she gave her direction, and in the end she got what she wanted. Tatiana's dead body and revenge on Bambi.*

*Bambi passed out cold.*

We are back from the hospital. I just got off of the house phone in the kitchen from talking to Cloud. I walk toward the living room. I'm standing in front of my sisters while they're sitting on the sofa. My hand is bandaged from the gunshot wound the shooter landed in me earlier that night. I'm in a lot of pain, but it doesn't bother me as much right now. I'm use to pain.

I look at all them. "I just got off of the phone with Cloud. The dude that was arrested for shooting me is named Dixon."

"How Cloud know him?" Denim asks holding Jasmine who is sleep in her arms. Her leg is in a cast, and Denim refuses to put her down. "He's not even in the drug game."

"Cloud runs one of the most popular auto body shops in DC and Maryland," I remind her. "His prices are through the roof, but his service is impeccable. Who do you think his major clientele is? Drug dealers."

Silence.

"I'm scared," Race says. "We can't defend ourselves if every time we walk outside, someone is trying to shoot at us. I mean how do we know it won't happen again?"

"I don't. But, you're going to learn to handle a weapon, and you're going to learn before Saturday."

"Bambi, I'm never letting you teach me how to shoot again," Denim replies. "The last time I let you, you got mad at me because I didn't hit the target in the head. You even slapped me in the face…remember?"

"Yeah but you're shooting is not to be fucked with now," I tell her. "I just want you to be the best," I hold my wrist so my hand doesn't throb so much.

"But I hit seven the entire time on the target. Which is the upper body," Denim continues.

"Not good enough," I tell her. "Hit the head and save your life."

"So what does all this mean for us?" Scarlett asks. "Are we on the run? Do we have to hide out? What's going on?"

Denim rolls her eyes the moment Scarlett opens her mouth. Every time Scarlett opens her mouth now she rolls her eyes. I hope they can get it together before Saturday. We can't afford this type of drama right now.

"It means that we are going to have to leave this house after the meeting with The Russians. Because, something tells me if our husbands didn't deliver to Dixon, there will be a lot of other people expecting packages, and coming here for the payout." I pause. "Some of which are legitimate, and others that are fake and trying to extort us. It's not safe. Maybe we'll have to break this one hundred million dollars down, buy a package and settle our husbands' debt," I say. "Basically, I might have to forge a *business* relationship with Mitch, but in the meantime I need to be sure that everyone is safe."

Denim's eyebrows rise. "Bambi, after we meet the Russians that's it right? You not trying to stay in the drug game are you?"

Silence.

"Bambi...we out of the business after that right?" Denim repeats.

After my best friend Tatiana was murdered in Saudi, there was one man who looked out for me later on. Much later on. His name is Jim Blazer, but I call him Sarge. He's an E-9, a sergeant major of the army, which is the highest level in his category. I went downhill mentally after that scandalous bitch murdered Tatiana. And a lot of things happened before Jim got into my life, but once I met him I was better for it.

I change out of my tight jeans and slide on my army fatigue pants. Then I sit on my bed and grab my phone. The gunshot wound is throbbing, but I take my mind off of it, and it doesn't hurt as much for now. I call Sarge and he lights up the moment he hears my voice, "Is this, Private Bambi?" He sings.

I laugh. "No, I'm more like Dishonorably Discharged Bambi."

"Not in my book," he laughs. "You'll always be honorable to me."

I love him. So much.

"Where have you been?" He asks me. "I've been calling you like I'm crazy. I was about to take a trip over there if I didn't hear from you tonight."

"I'm fine," I sigh. "How was your trip?"

"That's what I want to talk to you about," he tells me.

"Not right now," I tell him. "I need something else from you, and it's very important."

"What's up, honey?" He asks me, "And, before I go any further, congratulations on having..." He gets quiet. "You've been drinking haven't you?"

The thing about Sarge and me is this; he knows what I'm about to say before I even open my mouth. He also taught me some hand, and eye signals that we both understood and used in the military to communicate in private. He's like a second father to me, except I can tell him anything without feeling like I'm letting him down. He loves me unconditionally.

Instead of responding the way he wants I say, "I need you to come visit, and teach my sisters how to use a gun."

"Are you in any trouble?" He asks me. "Because I can bring some of my platoon brothers over and we can—"

"No," I tell him. "You've done enough for me. I just need a little training for them, that's all."

He sighs. "Consider it done," he tells me. "And if you need anything else in the future, count me in for that too."

THURSDAY
NOVEMBER 8<sup>TH</sup> 2012
3 30 PM

# BAMBI

I'm sitting in my doctor's office as my doctor goes over my chart. The bed under me is hard and uncomfortable, but so is my doctor's attitude towards me today. He isn't pleasant like he usually is, and I know why. I need something from him he doesn't want to provide. I can tell by the way he tightens his shoulders as he recalls my past through my health chart that he's hesitant to help me.

He's biased. By all the times I crashed my bare fists into windows when I woke up in cold sweats in the middle of the night. By all the times Kevin battled with whether to commit me when I wouldn't leave my closet for days, because I thought the Iraqi's were in my house out to get me. He's also biased by how the sounds of helicopters flying above send me in a frenzy that only heavy sedatives and unconsciousness can take me out of. He thinks I'm crazy…maybe I am.

Although, I can't say I don't understand why he doesn't want to write me a prescription I'm in pain, and need something now to make me feel better. Ignoring the sting of the bullet wound doesn't work anymore. I was up all last night. I need the best meds money can buy.

"Mrs. Kennedy, I checked out your hand, and I realize you're in great pain," he sits my chart down on the table. "But, I don't feel comfortable prescribing you anything stronger than Tylenol 4. You have a serious condition that can be worsened by anything more potent."

I frown. Why doesn't he believe me when I say I'm not going to abuse the medicine?

"Not only are you a recovering alcoholic," the doctor continues, "but, you also suffer from PTSD (Post Traumatic Syndrome Disorder). Now I took an oath to prescribe medicines to my patients in good faith, and I can't do that for you now. I'm sorry."

"Dr. Bred, I know I suffer from Post Traumatic Syndrome Disorder. But, I haven't been taking my medicines so it shouldn't be a problem."

The army said I had PTSD after I was gang raped and beaten, which I don't want to get into now. In my opinion I think the term they use is an easy answer for unorganized chaos. The worst part about all of this is outside of the doctor, nobody but Kevin knew I had PTSD. I didn't tell my parents and I definitely didn't tell my sisters. Only Kevin and Dr. Bred knew that under certain circumstances, I could be pushed to the brink and snap.

His eyebrows rise. "What do you mean you haven't been taking your medicine, Bambi?" He moves closer to me. "You have to keep your disorder at bay. And, you do that by taking your meds everyday. Not when you feel like it."

"And, I'm doing just fine without them, Dr. Bred," I respond. "But, I still need help. You wouldn't begin to understand how it feels to be shot, and not take anything for the pain. If I were all about the medicine, I would've accepted the prescription the hospital tried to give me." That's a lie I actually forgot my prescription after everything happened. "But, I didn't. That should show you right there that I'm responsible. Right?"

"How long haven't you been taking your meds, Bambi?"

I reposition myself on the bed. I want to say since my husband was murdered, but instead I say, "Since Sunday. I think," I clear my throat. "Although, it could be longer."

He places a hand on my shoulder. I knock it off, and he steps back. He's never touched me before with so much pressure and it makes me uncomfortable.

"I'm sorry, Bambi. I didn't mean to violate you." He walks across the room and sighs. "I don't know why you've chosen to stop taking the medicine suddenly. And, it's obvious you don't want to tell me." He looks into my eyes. "I mean, did something traumatic happen recently? You can tell me anything. I promise."

"My hand, Dr. Bred," I raise it in the air and it throbs more. I need him to refocus, and stay the fuck out of my business. "Are you gonna give me the medicine or not?"

He opens a drawer, pulls out a white pad and writes a pre-scription. "Take this to the pharmacy on the fourth floor," he looks over at me. "It's for one bottle of Vicodin. No refill." He walks over and hands it to me. "Are we clear?"

I smile and take the prescription from his hand. I walk out of the room.

After getting the prescription filled at the pharmacy inside the hospital, I grab the white bag holding my meds and I walk away from the counter. I bump into a cute black chick. "Excuse me," I smile. "I wasn't looking where I was going."

It's cool," she says as I'm walking away. "But Bambi, I was wondering if I could talk to you for a minute? It's funny I'm even seeing you here."

My face twists up. I turn around, and my heart drops when I see her narrow face. "Who the fuck are you?"

"I know all about you, Bambi," she smiles. Now that I look at her hard enough, I can see she isn't cute at all. Her brown skin looks touched with too much blush. She looks kind of fake. "You are a celebrity. You're Mrs. Kevin Kennedy. But, I also know that you know me. Let's keep shit real, and move this along."

I'm angry. I can feel the blood rush to the surface of my skin, and boil. "What do you want?"

"Can you tell me where Kevin is? I've been looking for him since Sunday."

My lips pierce. I bite down on my bottom lip. I gotta stop doing this. "Why are you asking about my husband?"

She sighs. "Kevin hasn't contacted me or his son since Monday. Now I don't know what the fuck is going on, but I don't feel good about it either. I told him if he missed one day without calling us, I would contact you. The thing is, I didn't have to find you, because I'm running into you here." She grins and looks like the joker. Thoughts of murder occupy my mind. "He may have thought it was a game, but I was dead serious. Kevin has a son and you need to be clear on this. We deserve to be financially cared for at all times."

I feel small bumps rise all over my body. "What did you just say?"

She takes a defensive stand. "Your husband is my son's father. If I was speaking a different language earlier, that's English for you now. He fucked me and we had a child. I need him to honor is responsibility. Do you get it now?"

I look around, and everybody's head is tilted in our direction. She has an audience, and I'm embarrassed. I'm sweating again. On my forehead and upper lip. I tell myself I don't believe her, but of course I do. Lately I was discovering that there were a lot of things about Kevin I didn't know. Still, I must stand strong in the face of sluts. Whether Kevin fucked this gutter bitch or not, I'm a Kennedy, and she's gotta respect the name.

"I think you have it wrong, honey," I respond with a strong voice. "Kevin doesn't have any children outside of his twin sons who I gave birth to. And, since you referred to me as Mrs. Kevin Kennedy, I know you know me already."

I turn to walk away until she says, "I think you better take another look at my child. And, then make your statement again. You may be uninformed, but you're not blind. Use your eyes, this is Kevin's child."

I spin around. I grit on her, and then my eyes roll over her son. He has the same long lashes as Kevin and the same thick eyebrows. Of course he belongs to him. I feel myself tremble. I'm sweating harder, and my legs buckle at the knees. I fall forward, but when I do I'm grabbing the girl's hair with my good hand. I take her down to the dirty floor with my body weight. I use the arm with my gunshot wound to press my forearm against her throat. My other fist becomes magnetized to her jaw, and I strike her over and over again. Her skin opens up like a wax doll exposed to heat. Her warm blood lotions my hand. She's no match for me. But, then again most bitches aren't.

She's flailing wild arms in my direction, but isn't landing anything that causes me serious pain. Her son is a different story. I can feel his knuckles slam against my right ear repeatedly as he tries to help his mother. My ears are ringing. His annoying blows distract me, and I push him toward the wall where he stays.

When I'm done with her, I stand up, and throw the metal trashcan down on her face. It strikes her chin, and blood sprays up like a water fountain. Having damaged her face for what I predict is permanent, I spit on her and say, "Stay the fuck away from me and my family. Do you hear me, bitch?"

She rolls to her side, curls up in a ball and weeps. "You a crazy, black bitch! What is wrong with you? All I wanted to do was talk."

I look at her son and say, "Your daddy is dead, kid. Get use to it. I have to."

I storm away.

My tears fall down to my jeans as I sit in the driver seat of my Rolls Royce. My bandage is wetter with my blood. I guess the wound reopen. The teardrops cause the blue in my jeans to darken with tiny circles. The harder I wipe them away, the more I cry. How could Kevin betray me like this? Who did I really marry? If you fuck a bitch on the side, why you have to be a dirty-dick-ass-nigga about it and slide up in her raw? He has no respect for me, and my body and I'm glad he's dead. I wish my heart believed my mind.

I remember about four months ago I had a bad case of crabs. At first I didn't know what was happening because my panties had red dots everywhere, from the crabs sucking my blood. When I picked one off of my pubic hair one day, and saw it move, I almost fainted in my bathroom. Instead of telling Kevin right away, I avoided sex for one day by telling him my period started early. When I couldn't deny him my body any longer I told him the truth. I went through so many scenarios in my mind on how I could have gotten them, but I never thought Kevin went outside of our marriage once. It wasn't even in my thought process.

Kevin told me that I must've gotten them from the toilet in Las Vegas when we went to see Kanye West. And, I believed him because we went through hair after hair on his body, and there was not a crab in sight. I felt dirty thinking I could've given them to him, but he made me love him harder when he held me in his arms, and told me not to worry. I'm such a fucking idiot! That nigga gave them creepy-crawlers to me. To hell with Kevin Kennedy!

I remove his picture from my glove compartment, and look at his smug face. No wonder he didn't allow me to have any friends, or hang with anybody else without a Kennedy name. I would run the risk of meeting one of his whores. I wonder how many other kids he has out there. I throw the picture down on the floor, and it floats to my feet.

I remove the pill bottle from the prescription bag, and twist off the cap. I push two out, toss them into my throat, and wash them down with the Corona hidden in the paper bag between my legs. I take two more for good measure. I can't wait for the feeling I know is coming. The feeling that nothing matters. The feeling that all is okay, when the world is going to hell around me.

Suddenly I feel like I'm being watched. When I look out ahead of me, I see a white man in a navy blue Honda Sedan. He's staring in my direction. Who is he, and what does he want with me? Without moving my upper body too much, so that he could see me, I reach to my left to release my hammer under my seat. Slowly I raise it up, so that the barrel is facing in his direction. I roll my window down and aim at him. He can see me now. I wink, fully prepared to fire, but he speeds away from the scene.

My mind is racing until, well, until suddenly I feel light and don't feel anything anymore.

# DENIM

I stand in the kitchen with my hands on my hips watching Scarlett drink ice-cold water. Bum ass bitch! I'm expecting her to give me a real answer about what happened to my baby girl. Right now Jasmine is upstairs sleep, because the medicine they gave her for the pain makes her tired. She suffered a broken hip and leg, and the doctor doubts she'll walk the same again.

"Scarlett, when are you finally going to tell me what really happened to my little girl?" I ask leaning against the stove. "I went in your bathroom yesterday, and noticed there's a carpet right in front of the tub. So how could you slip? It doesn't make any sense to me."

Scarlett's face reddens. "Why do you want to make me so guilty, Denim? Why can't you believe that I didn't mean to hurt Jasmine?"

"Because something is up with you," I point at her. "Camp use to tell Bradley all the time how violent you were. Said you got real jealous whenever he would go out, and hit him in the face sometimes when he came home late at night. He said half the time he wanted to stay out, and that he despised being married to you. Camp told Bradley that he was even thinking about divorcing you and everything."

Scarlett slams the water glass down. "How did you know that? About the divorce?"

"I just told you," I respond. "I never said anything to the girls, because I respected your marriage, and I didn't think you were abusive. But, now I'm wondering if I was wrong."

Scarlett pushes past me and walks into the living room. "If you can blame me so easily for something like this, Denim it means you've never trusted me in the first place."

"Bitch, I'm not trying to hear none of that shit. Bambi and Race may be blind to who you really are, but I'm not anymore. If it slithers like a snake kill it," I yell. "For real, I would respect you more if you just came out and told me what you did to Jasmine. For once since this shit began, just be honest."

Scarlett stops in the foyer, and I stand in front of her. Her cheeks redden. She's under pressure. Good for the bitch.

"I'm gonna be straight with you, Scarlett," I say. "I know watching an autistic child is hard work. Trust me I do." My voice is softer. "There are plenty of times when I question God as to why he gave me an autistic baby. And, sometimes I even curse him for it. Especially, when I'm trying to connect with her, and she acts like she doesn't see me. It's normal to feel overwhelmed with autistic children, Scarlett, and I can understand if you lost it when you watched her. I just want the truth. I promise you, that if you tell me what really happened now, I will trust you again. But, if you lie to me, I will eventually be the death of you."

When she doesn't respond, and appears to be thinking, I'm hoping that the truth will come out of her thin lips. Instead I see headlights brighten the curtains in the living room.

Scarlett grabs her coat. "I never meant to hurt Jasmine," she tells me while twisting the doorknob. "I hope you can forgive me."

When she runs out I walk up to the window. It's dark outside but I can see Bunny's black BMW in front of the house. Scarlett hops inside and they pull off. What the fuck is up with that? They don't get up like that with one another. So why are they together?

I walk to the house phone on the wall to call Bambi. It's evening and she hasn't been home. I hope things are okay, since I know she's drinking again, despite telling us at dinner the other day that she quit. I want her to get help. When I dial her cell phone number, instead of her responding the call goes to voicemail.

I smile because the voicemail is in Kevin's voice and he says, '*You have reached the love of my life...Mrs. Bambi Kennedy. She's probably with me, but will get up with you when she can. Leave a message.*'

How cute. I don't leave a message because I want to talk to her about Scarlett's skunk-ass in person. I just hope Bambi finally believes me.

My mother smells funkier than ever today. She's on the bed, naked from the waist down. A piece of plastic is beneath her ass to catch the wetness. I dip the orange sponge in the warm soapy water, open her legs and wipe her vagina. The smell is sickening. White shit is caked up around her clit so I have to get it good.

"Ouch, Denim...not so rough," she tells me as she flips the buttons on the remote control. "I tell you all the time that you're too heavy handed."

I frown. "Ma, if I don't wash you good you're going to get an infection," I reply dipping the sponge back into the murky water to wash her asshole. "If Grainger would wipe you every other day like I asked, it wouldn't be so bad when I do it." I spread her beefy ass cheeks and wipe her ass hole. Shit is caked up everywhere in there also. But, when I see something plastic in her asshole, and pull it out, I'm grossed out. It's a used condom. I throw it down on the floor and throw up what I ate yesterday. I wipe my mouth on my arm. How disgusting. "Ma, why would you let a nigga fuck you and leave that in your body? What's wrong with you?"

She looks embarrassed. "Denim, stop making everything a big deal, it happens to the smallest of girls." She focuses back on the TV and I cut it off.

"Ma, you can't leave foreign objects in your body! What the fuck!" Her body is spread out all over the bed and seems to melt into the mattress. I can't tell where she ends or the bed begins. "They don't even have enough respect for you to throw the condom in the trash." Frustrated, I lean against the wall across from her bed.

"Denim, I got enough on my mind. I don't need you fussing at me for getting a little dick from time to time." She tells me trying to get her upper body comfortable. "These white doctors trying to take my leg, Denim. I need my leg. That's the only thing on my mind right now."

She loves to turn shit around. "What difference does it make if they do take your leg? You don't use it anyway."

She pouts and I can tell she's about to cry. I'm sick of her fake crying games. Even as I look at the two dressers that sit on the left and right of the bed, they're filled with cookies, candies and sweet sodas. She has diabetes and the doctor told her to eat right. I spent thousands of dollars in vegetables to help her eat healthier, but when I open the refrigerator everything is rotten and spoiled. Then this bitch had a nerve to have me washing her funky ass, with a condom in her body? She can cry if she wants to, but I don't care anymore.

"Why would you say something like that to me," she sniffles. "When you know how hard I'm trying."

"Ma, you don't do anything but suck dick and eat! How is that trying?"

"Denim," she screams at me. "Watch how you talk to me. I'm still your mother."

"I'm being honest, ma. You allow these men to come over here, put whip cream and shit on their dicks while you suck it off, and you think shit is sweet. I'm keeping it one hundred with you, you're playing yourself like a fat whore."

"Denim, you don't know how it feels to be immobile."

"That's right, ma. But, do you know why?" I pause. "Because, unlike you, I didn't allow a man to bring me down. I didn't allow a man to stuff my face full of food until I was too fat to get out of bed when he was done with my body. I didn't allow a man to make me feel like dying when he was through with me, ma." I walk up to the bed. "Ma, you gotta get your life together. I'm not gonna always be able to take care of you."

"What do you mean?" She asks with wide eyes. "I can't afford my health insurance or my medications without you."

This type of pressure makes me feel the need to do stuff I don't want to. I agreed to help Bambi facilitate the meeting with The Russians for three reasons. First, I know my mother needs my financial help. Secondly I have an autistic daughter. And lastly, I do not want to give Grainger the satisfaction of knowing I failed with Bradley. But, I'm starting to not give a fuck no more.

"I'm going to help you for as long as I can, ma. But, I'm starting to feel like you not appreciating what I do for you."

"Baby, that isn't true. Of course I appreciate—,"

"Then start taking care of yourself, ma," I cut her off. "I want you to start eating right, and I want you to cut these men off at the door."

"You don't understand, Denim. I need them."

"Even at the expense of your own health?" I look down at the floor again. "A nigga bust off in you and left a condom in your body. That's not good, ma!" She looks away from me. "Ma, are you saying that you need these men even at the expense of your own health?"

She stares into my eyes. "I'm saying that whether I'm fat, skinny, ugly or beautiful, it doesn't matter if I don't have a man to make me feel like a woman. You have Bradley, Denim." I can feel a cry coming on realizing my husband is dead, but I push it down deep. "I'm trying to get that. And, if it means letting a man rub on me, grab on me, spit in my face, slap me around and take pictures of me while I'm like this, than so be it. Because at the end of the day, at least he's here."

My heart breaks, because my mother use to be so strong. When my sister and me were kids she was the one who would take a dollar out of our allowance every time she saw us with our heads held low. Now she's different. Weaker. Fatter. Uglier. And, I hate her for all of those reasons and more. Maybe she's more alike me than I realize and I'm scared.

"Ma, you can't presume to know the things about my life I don't tell you. I might not always have the unlimited access to money. Things change. People change, and situations change."

Her eyebrows rise. "Oh, my God! Please don't tell me that Bradley has finally left you. I knew it was coming, but I always thought that you would have more time. I hope you saved up some money for us because we're going to need it."

My nose twists up. "What do you mean has Bradley *finally* left me?"

"Baby, I didn't mean it that way. It's just that me and Grainger always said it was just a matter of time before he left you. Seeing as how he was her boyfriend first and all. I figure that he's still in love with her, and I was always afraid he would hurt your feelings."

I'm consumed with anger. I do everything for this bitch. Wash her pussy when she can't do it herself. Shop for her. Buy her expensive clothes to fit her large body, and still she takes Grainger's side. And, then this bitch got the nerve to think my husband would want a fucking drug addict? As good as my juicy is? She got us all fucked up.

"You know what, ma, I'm done with you. From here on out have Grainger take care of you and wash your funky pussy. I'm out." I walk toward the living room to get Jasmine. I'm crying and I hate myself for it. So ungrateful, my mother is.

When I walk into the living room, Grainger has Jasmine in her lap while she's stroking her hair. Jasmine is sleep. It seems odd, and I snatch Jasmine out of her lap. I sit Jasmine in the loveseat and say, "What you doing holding my baby?"

Grainger shakes her head. "Look at what God did to you," she looks at Jasmine who is sleeping again, "that's what happens when you betray your sister. You have a monster for a baby."

The hairs all over my body feel like they stand up. "I'm telling you right now that you're pushing your luck with me," I say to her. "What you want me to do, fuck you up in this bitch again?"

"I didn't mean it that way," she says. "Besides, Jasmine is cute even with her slow brain."

She's doing all she can to push me and I hold back. I don't want to give her the satisfaction. I think she wants me to fight her so that she can feel alive. She's a zombie, so I'll leave her that way. "What do you want, Grainger?"

She steps up to me. I can smell the dirt on her skin. "Word has it that the Kennedy Kings aren't making deliveries," she says with a smirk on her face. "Heads are gonna roll."

I try to keep a straight face. "Well whoever has the word doesn't know what the fuck they talking about. My husband don't miss no deliveries, sweetie-pie."

"Your husband huh?" She giggles. "You just love throwing that shit in my face."

"I'm not throwing shit in your face," I say with my hands on my hips. "The last name is Kennedy, bitch. Deal with it. It's really time to start doing that."

She looks angry now. "Where is Bradley?" Grainger continues. "How come I haven't seen him in days? Normally he checks on ma at least once a week."

I wake Jasmine up, grab her coat off of the chair and place it on her body. "How 'bout my husband has better things to do then to come around here and worry about ma."

"I hope he's okay," Grainger says shaking her head. "Because from what I'm told, niggas is looking for him too. He might be lying in a ditch somewhere. Are you sure he's still alive?"

"You swear you know everything," I grab Jasmine's arm and slowly walk her to the door. The cast on her legs makes it awkward for her to move. "Instead of trying to sell them fake ass purses you be pushing, you need to get a fucking job, and go wash ma's funky ass. I left it in there for you."

"People who are almost dead shouldn't give directions," Grainger continues. "Because they also said unless they get their delivery, women and children can get the business too. Watch your back, baby sis. And your slow daughter's too."

I move toward my car without responding. When I strap Jasmine into her car seat, I call Bambi again. She still doesn't answer the phone. What the fuck is she up too?

# BAMBI

I wake up to extreme pain. When I open my eyes I'm still in my car. My head feels heavy and loopy. The sky has turned dark purple and the stars are out. My jeans are down at my thighs along with my white silk panties. I feel a piercing pain between my legs again, and I wonder what it is. When I look down I see a man wearing a filthy tan trench coat. His face is stuffed between my thighs. The smell rising off of his body resembles dry piss, and dirty skin. I'm about to yell, but my mind immediately goes into survival mode.

The pain is the worst I'd ever experienced. And, I say that despite the gunshot wound in my hand, and the things I experienced in Saudi Arabia. A bum is nibbling on my clit so hard, that it feels like he's slicing into it with his teeth. I don't want him to know I'm awake, because I don't know if he has a weapon or not. I have to be easy before I make my next move.

At a snail's pace I reach down to grab my gun in the driver's side door. Just as I feel his dry tongue slither into my pussy hole, I grip my gun. With the handle firmly in my palm, I raise it, press it down to the back of his head and pull the trigger. Red jelly-like substance splashes on my face, windows and dashboard. I wipe it away from my mouth and eyes. I hope he doesn't have AIDS. The smell of blood and gunfire reminds me of the worst times in my life.

I haven't killed a man in over 17 years. I'm breathing so hard now, I'm shivering. What the fuck is happening to me? Why did this person come into my car, and violate my body?

I push his limp body out of my lap and into the passenger seat. From what's left of his face, I can see he's about forty years old. He's black. And, now he's dead. I guess he won't be raping another person anytime in the near future.

I continued to wipe his guts out of my eyes so I can see better. I can't believe this shit just happened to me. I guess the four Vicodin pills mixed with the beer I drank put me in a deep sleep. And, because of it I let my guard down.

I look around to see if anyone is looking in my direction. Or if they witnessed the crime I just committed. But, everything looks vacant out here, which is probably why he chose to rape me. I don't even know how I got here.

I pull up my jeans and pull down my shirt and look in the backseat of my ride for my purse. I notice immediately that it's gone. My heartbeat kicks up speed. I can't believe I was so high that I wasn't aware of my surroundings. I need to be careful, because if I would've waited a little bit longer it could've been me dead instead of him.

I take a deep breath and try to get my mind right. What am I going to do, to get myself out of the situation? If I call the cops, they might investigate me, and possibly want to talk to my husband. Kevin's absence might bring attention to where he was, and who we are. I can't go home, and I can't get the police involved. I need that money first.

Using the phone in my car I call Denim on her cell phone. It rings twice before she answers. "Denim, I need you and the girls to meet me at the *H* motel." I reach across the corpse, open the door and push his body out.

"Which one?"

"The one off of New York Avenue. This is important so you gotta come now." I close the door and pull out of the parking space.

"I'll let the girls know," Denim says. "Are you okay?"

"Just hurry up. I'll explain everything later."

# DENIM

The first thing I feel when I walk into Bambi's motel room is the heat. I'm the first person to see her condition. Her clothes are covered in dry blood, and her hair is snatched back into a messy ponytail. At first I was worried that the blood belonged to her, and that she had possibly been in an accident, until I see the gun sitting on the table in the room.

Once we're all inside, Scarlett latches the door to make sure it's locked. I hate that bitch. Every time I see her it's hard not to think about Jasmine, and what I know she did to her in that bathroom. Jasmine is with Bambi's mother so at least she won't have to see her face right now.

"Thanks for coming, ya'll." Bambi walks toward us. "I been beating myself up ever since that shit happened tonight."

"Can you start by telling us what's going on?" I ask her walking up to her. The moment I'm within her breathing space I can tell she's been drinking.

"I killed a man," Bambi says pacing. "He was in my lap, and I blew his fucking brains out." She stops and looks at all of us. The way she gives us the news sounds regular, and I wonder how many people she has killed before. "And if I could do it again on my mother's life I would."

Scarlett approaches her. "Bambi, I am so happy you are alive. If we would have lost you I think I would've lost my mind." She places a hand on Bambi's shoulder. "Can you tell us what he did to you?" She asks looking over her body.

I know we here for our girl, but just the sound of Scarlett's voice does something evil to me.

"He raped me," Bambi says holding her head down. "And, I said nobody would ever take anything from me again." She looks at Scarlett. "The nigga didn't get the memo so he paid for it with his life. He actually...he actually...oh my God!"

I have so many questions, but I don't know where to start. First I want to know what she meant by saying that no one would ever take anything else from her. Secondly, I want to know who violated her tonight.

"Bambi, what are you talking about?" I ask softly. "When you say he was in your lap?"

"I was in my car sleep," she says sitting down in the chair at the table. "I guess I was tired after being heart broken by Kevin once again," she pauses and looks as if she wants to cry. "Anyway my mind was heavy and I dosed off in my car. When I woke up, some nigga was in between my legs chewing on my pussy."

We all frown. I don't know what disturbs me most, some strange man touching her, or chewing on her pussy.

Although we were all probably taken at her response, Race was the loudest. "Yuck," she screams. "What do you mean he chewed on your pussy? And are you okay?" She looks in the direction of her crouch.

"I'm still sore, but I'm alive," Bambi responds. "The shit was a nightmare."

"Bambi," I say, "something doesn't make sense. How was he able to get to your lap? It's like you're missing a step."

She sighs and rolls her eyes at me. I know right away I'm on to something. "My hand was in pain so I went to my doctor's. He gave me a prescription, and I took a few Vicodin and drank a beer. I must've dosed off because when I came to, he was in my car."

"So your car door was open?" I continue. "That's what you're saying to me?"

"Yes, Denim. I'm saying that I made a mistake."

"Bambi, you drive a fucking Rolls Royce! What is wrong with you? You better be glad you still alive. You could've gotten car jacked! The shit you been doing lately is dangerous," I yell. "The blackouts, the drinking...all of this shit has gone on too far."

"Tell me something I don't already know, Denim," she responds.

"Do you realize that it's Thursday? And, that we have a meeting with the Russians on Saturday? We can't have you running around doing dumb shit when we days away from completing something you started."

She stands up and approaches me. The look in her eyes is deadly. We all had our opinion about what happened to Bambi in that war. Race and I said she might have been raped. Scarlett said she might have seen senseless violence. But, none of us knew for sure. Yet here I am standing in front of her, scared for my life. I have no doubt that if I pushed too hard, she could hurt me too.

"What the fuck do you mean running around doing dumb shit," she asks. "Denim, I'm having the worst week of my life—,"

"And we are too," I yell cutting her off. "You aren't the only mothafucka who lost a husband this week, girlie. We all have," I continue. "I want to cry so badly my chest aches from holding it back all the time. But, just like you told us the other day I'm telling you the same thing. You must toughen the fuck up. Be glad that the only thing he chewed was your pussy. He could've taken your life too."

"How could you say something so callous to me?"

"Callous?" I scream. "There's nothing callous about the shit I'm saying to you. I'm speaking the truth. My husband is dead, your husband is dead, all of our husbands are fucking dead! That's our reality," I say out of breath. "But, there's still work to be done, and there will be plenty time for crying. Right now you have to toughen up, and you have to do it now."

Bambi laughs at me. "Toughen up? Bitch, I lost my husband, was shot in my hand, and found out that Kevin had another child outside of our marriage. And, you know what, I'm still

137

breathing. So name a bitch who's tougher than me right now. I want to meet her!"

We all gasp upon the news of the baby.

"Baby," I say in a soft voice. "I'm so sorry. I didn't know Kevin—"

"How could you?" Bambi turns to walk away. "I didn't know about his son either."

She sits on the bed, and drops her head. I want to hold her, but Bambi's actions can be sporadic and violent if touched suddenly. "He had a little boy," she continues shaking her head. "And, he was so handsome that I knew it was his son the moment I saw his face. I knew he was Kevin's son before she even told me."

Scarlett walks up to the bed and sits next to her. "Bambi, this is fucked up." She looks up at Race and me, but I look away. "I don't know what the fuck was on Kevin's mind, to step out on you, but he's dirty as shit for this move," Scarlett continues. "I don't think any of us are dumb enough to think that every now and again, the boys wouldn't step out. To be honest, that's the nature of the beast."

"The nature of the beast?" I yell at Scarlett. "That's you white girls' problem today. And, then they say black bitches yell too much. You accept too much shit from these niggas, and make it easy for them not to face the music. A dog is a dog. A cheat is a cheat and a bum is a bum. And, if any of us accept disloyalty something is wrong with us not them."

"I'm not white and I agree with, Scarlett," Race replies. "We all know our men cheat. I think the difference is we get mad at them when they don't do a good job of hiding it. The white girls just accept it and move on. That's just my opinion."

"So you saying Bradley cheated on me too?" I ask Race.

"I'm saying you're not immune to the deeds of a nigga with money and power," Race replies. "Yes we are wifed up. Yes we were given the ring, but at the end of the day they held all of the power."

"Not anymore," Bambi says to us. "Not anymore."

Race walks up to Bambi, drops to the floor, and lays her head on Bambi's knee. Instead of saying anything to Bambi, Race just cries in her lap. Her tears roll out of her eyes and dampen Bambi's jeans.

"I loved that nigga more than anything," Bambi says with glossy eyes. I can tell she wants to cry harder, but she doesn't. "He made me sleep with his dick in my pussy every night. There were nights where it was too hot, and I wanted to move to the edge of the bed just to breathe. I didn't because he would think I was cheating, and argue with me about it for weeks at a time. I'm talking about the silent treatment." Her head hangs lower. "I gave him two of the greatest sons in the world. I loved and encouraged him throughout his journey. And, I stood in his shadows. And this is how he repays me? Why would he do this shit to me?"

I want to hug my sister, because I can tell she needs me. But, there's no room for me next to her. Scarlett is to her side and Race is on her knees. Instead of trying to find my space around her I pull up in front of her. She needs a lieutenant. Not a weakling. I'll leave them to the bullshit. When I'm in position, I look dead into her eyes.

"Bambi, Kevin's done for," I say to her. "He's dead. He can't love you anymore. He can't come back and answer to what he did to you, and he can't take away the pain. You have to pick up the pieces, because we need you now. You were the one who told me that if we didn't get stronger, and pull ourselves together, we were going to run the risk of not being able to take care of each other, and our families. You had me on that shit, and I need for you to follow through. There's nothing more important right now than this meeting on Saturday. And, if afterwards you want to grieve, then we won't stop you. As a matter of fact, I say when that time comes that we open one of them packs of cocaine, grab some champagne, and some sexy ass young niggas and have a proper grieving party. But, right now is not the time."

Bambi smiles at me. "I guess you my little sergeant at arms now."

"I'm your family, and the bitch who will keep it real when the other suckers won't," I say looking at Scarlett.

"She's right," Scarlett says adding her two fucking cents. "We need you strong, but you gotta stop drinking too."

My face tightens. Oh how I hate that bitch. But, then again what's new? But, as much as I talk shit, Camp chose. He chose her as his wife, and for now I would have to stay true to the Kennedy name. But, on everything I love we are going to have a proper discussion about what happened to my little girl when the time was right.

In the mean time, I'm not going to be fake sisters with her any longer. And, I plan to dig deeper into her past. We didn't know much about Scarlett. She came into our family bare. I never met a cousin, her mother, her father or anybody else on her side of the family. I can't help but wonder why. If they are ashamed of a daughter who married black, I can understand that, but Scarlett walked away whenever the subject of her family came up. No worries though, I'll get at her later.

"I'm going to stop fucking with the bottle," Bambi says yet again. "But, when I went to sleep in my car, I had a dream about us. All four of us."

"What was it about?" I ask.

"I had a dream that the four of us became the biggest drug kingpins the world had ever seen."

Race laughs and says, "If you had that dream, I couldn't have been anywhere near the picture."

"You were there, and you were great too," Bambi responds. "You were handy with them weapons."

"That's the future," I say. "For now, we need to prepare for the greatest moment of our lives. The meeting with the Russians on Saturday."

"Now you talking," Bambi says. "Now you talking."

# FRIDAY
# NOVEMBER 9$^{TH}$ 2012
# 6 00 PM

# RACE

As I park my pink Porsche in front of Carey's house, I can't help but smile. Carey is the type of person who I can talk to about anything. She knows Ramirez and me are married, but doesn't try to take my place, despite sharing a bed with him when he gets in the mood for something different.

There were even a few times when Ramirez was over her house too late, and Carey would send him home not wanting to destroy our marriage. So yes she was the side chick, and yes she loved my husband. But, at the end of the day she loved me too, and it was something I could feel whenever I was in her presence. I know my sisters would never understand. So Carey remained me, and Ramirez's best-kept secret to a happy marriage.

I get out and knock on the door. It opens and Carey appears wearing a pink silk nightgown. Her hair falls on her shoulders. "Hey, Race," she says bringing me into her warm arms. "Why is it that you get prettier every time I see you?"

"Not prettier than you," I respond. I feel light on my feet now. Not sure why.

"Girl, you're so silly," she continues. She runs her fingers through my light brown hair. "Your beauty runs rings around mine."

I don't believe her. How could I? She's gorgeous. She stands five foot two, which is shorter than me, and she has triple D breasts. Ramirez was a titty man despite his telling me repeatedly that mine are *okay* and cute. He even tried to coerce me into the doctor's office for an upgrade. And what my sisters don't know was that next month; I was going to go under the knife for him. But, that was before someone killed him, and took him away from me.

When she releases me I can see a cute smile spread across her honey brown face. I really like this girl...so much. Don't get it twisted, I never had sex with her, but I can only imagine how great it must be when Ramirez is inside of her.

"You don't know how much I've been worried sick about you," Carey tells me. "How come you haven't been answering my calls? I haven't spoke to you since Saturday."

I swallow. She makes me jittery and nervous. "I know and I'm so sorry," I walk into her beautiful home furnished and paid for by us. "I know you were worried, but I couldn't get away to come see you or talk to you."

She rushes into the kitchen, "Please don't do that again, Race. I care about you. I know our situation is weird, and doesn't make sense to outsiders, but you and I have an understanding. If I don't speak to you my day is fucked up. You know that."

Her voice sounds like a smooth duet from Mariah and Luther Vandross. It was something I wanted to hear over and over again. "Why you say that?"

She digs into cabinet after cabinet. She's busying herself with something, but I can't see what she's doing because I'm staring at her body. She moves around like a dancer. A ballerina. Maybe it's because she's a stripper. How does she do that?

"We've had this conversation over and over again," she starts. "I swear, Race, sometimes I think you ask me questions just to hear me talk."

I feel like she can see right through me. How does she know? I didn't even know before that moment how much I idolize her. But, yes it's true...I love hearing her voice.

Instead of telling her that most nights I want to stay in her bed, instead of my own I say, "I really want to know what you meant, when you said we have an understanding." I take off my brown leather jacket. I keep my sexy Christian Louboutin high heel boots on, because I think she likes them. She says they make me look taller and sexier.

When she finally comes out of the kitchen she's carrying a hot drink in a red coffee mug. The moment the smell slithers up my nose I know what it is. My favorite …Colonial Hot Buttered Rum. I can see the white whip cream just oozing alongside of the cup. I'm afraid the cream will fall onto the Italian carpeting until she takes her pink tongue and laps it off. My pussy jumps. Why does it jump?

She walks me to the plush pea-green sofa. I sink into it, and it feels like my grandmother who passed when I was ten years old is wrapping me in her arms again. When I'm comfortable she hands me my drink, and I sip it slowly. The heat burns my upper lip, and I'm about to cool it with my own tongue until she runs her wet tongue over my mouth instead. I'm shivering.

"You always burn yourself whenever I make this drink for you," she rubs her hand over my face and looks into my eyes. "Honest, Race I don't know how you drink such a high calorie drink and not gain weight. You're so fit and in shape."

I'm tingling all over. I'm stunned. I can still smell the scent of the watermelon Starburst she ate earlier on my mouth. I wonder if her tongue is sweet. Carey is not doing anything different. She's this way every time I visit, which is why I make it my business to see her twice a week. But each time I come here, and she treats me like this it feels new. It's sorta like my favorite movie *A Girl's Love Story*. I can watch it a hundred times and it never gets old. She…never…gets…old.

"Thank you," I look down at my brown boots again. "You're so sweet to me."

"Tell me where you've been," she sits so close to me, her right titty is rubbing against my arm. "And, why haven't you or Ramirez called? Don't lie, Race. You know I can see right through you," she places a warm hand on my breast.

"You haven't spoken to Ramirez?" I ask.

Her hand drops into her lap. "Race, in the years we have been playing this game together, name one time I've spoken to Ramirez, or have seen Ramirez when you weren't aware?"

I couldn't recall. "I don't know," I tell her, for fear of sounding dumb.

"Listen, beautiful," my pussy jumps again. "I love Ramirez, and I've never lied to you about it, but I will drop him dead if he tried to have a relationship with me that didn't involve you. I fuck Ramirez, and see to it that his needs are met, but I need you in my life." If she's running game on me she's the best.

Since Kevin has had a baby on Bambi, I have to ask, "Has he ever tried to have a relationship without me?"

"Never," she says running her fingers through my hair again, "and if he had, I would send him on his way. I don't play that shit. My position is to keep your marriage together, not pull it apart."

I think about when she made my drink earlier in her kitchen. At some point, when she was opening and closing the cabinets I noticed all of my favorite foods were stocked up in her house. *My favorites*...not Ramirez's.

"Thank you for your loyalty," I say. "If I told anybody about us they would call me dumb or stupid."

"Then don't tell them about us," she says. "Why we gotta be validated by what other people think? You love me and I love you both," she smiles. "And don't worry about my loyalty, because it will always remain with you," she kisses me on the nose and this time I can feel my syrup leak out of my pussy. "Its just important for me to make things clear. Your place with me is firm, and I put you first."

I can feel her riding for me like the steering wheel to my Porsche. So I feel comfortable. Comfortable enough to tell her about Ramirez's death. After all, she's part of my family too. No she doesn't bare the Kennedy name. And, no she won't be welcomed into the Kennedy home. She's still a part of me and Ramirez's world, and I love her all the same.

"Carey, I have something to tell you," I say firmly like I heard Ramirez do many times before. Look at me rising to the occasion, and being all strong and stuff. Ramirez would never believe it if he didn't see it with his own eyes. I'm sure of it.

"What is it?" She looks worried, and I feel bad for her.

"Something terrible has happened to Ramirez. When he was out of town—,"

"What are you talking about?" Her eyes widen when she cuts me off. "Was he in an accident or something?"

I wish I could tell her that was the case, but it isn't true. "No, it's much worse." It's ironic, my being strong for her forces me to be stronger for myself. I don't feel as weak as I usually am. I feel like a protector.

"Race, you gotta tell me now, or else I don't think I can hold up my body. What is going on with my sweet Ramirez?"

I certainly don't want her falling forward, or shitting on herself like I did the first day I found out he was killed. So I take three deep breaths and say, "He was murdered."

Carey's eyes widen larger. At first I'm afraid that her eyelashes will get tangled in the soft curls that surround her face. But, then she falls forward, and presses her face into the palms of her hands. I'm supposed to do something. I'm supposed to protect her right? So I put my hand on her right shoulder. It's only there for a minute before she falls into the center of my lap. I can't hear what she's saying at first, although she's clearly speaking. Instead I focus on the way her body jiggles, causing her breasts to dance. The heat from her body causes my pussy to warm up like a Crock-Pot. I'm horny during the worst time in my life. Something is wrong with me for being turned on by her vulnerability. Something is terribly wrong with me.

And, then it all makes sense. I'm taken back to the period when I first met my husband.

# 8 YEARS EARLIER

*Race was on her knees sucking Diamond's clit in the stall of the girl's bathroom in high school. Diamond belonged to Ramirez in public, but Race behind closed doors. Diamond was gripping Race's hair so hard as she sat on the toilet while getting her button flipped, that Race's eyeglasses were smeared with Diamond's pussy juice. Race had eaten pussy in the past,* but she never tasted a button as sweet as Diamond's in her young life.

"Flip that tongue you nerdy, bitch," Diamond supervised, gripping Race's hair so roughly she was snatching it out by the roots. "Yes, yes, yes, you doing that shit, girl."

As Diamond dropped all of her cum into Race's waiting mouth, she received a page from her boyfriend Ramirez on her beeper. Having gotten her rocks off, she pushed Race's face back and spun the toilet tissue roll. Taking a heap of tissue in her hand she wiped the syrup from her clit knowing that since school was almost out, Ramirez would be pounding her back out within the hour.

"You can leave now," Diamond said since Race hadn't made an exit.

Race stood up and wiped her knees. "You coming to my house later right?"

"I don't know," Diamond shrugged. "It depends on what Ram wants to do with me."

"But, I haven't seen you in—,"

Race's sentence was cut short by the grip Diamond had on her throat. "Let me tell you something, bitch, what we do in here stays in here. If I ever find out you told Ramirez about us I would deny you and then kill you? Now get the fuck out of here. It's too crowded."

Race opened the stall door and trooped to the sink to wash her cum soaked face. She was tired of Diamond fucking with her feelings. Race didn't even understand what was going on with herself. Race had feelings for Ramirez and Diamond and both of them seemed to treat her the same way, like she didn't exist. Was she gay or not? She didn't know.

When the school bell rang, Race went to the school's office for a letter she was told was waiting on her. She learned she was valedictorian and was so proud of herself. When she came out of the office she accidently bumped into Diamond. Diamond decided to make fun of Race in front of Ramirez, to conceal how she really felt about Race. Race's tongue was the only bath Dia-

*mond's pussy had seen for the day, yet she acted as if they were strangers.*

*Diamond, slapped the books out of Race's hand with Ramirez standing right next to her. Then in a rage filled fuel, she kicked her repeatedly in the stomach. Race was hurt and devastated at her actions. Why was the girl who she treated so kindly in the bathroom trying to kill her now?*

*Race vowed to never mess with a female again. Of course that was before she met Carey.*

After crying for what seemed like two days in my lap, Carey raised her head. Her brown cheeks were red as my favorite lipstick and she looked distraught. "I'm so sorry, Race," she tells me. "I'm sitting here crying my eyes out, and here it is you are the one who has lost your husband."

"We both lost, because we both loved him."

She sighs and wipes her face with the back of her hands. "So what are we going to do now? I mean, who is going to take care of us?"

I shrug and look into my hands. I don't have a solid answer. Although we had a plan of action to meet The Russians, I'm not sure where life would take me from there. I'm not even sure if the plan will work. I mean dressing up like men? It sounded far-fetched to me.

"I don't know," I tell her picking back up my drink. "For right now Bambi says we can't tell anybody that the guys are dead. Pending this meeting with some important people on Saturday," I sigh. "But, I might have to take on more work from independent movie companies who hire me."

"Independent movie companies," she frowns. "You still doing that shit?"

Her comment stings a little but I let it slide. The movie makeup and props I make are my life's work. It's something I adore and always wanted to do. "That's what I've always done even with Ramirez taking care of me."

"But, what about me?" She points to herself. "Who's going to take care of me? I stopped dancing at the club for you guys. My rent alone is $1,400, Race". And, that's not including my car note, my clothes and stuff like that. Ramirez gave me an allowance of ten thousand dollars a month...minimum."

My eyes widen. "Carey, I'll do what I can, but I can't afford that type of money a month right now. I spend most of my cash on my supplies, because Ramirez always had me financially."

Carey gives me a look that can kill. I saw it one other time in the bathroom in high school. When Diamond grabbed me, and threatened my life.

Carey wipes the tears off of her face again and her entire demeanor changes. "You are going to have to take care of me, Race. I...I can't do it by myself. I need your help."

"But I can't afford this lifestyle," I tell her looking around her home.

Carey stands up, walks to the door and opens it. "Race, I love you, but if you deny me the exact same lifestyle I am accustomed to now, I'm going to be your best enemy. I'll also tell your little friends and family about our arrangement. Now you get in your little pink Porsche, and find me some money. And, don't come back here until you do."

# SCARLETT

Bunny is sitting in front of me with a knowing expression on her face. I hate this woman, but I also realize we are connected forever. She owns me now and it's all because of what I'm about to tell her. As her big lips move, I run my hand over my stomach. I'm trying to see if the baby is still inside of me, even though I tried to kill it after I hurt Jasmine.

I sat in the car after dropping Jasmine off at the hospital, and slapped myself over and over in the stomach with a piece of plywood. That's how I got the horizontal mark across my belly. Can a baby live inside of a monster? I hope not.

"Why did you hurt your daughter?" She crosses her legs and smirks at me. "I mean what would make a woman do something so callous to a child?"

The shame washes over me like quicksand. No matter what I say, I won't be able to take back what I did. And, as long as people like her know about it, I won't be able to forget either. "She wasn't a baby," I clear my throat. "She was four-years old."

"She was still a child," she grins. "So why would you do it?"

"Because I couldn't stand the sound of her crying," I look into her eyes. "I couldn't stand the annoying ring of her sobs. So I wanted her to stop." I'm filled with anger and I look around the room to see what I can hurt Bunny with. But, her home is so bland, and drab that there is nothing in view to pick up.

"Is that what you did to Denim's baby?" Bunny persists. "Did you stop her from crying too?"

Changing the subject I say, "How long have you been fucking your own nephew?" I sit across from her and cross my legs. "Has it been all of his life, or just most of it?" Bunny isn't smiling anymore, but I am.

"You don't know what the fuck you are talking about, little white girl."

I laugh. "It's funny how people claim that whites are racists, when I've been called out of my name more times than I care to remember by blacks this week alone."

"Blacks," she laughs. "That may be true, but that's because we welcome you into our homes, and you hear our personal business. We are real green that way. But, I can only imagine the evil things whites say behind our backs."

"You're hilarious," I laugh.

I think laughing in her face upsets her. "If you knew me, I mean really knew me, you wouldn't be chuckling so hard."

"How long have you been fucking Kevin?" I repeat. "Or maybe you'll understand me better if I say, how long have you been fucking Bambi's husband?"

The anger rolls down her face and is replaced with strength. "I didn't fuck Kevin, I made love to him. It was me who taught him how to kiss a woman. It was me who taught him how to hold a woman, and it was me who taught him how to eat pussy. Bambi needs to be on her knees and thanking me for the boss I am." She rubs her arms. "Before Bambi came along Kevin, and I had an understanding. I would continue to love him in private for as long as he kept me first. He violated that when he married that bitch." She points at me. "He belongs to me!"

I laugh at her. "Bunny, you're eight feet tall and shaped like a bullet." I giggle harder. "Kevin was never yours. All you did was brainwash him into thinking that he owed you something. That's the only reason he kept you around."

"How did you know about me and Kevin?" She places her hands on her hips. "I never told anyone. Did he?"

I can't be sure, but something tells me via the looks in her eyes that she hopes that he did tell somebody. "I didn't know before now. It was a guess that you just confirmed."

She isn't smiling anymore. "Where is Kevin?" She asks firmly.

"Kevin is dead," I say trying to get comfortable on her sofa. "Camp, Ramirez and Bradley are too." I swallow trying to wash the deceit down my throat with my own spit. "Bambi didn't want to tell anybody, because we have to take care of something first."

Bunny is quiet, and I can't read her facial expression. Instead of saying anything to me, she gets up, and walks over to the breakfast nook. "Did she have anything to do with it? Did Bambi kill my sweet baby?"

I frown. "Of course not. Why would you think something like that?"

"Well why did she lie?" She yells at me. "If she didn't have anything to do with his death, why not tell me the truth?"

I sigh. "Bunny, please just drop it."

"Bitch, don't tell me to drop shit! Why would she lie?"

I get up and walk closer to her. "I told you why already. We have a meeting with The Russians on Saturday. Bambi thought it would be a good idea to keep their deaths a secret, until after the meeting is over."

"For what?"

I'm quiet, because what Bambi wants us to do sounds so ridiculous it's hard to articulate it to another person. "Because we have to go to the meeting, and make a drop. Plus we don't know who has a stock in the money. The plan was to divide it four ways." I leave the most embarrassing part out.

"And," she continues. "I know there's more."

"We have to dress like men," I swallow. "We have to *be* our husbands."

She laughs so hard a silver button pops off of her shirt and drops to the floor. The funny thing is, she doesn't seem the slightest bit sad that Kevin is dead. She seems like she's in revenge mode more than anything else.

"I don't know what's going on, Scarlett, but I can assure you that you won't be able to pass for men." She wipes her tears. "So if Bambi has convinced you all to do that, it will be a great mistake."

"Since you know now, I guess I'll tell them that I told you," I sigh, throwing myself into the sofa. "They're going to kill me anyway." I close my eyes, and think about how life will be without my sisters. "This is the ultimate betrayal."

"Stop the fucking violins, Scarlett. Because if you thought there was a one hundred percent chance that I would tell them about you, you wouldn't have told me. You told me because you are hanging on to the hope that I won't tell them about your life. Right?"

"Bunny, you told us that Bambi was drinking again, even though she didn't want you to. Why wouldn't I think that you'd do the same thing to me?"

"Because I want that deal to go down on Saturday," she points at me. "As a matter of fact, if the meeting goes down, I can get my cut and we will benefit. How much is the package worth?"

"One hundred million dollars," I say.

I could have sworn I saw diamonds gleam in her eyes. "Kevin left her in hold of that much cocaine?" She asks with raised brows.

"I don't know how Bambi plans to pull it off." I can hear the money machine going off in her head from here, and it's making me mad. "Do you even care that Kevin is dead?" I ask in disgust. "To me it seems that the only thing you are worried about is money."

"Little girl, let me tell you something sweet. Bambi will pay for lying to me about my nephew. But first she's gonna pay in cash." She points at me and says, "And if you keep your mouth closed today, tomorrow you'll be a very rich white woman. Free to steal another black man."

I frown. "If I follow Bambi I'm going to be a rich woman anyway."

"Let me explain something, if Bambi finds out you told me about that deal you're cut off for good. Giving you a piece of the pie will be the last thing on her mind. I don't know if you are aware or not, but Bambi is a trained killer. A murderer. Now that I think about it you may want to give some serious consideration to taking her out before she gets you. Because even when I break you off, once she finds out about your betrayal, you're dead to her. She'll see to it."

"I don't want any money," I tell her trying hard to not think about life without my family. "I just want to go on with my life."

"Than you're a fucking fool," she tells me. "You need this money to start all over, and there's no shame in that." All I can do is cry. "Scarlett, relax. There's no need in you crying anymore, you made your decision, and you've chosen sides. It's time to play ball now."

When I remember how Bambi killed that man in her car, I think I'm in way over my head. Not only that, but she took a bullet in the hand like a G. I'm not sure about this. She is a soldier. What was I thinking? I don't have anything to protect myself with if Bambi does step to me. Prior to her soldier friend showing me how to shoot a gun, I didn't even know how to use one. I realize immediately that I need protection.

I clear my throat and ask, "Do you have a gun?" I look into her eyes. "I need to be able to protect myself from Bambi."

"Of course I do," she grins. "And, if you decide to use it, it will be our little secret."

When I walk into the abuse meeting the room is dark and dank. Nothing about it is welcoming and I wonder if the participants prefer it like that to hide their shame, and guilt. I know I do.

I walk past an older white lady and a man, and sit in the seat in front of them. Everyone seems to be looking at the lady who is speaking in the middle of the floor. She's black, probably about my age. She seems scared and I focus on her voice.

"It started when I was fifteen-years old, but continued all the way up to my eighteenth birthday. My mother came home drunk most days, and I can't recall any happy days in my household." Her head drops along with her voice. She looks out into the crowd. "At first she would tell me to slap her, for no reason at all. When I would do it, she'd ask me to do it again, and again. She would smile when I would do it too, like she got off on it or something," she's crying. "I think she loved pain. But about fifteen slaps later, she would hit me hard and ask me to fight her. I-I can't do this…" her voice trails off.

"It's okay, honey," the older lady behind me says. "It's okay. Let it out."

The talking girl looks back at the older lady behind me and smiles. "Thank you," she says. She clears her throat and starts talking again. "My mother would make me kiss her, and stuff like that. Her mouth always smelled like cigarettes and dirty men. I can still smell her now." Heavy tears exit her eyes and she swipes them away. "When I was eighteen I left her house, and moved in with this older man. He was nice to me, he just drank a lot like my mother. I was use to it by then though. I guess you can say I had experience in how to treat drunks. But after six months of staying with him I got pregnant. I loved my baby more than anything at first. That was until she started crying all the time. I couldn't take the cries," she places both hands over her ears. I immediately can identify with the feeling. "So I shook her hard. She was only five months at the time. She died the next day...on a Sunday. That's all I can say for now," the woman quickly walks away and a few people touch her softly as she rushes by on the way to her seat.

A white man with a long gray beard stands up next. "Anybody else?"

I feel like he is talking to me. There is nothing more I want to do than to talk to someone about my experience. I didn't even know I was standing when I first got up. I move to the middle of the floor and turn around and face the crowd. Everyone seems nice and welcoming and I appreciate it.

"My name is Carolyn Wells," I say. I know it's a lie but I still feel the need to protect my identity. "When I was younger, around ten years old, I was sent to my aunts house while my parents were out of town. For reasons I still can't figure out today she hated me. Very much. She did a lot of things to taunt me, but one of the things I remember was how she use to drown me.

I clear my throat. "She had this big silver sink in the basement. She use to fill it with cold water and ice cubes. I can't understand why the ice cubes. Never could. She would put this step stool in front of the sink, and make me step on it. I begged her not to force me to do it but she never listened. She'd put my head over the sink, climb on the stool and sit on the back of my neck. A few times she would have to revive me because I would pass out and couldn't breathe."

Suddenly the memories make me scared and I feel lightheaded. I'm trying to stay on my feet, but my legs feel like Jell-O. I black out.

# BAMBI

I'm already irritated before going into my house. Why, because I see Bunny's car parked in my driveway, which means she's inside somewhere. When I open my door, I notice two navy blue suitcases in the foyer. I throw my keys on the table next to the door, and walk toward my bedroom. On the way there, I catch Bunny walking out. Luckily I predicted that she might be coming back to snatch some more money, so I transferred it from Kevin's safe to mine. Although I would be a millionaire soon, if something went wrong I needed that cash to get on my feet.

"I see you took the money out of the safe," she says.

I try to conceal my pleasure, but I'm smiling anyway. "What are you doing in my house, Bunny?" I ask. "You got your allowance already."

"Correction," she grins walking around me. "What are you doing in my house? My name is on this deed, remember?"

"Unless the house is transferred out of Kevin's name, then this house belongs to me."

"You're right, but I spoke to Kevin today and he said it was okay for me to move in until they finish the renovations on my home. So I'll be here for about a month."

"Bunny, what the fuck is wrong with you? I know for a fact that Kevin didn't say you could move in here. Why do you get a kick out of antagonizing mothafuckas? Go back to your own miserable life and leave ours alone already."

"What do you mean when you said Kevin didn't say that I could move in here? If you don't believe me, call him."

I don't move. She has me in between a rock, and a hard place. But, if she knows he's not alive why isn't she telling the rest of the family? Or the police? What does this bitch really want?

"I'll call Kevin tonight, Bunny," I say. "In the mean time you need to back off. Way off. Because you don't know the kind of person I can be. I'm warning you but to tell you the truth, I'm getting tired of talking to you."

Bunny clutches the blue Celine bag on her shoulder and says, "I'll be back later to bring the rest of my things. So you and the girls need to make room." She smiles at me. "I'm not sure, but something tells me we're going to be the best of friends." She leaves out of the door and slams it behind herself.

I grab her suitcases, and surprisingly they are very light. I walk them to the back of my house and toss them into the back-yard. Because even though we are going to move out of here, and get another house, I don't want her shit near me before time. I can't sleep one night with her here.

When my personal phone rings in my room I rush to an-swer it. "Hello."

"Hello, baby girl," my father says. "Your mother told me you picked up Jasmine from her house the other day but I missed you. I was in town from Japan and was sad about it. How are you?"

My father's voice sounds more loving than it usually is alt-hough still stern. He's very serious and his example of love and my mother's is two totally different things. Although my mother has moved in with a woman, which I despise, and he's remarried, they are still best friends who speak everyday. I wish I had that kind of bond with my father.

"Hey, daddy," I say dryly. I really don't want to talk to him.

"How are you?" He repeats. "Your mom says you were shot."

"So you're calling to ask me about mom? Or my gunshot wound?" I sigh. "If you are don't worry about it. I'm okay. Besides, I haven't spoken to you in almost a month."

"I want to talk to you, but–"

"But what, daddy?" I cut him off. "You were avoiding me all my life. Why talk to me now? I know you blame me for what happened in the army, and I can never forgive you."

"I'm not blaming your for anything, Bambi," he says. "I just think you have the facts wrong. For heavens sake, it's been seventeen years already. You have the home and the lifestyle you always dreamed about. Why are you still crying over spilled milk?"

"Spilled milk? Spilled milk?" I yell louder. "My life was ruined by twenty-two men, daddy! Twenty-two! I had to have my vagina reconstructed, and its still not right—,"

"Bambi, I don't want to hear this—,"

"You will hear this," I cry. "Twenty-two men violated me in the worst way imaginable! And I called on you for support and you let me down. You know who came to my rescue, Sarge! It's because of you I will never be the same."

"So you're blaming me for the PTSD you suffer with too? Or let me get this straight, you're blaming me for the black outs. No I know what you're blaming me for, for being discharged from the military."

"You need to know for as long as I live, that I will never forgive you for abandoning me. Ever."

# SEVENTEEN YEARS EARLIER
# SAUDI ARABIA

*It had been three weeks since her friend Tatiana Clark was murdered by Desseray. All Bambi wanted to do was go home; instead she was transferred to another platoon to complete the mission. This was one of the largest platoons with over thirty soldiers.*

Bambi hated her new platoon mates mostly because of the lustful looks they gave her when she walked around. Unlike Desseray she didn't socialize with any of them. She kept to herself and she liked it that way.

After a long night, Bambi was sitting on the side of a tank thinking about her life. She was depressed, because at Chow-Time one of her platoon mates received some pictures from her family and they appeared to have a fabulous life. Now she wanted the same, and wondered if enlisting in the army was in vain after all. Her thoughts were halted when she was tapped on the shoulder from behind.

Bambi looked up and was staring into the blue eyes of Private Harvey. "Hey there, soldier. I been looking all over for you." Without warning he struck her in the face with a closed fist, and when she woke up she was in a different place.

Bambi was inside of a tent, naked and on the sand floor. Her wrists and ankles were tied with four separate ropes, which four soldiers pulled to hold her down. A green sock was stuffed in her mouth, and rope held it in place. Every time she tried to move, they pulled on the ropes harder and she felt as if her limbs would be torn out of the sockets.

One by one the soldiers boarded her body as they took swigs from the liquor bottle being passed around the tent. This was happening for many reasons. First some one paid them, and secondly Bambi was what they considered a tease. She would walk around the camp like she was cute, and better than everybody else, and would not speak to them. They figured this would put her back in place.

The first soldier wasn't as rough. He took time prodding her vagina. When he lay on top of her he shivered, and said I'm sorry in her ear persistently. His kindness was the last compassion she was shown, before the rest of them ripped her apart. Some went into her vagina and released their semen into her body, while others took her anally.

One flipped her over, and stuck a metal pole into her rectum, while he raped her vaginally. Two soldiers thought it would be cool to rape her together and take pictures, so they did their *thing. She was burned with cigarettes, pissed on, shit on and humiliated. When she looked across the room, she saw Desseray standing observing everything. But instead of enjoying the view, Desseray looked horrified at what she was seeing the men do.*

*"Help me," Bambi said in a weak voice.*

*Instead of helping Desseray turned around and walked out of the tent.*

*After they witnessed how much damage they caused, they made plans to kill her. So they beat her until she was unconscious. They took her body to a remote part of the camp, and dug a sand hole. They threw her body inside. She was left for dead, until Sarge found her alive.*

Fuck my father! He will never understand or accept what happened to me. My father was a lost cause. I'm tired of begging for his love, or needing him to validate me. If he wanted to choose the army over me, than he needed to live with his decision.

"Dad, don't call me again. I'm done with you. Stay the fuck out of my life."

"Bambi, be careful with me because whether you like it or not, I'm still your father and I deserve respect."

"You deserve nothing from me," I tell him. "So stay the fuck out of my life."

# BAMBI

I'm in my closet on the floor thinking about tomorrow. I just removed a cool bottle of vodka from the freezer and downed half of it already. I don't know what it is about drinking, but nothing comes close to the sensation I feel when it rolls over my tongue, and slides down my throat. Immediately my problems go away.

I'm just about to take another swig when I hear our doorbell ring. Where the fuck is everybody? I stand up, and at first lose my balance, and fall into the clothes inside my closet. When I try to get myself together, some of my clothes come down and topple on my head and floor. I pull myself up again, and the entire gold rod holding the rest of my clothes come crashing down. Finally I crawl out of my closet and to the door. Maybe I'm drunker than I realize. Let me keep it real, I'm a fucking mess.

When I open the front door, Cloud is looking down at me. "Bambi, what the fuck is going on?" He picks me up and walks me to the couch in the living room. "Why are you on the floor?"

I don't answer him. Instead I put my face into my hands. My head hurts. My temples throb. "Cloud, now is not a good time for you to be here." I look up at him. "Can you come back later please?"

"I'm not going anywhere, Bambi so don't even ask me. Have you been drinking again?"

"If I did, would it make you feel better about yourself?" I ask him.

"Why would you say some slick shit like that to me?" He asks. "I'm asking you if you're drinking because I give a fuck about you. Ever since that shit happened four weeks ago you've been carrying the shit out of me. Like you don't have love for a nigga no more. And, I'm sick of it." He looks at my hand. "And why isn't this gunshot wound bandaged? Covering it with a big ass Band-Aid is not sanitary or safe. It can get infected."

"Cloud, can you please leave?" I beg him. He's so annoying. "All I want to do is be left alone right now. I don't need all of this bullshit from you or anybody else. Besides, I heard enough from my father already." It's funny; two of the most important men in my life, my husband and my father, broke my heart.

Cloud sighs. "Okay, before I bounce I need to know where Kevin is? A few dudes been by my shop that I haven't seen before. They didn't seem too nice."

"What were they saying?"

"That the Kings ain't been making deliveries. Shit like that," he looks at me. "So you see that it's important that I get a hold of him."

"Why don't you call him yourself?"

"I did but he wouldn't answer the phone for me. So I figure he'll answer the phone for you," he touches my leg, and I push his hand off. "I'm sorry, Bambi. I wasn't trying to violate you."

I get off of the couch and rub my forehead. "Cloud, you aren't violating me. I'm just trying to get my mind together that's all. I have a lot of things going on and I don't need this right now." I walk to the door and open it. "Can you please leave?"

Cloud slowly walks toward me. "Not sure what's going on, but I'll say this, I'm here for you, Bambi. But, I can't be if you don't allow me." He runs his hand across my face and I slap it away. I don't deserve affection right now so I don't want it...from anyone, especially him.

"What is it with you, Bambi?" He asks.

"You already know," I tell him. "I needed you that night."

"The night you were dressed as a dude, and I found you in the club?"

"Fuck no," I yell. "And, stop playing with me because you know what I'm talking about. I needed you that night and you chose Kevin over me. I thought we had a bond, I guess I was wrong."

"I know, Bambi and I regret my decision for turning you away every day of my life," he says putting his hand over his heart. "Kevin is my cousin. But, it doesn't stop me from being in love with you though."

I'm stunned. I was going to say one thing to him but now I'm stumped. I gotta tell him the truth now, because I never looked at him like that. "I don't love you back, Cloud. I'm sorry and I hope I didn't leave you with that impression. The only thing on my mind is Kevin and my family. I hope you understand."

"I never meant to pull you away from him, I just figured after what we shared the night I found you in the club, things would be a little different that's all."

"Cloud, I didn't even finish you off. Get over it already."

He turns around without another word leaving me alone. As I walk back toward my bedroom, all I want to do is take a bath and jump into bed. Instead my phone rings. When I answer its Avery. "Bambi, I'm sorry to bother you again, but is Kevin available? I been calling him for days and he hasn't answered the phone."

"Kevin stepped out, I can take a message."

"Can you tell him to give me a call? It's very important."

"Avery, I'm gonna be honest with you, Kevin doesn't have time to talk on the phone these days. So whatever you want to tell him, you might as well tell me instead."

"I understand, it's just that...well...I need to make sure he's at that meeting tomorrow. Because I won't be there."

This the type of nigga who thinks he can bypass me. Kevin took his mouth play more times than he should have, but I won't. "Let me tell you something, mothafucka, I'm Mrs. Kennedy, not some bum ass hood rat. Now if I say Kevin will be there you can set your watch to that shit. Are we clear?"

"Bambi, I just—"

"Are we clear?" I yell cutting him off.

"Yes, we're clear."

"Like I said, the meeting is going down as planned. I'm out." I wonder what's Avery's cut in this transaction and why he's being so pressed. Whatever he's broken off, won't come out of the one hundred million we receive. I can tell you that.

After hanging up on him, I walk to my closet. The bottle of vodka is singing to me again, and I want it so badly I can taste it. But, remembering the meeting tomorrow, I bypass the liquor to move to my closet. I want to check the envelope Kevin left in the safe for the cocaine delivery. It was the only thing remaining inside of his safe since I took the money out and put it into mine.

I transferred the money, and left the note because I knew the note was of no significance to Bunny. She was all about the cash, and I wanted her to know I did it on purpose. I would've loved to see the look on her face when she saw that the money was gone. Greedy-ass- bitch.

When I turn the knob to the safe and it opens, I feel light headed. I am staring at an empty rack. I leap up and look on the floor. Where is it? Where the fuck is the note that held the number of the driver bringing the cocaine? I quickly open the pink safe, although I knew I hadn't placed it in there. Just as I thought it was empty too.

"Oh no, please don't! Please, God don't say she took that shit," I yell moving to the phone.

I called Bunny's house five times, and each time she doesn't answer. All that shit she did earlier today, by fake moving in was just to throw me off. I knew something else was up. If I wasn't drinking I would've been smarter.

I rush to the backyard, grab one of the suitcases and look inside. The first one is empty. I fall to my knees because I can hardly breathe. *What the fuck is this bitch up to?* I move to the other suitcase, and open it. There's nothing inside but a letter. I snatch it out, crawl up against the side of my house and read it.

*'Dear Bambi, feel free to use these suitcases for when you're put out on the street. When I'm done with you, they will be the only things you have to your name.'*

I feel like I'm spinning. I have taken Bunny's verbal abuse for the seventeen years that I've been married to Kevin. I allowed her to intrude on our marriage. I bit my tongue when she tried to tell me how to cook for him, talk to him and be his wife. I'm done with her, because on everything I love if she fucks up this business deal tomorrow, she's as good as dead.

# AUNT BUNNY

*B*unny is sitting in her living room with a glass of Merlot in one hand and the phone in the other. She felt like the late Griselda Blanco, the Godmother of Cocaine, as she handled business. "Why would you even come at me like that, Donatello? You know who my nephew is. All the good shit pumping through this city has the Kennedy brand on it. You know what they call it... Virgin Pussy. So if I tell you I got a deal for you of a lifetime, the only question is how much can you afford?"

"You not even telling me how much you got," Donatello responds. "The least you could do is tell me what you working with."

"Listen, son, I don't know who you think you dealing with, but I don't have to tell you shit about my supply. Keep in mind our shit is not stepped on, it's pure. With this type of quality what comes to you in a kilo can easily be turned into more. That's totally up to you. You just tell me your order and we'll go from there."

"And, Kevin is gonna allow this?"

"Kevin?" She asks sitting her merlot on the table. "Let me explain something to you, you're running this deal through me, not my nephew. Now what the fuck you want to do?"

"Three kilos," he chuckles, "you drive a tough bargain. When will it be ready?"

"Tomorrow, and let the streets know whose in charge," Bunny continues. "While Kevin is out of town, I'm handling all Kennedy business."

"You got it," he says.

"But have my money ready, Donatello, I'm not fucking around with you."

"Come on, aunt Bunny, you and my mother are best friends. You act like you don't even know me. I'm good for it."

"Nigga, the fact that me and Therese share a drink here, and there on the weekends ain't got shit to do with how I collect my bread. Have my money when you come see me tomorrow or don't come at all."

He laughs. "Damn, Bunny, you cold blooded."

"It is what it is," Bunny giggles sipping her wine. "Don't let the age fool you, unlike the Kennedy wives I'm about this life. I don't let nobody take shit from me like they do," she continues feeling herself because she was stealing Bambi's money under her nose.

"They be letting niggas take from them?" Donatello asks.

"Them bitches are weak," Bunny continues. "Without the Kennedy Kings to protect them, they open bait over there," she laughs. "But, fuck all that, come see about me tomorrow, and I'll have your work."

When there is a knock at the door, Bunny ends the call and walks toward it. She laughs when she sees Bambi on the other side through the peephole. Bambi is wearing army fatigue pants, and a black leather jacket. Her long hair his hanging down the sides of her shoulders, and although beautiful, she looks distraught. Bunny opens the door.

"I still can't believe they shot you in the hand," Bunny says looking at the huge band-aid covering the gunshot wound. "Too bad they didn't get you in the heart instead. Then again you can't send a boy to do a woman's job," she laughs at her own joke. "What the fuck do you want with me, Bambi?"

Bambi steps into her house carrying a Hermes green Clemece duffle bag. "Bunny, is anybody in here with you?" Bambi looks around.

*Bunny folds her arms over her warped breasts and asks, "What you gonna do? Kill me? Like you did Kevin?"*

*"Bunny, I don't know what the fuck you talking about," she says. "I would never hurt Kevin. That nigga is the love of my life."*

*"Then why are you lying about where he is and what happened to him?"*

*"I'm not here to argue with you," Bambi says in a soft voice. "I know you and I haven't had the best relationship. Maybe it's because we both love Kevin and want the best for him. I don't know what the reason is. I just want you to know that I'm sorry for my part in everything. I truly am. All I want to do is put the bullshit behind us, and move forward. I want you in the twins lives, and I know you want to be in their lives too."*

*"What about Kevin?" She asks. "What about me being in Kevin's life?"*

*"He's gone, Bunny," Bambi responds crying. "He died on some fluke shit in LA. Check the news, a nigga came through and killed a bunch of innocent people at a casino. The Kings were there. They were there under fake names so the bodies couldn't be identified. I was going to tell you and the entire family, but I couldn't do it right now. There is a very important meeting that's going down tomorrow. But, on everything I love, including my boys, when the meeting was over I was going to tell everyone."*

*Bunny looks her over. "You have on your fatigue pants," she points at them. "Everyone knows when you wear the fatigues that either you're thinking about something or up to no good. Which one is it? What you here to kill me or something?"*

*Bambi raises her arms and spreads her legs. "Check me. I'm not strapped."*

*Bunny quickly moves toward her and runs her hands over Bambi's breasts, pussy, ass cheeks and every other meaty parts of her body. When she is done she says, "Maybe a gun is in the bag."*

*"Money is in the bag, Bunny," she nods towards it. "Open it."*

*Bunny grabs the duffle, pulls back the gold zipper and looks inside briefly. True to Bambi's word it has money inside, but its light.*

*Bunny laughs. "And what the fuck am I supposed to do with that?"*

*"I'm giving you that money in exchange for your life,"* Bambi pleads with her. *"I don't want to hurt you, Bunny. I swear I don't, but if you don't give me back the envelope with that number, I'm going to beat your ass, and then I'm going to tie you up."*

*Bunny chuckles. "Wait, you are going to beat my ass?"* She points at herself. *"You and what army?"*

*"The Bambi Army,"* she replies. *"And, after I beat your ass, and tie you up I'm going to grab the dullest knife in your kitchen, and gut you. If you give me what belongs to me we can stop your fate, but you gotta do it now."*

*Bunny isn't laughing as hard. "You really have it all worked out in that head of yours don't you? Tell the truth, you've been thinking about killing me for awhile now?"*

*Silence.*

*"You don't have to answer me, Bambi. I already have the answer. It's all in your eyes,"* Bunny raises her shirt. *Next to her stretch marks is the handle of a chrome .45 handgun. "But, I been ready for birds like you since the day I was born." She releases her shirt, grabs the Hermes bag and throws it in Bambi's chest. "That money is too light for me, mama. I'm done begging for cheese, Bambi. I'm looking for the big bread now."*

*"Bunny, in this bag is everything I have,"* she continues.

*"Well keep it,"* Bunny laughs realizing by this time tomorrow, she stood to have a couple hundred. And, that's not even a percentage of what the entire cocaine shipment was probably worth. She knew all about the code words needed to get the work delivered, she worked with Kevin before.

*"Bunny,"* Bambi says breathing heavily, *"that money belongs to me and my family, and I can't let you have it. I'm sorry. But if you give me back that number, I'll give you five hundred thousand dollars, that's half of what the shipment is worth."*

"So the shipment is worth one million?" Bunny grins. "That's it?"

"That's it, Bunny, and you can have half of it if we can put this all behind us."

Bunny laughs like a hyena. "Bitch, that shipment is worth at least one hundred million dollars. Well, at least that's what Kevin was giving it to the Russians for."

The humbleness is wiped off of Bambi's face. "Who told you that?"

"Who do you think, darling?"

Bambi shakes her head. In her opinion there is no end to what Kevin would say and do for this woman. "How were you able to get so deep into Kevin's head that he would tell you anything? Even the code to his safe?" Bambi looks at Bunny's man-face and warped body. "What are you, fucking him or something?"

She laughs. "How else do you think he knew how to eat that pussy of yours so well, honey?" Bunny rubs her hand between her legs and cups her vagina. "I taught him."

Bambi is breathing so heavily it was the only thing that could be heard in the house. She releases the bag from her hand, but right before it hits the floor, Bambi yanks out the nine, cocks it and blows half of Bunny's face off. Had Bunny accepted the peace offering, she might've seen the gun tucked on the side of the bag. But greed and hope for a bigger cut of the money blinded her. Bambi knew she wouldn't take the bait. She smelled the bigger payout already.

When Bunny's blood poured out of her body, Bambi put one more bullet it in her head forcing her brains open. When she was done she wiped the brain matter off of her face, and ransacked the house. She needed that envelope. Bambi demolished the house on the hunt for it. Fifteen minutes later, her search ended in vain in Bunny's bedroom.

Her heart rate increased as she realized Bunny might have prevented her from getting the biggest payout in her life. One hundred million dollars was a lot of money to lose and to have never had.

*"Calm down, Bambi," she says to herself. "Think...where would she put the envelope?"*

*Bambi looks at the bed, the dresser and even the floor. Across from her sits a picture of Bunny and Kevin that was taken last year. Kevin had taken Bunny on vacation to Barbados. Since they went alone on the trip, Bambi could only imagine the things that they did to each other. She moved toward the picture to break it until she thought about it. Placing her gun on the edge of the dresser, she picked the picture up and removed the back.*

*She exhaled when she saw the note. It was the number she needed to call tomorrow. "Thank, God!" She says out loud.*

*Bambi rushes to Bunny's body, snatches the ruby chain off of her bloodied neck, and runs toward her Rolls Royce. She just got away with murder.*

# SCARLETT

I 'm sitting in the kitchen trying to force down a cup of ginger ale. I just finished watching the news. Apparently the man who came in and killed all of those people in Las Vegas was fired two weeks ago for stealing, and decided to come back and take lives. A disgruntled employee murdered our husbands. How did he even get a gun inside? There were still five people who were unidentified, but they weren't releasing their pictures yet due to the investigation. My life is a mess.

As I look at the gun in my lap that Bunny gave me, I wonder if I'm willing to use it on my sister or not. I thought about packing up all of my clothes and leaving, but having absolutely nowhere to go, and no money stops me. What a fool I am to get involved with Bunny's ass to begin with. So stupid.

When the door unlocks, I grab my gun, and tuck it in the back of my jeans like I saw my husband do a million times. I pull my pink sweater over the handle, and walk toward the door. Bambi comes into view and she looks angry. She knows I betrayed her. I know Bunny told her that I betrayed her, and there is nothing I can do about it now.

"H-hi, Bambi, are you okay? You look flushed," I say.

She stands in front of me and the time she takes to answer my question kills me. "No, I'm not okay," she responds. "I-I feel betrayed once again."

I swallow. "Bambi, love is a funny thing. Sometimes the love you have for a person prevents you from doing what is right, because you don't want to hurt their feelings." She hates me. I know she hates me.

"That sounds like a cop out to me," she says throwing her green Hermes bag on the floor. It's only then that I notice that she's wearing fatigues. "If you really love a person you honor the bond you have with them. You don't do anything that might hurt them. You cherish them and you protect the fact that hurting them is something you can't do, because they'd never be able to handle it." She rubs her hands over her face.

"Bambi, I..."

"You don't live with a person for year after year, look them in the eyes, tell them you love them, and stab them in the back," she cuts me off.

This is killing me. I knew my betrayal would hurt but I never thought it would feel like this. If God saw it fitting for her to forgive me, and for us to move past this, I will never destroy our bond again. I mean that on everything I love and everything I feel.

"Bambi, this is life," tears roll down my cheeks and I smear them away. "Do you know how often people hurt the ones they love? Don't you see that the ones you love get hurt first? It's not right but it's true. My aunt told me that," I swallow. "Just like Kevin had a baby on you, you're not going to tell me that he doesn't love you. He made a mistake. It happens. I'm not going to hear it."

"You really believe all of that shit you saying right now don't you? Camp really had you brainwashed."

"I'm not talking about Camp or Kevin," I tell her wiping more tears away. "I'm talking about our bond. I'm talking to you as a sister, and my only regret is that we didn't have this conversation earlier. People make mistakes, Bambi. I made a mistake."

"What are you talking about, Scarlett?" She frowns.

"Let me finish," I beg her. "I make mistakes, and I do things that are unforgivable. But, I'm trying to change. I'm trying to be a better person in the hopes that I can be a better mother." I rub my stomach.

Her eyebrows rise. "A better mother? You're pregnant?" She asks.

"Yes, I am." My response is flat and its only then that I seriously realize what I'm saying. I've thought about it before, but the magnitude strikes me as if someone dropped a big piece of iron on the top of my head.

"I don't understand," she shakes her head, "I mean, I thought Camp wasn't interested in having any babies."

"Who told you that?" I glare. Sounds like there was more talk about me around here than I was aware of.

"Come on, Scarlett, you know how them niggas talk," Bambi continues. "Camp told Kevin that he wasn't trying to have any kids, and Kevin told me."

"But, we weren't having kids not because he didn't want to, but because of me."

"You?" She says. "Why wouldn't you want to have kids with a rich ass nigga like Camp?"

I think about my abusive past and decide to lie. "Because I'm not ready for kids, but it seems that I don't have a choice right now, do I?"

"I hear what you saying," Bambi continues, "but I still can't condone disloyalty. Of any kind."

"What does that mean?"

She steps toward me and releases the gun in her waist. I move to grip the handle of mine that sits in the middle of my tailbone. It reminds me that I don't trust anyone, although I desperately want to.

"It means that I'm glad Kevin's gone," she places the gun on the table. "And, that if he was alive, I'd kill him again."

I take my hand off of my weapon, and pull down my sweater. False alarm. This isn't about me. She isn't talking about me. I'm more than relieved. "I'm sorry, Bambi," I whisper. "About everything Kevin has put you through."

"There's no need in you being sorry, you weren't the one who did me wrong, that nigga was." She shakes her head. "I found out today that he was fucking Bunny's ass. Can you believe that shit, Scarlett? The bitch is shaped like a bullet."

I laugh so hard, I grip my pregnant belly.

"What's funny she asks?"

I can't tell her that I said the same thing. That she was shaped like a bullet. Instead I say, "Bunny is a greasy bitch who will get what's coming to her sooner than later."

"I know," Bambi says under her breath. "I know." She looks into my eyes. "Anyway, I'm just glad that I have you all. Without you, I think I'd be a mess right now. You know what I mean? Money and cocaine will come and go, but the real asset in life is loyalty. You can get so much further with it. Our husbands had it, but they gave it up for selfishness." She shrugs. "I guess that's why they are gone and we're still here."

"I guess so," I respond.

"Anyway, Sarge is coming back later on tonight. He wants to make sure that we look the part for tomorrow. So be ready."

"You told him we meeting with The Russians?"

"Nope," she shakes her head. "I can't have anybody knowing about that money but us. He just knows that we all need to be convincingly male by tomorrow. He wants to help because he loves me."

"Must be nice to be loved by a man even with Kevin gone," I say.

"It feels good," she sighs. "But, I really wanted to be with Kevin for the rest of my life. Now I see that we were together for the rest of his." She grabs her bag. "Anyway, go get yourself together. Sarge will be here in an hour."

As she walks away I turn around to look at her as she enters the elevator. Even in her most evil she still looks beautiful. And the only thing I can think is damn, I'm glad I didn't have to kill her.

# BAMBI

When I see Cloud's car pull up in front of my house for the second time that day I'm annoyed. Because now I know what he's coming to tell me, that his precious aunt Bunny is dead. And, you know what, it's going too be hard to act like I give a fuck too.

"Where are the girls?" He asks when he steps into the house. "I got to talk to all of you now, and it's very important."

"Important like what?" I ask playing dumb. My face is straight but I can feel my left cheek twitch. My jaw trembles and I bite my lip.

"I really want to tell everyone all together," he looks into the foyer. "Where are they?"

I can feel my heart beating hysterically. I know as of now he doesn't know I killed her, but I'm afraid that my sisters will know I'm guilty when they see my face. They know first hand the beef I had with this bitch. It ran deep. I been wanting her dead for seventeen years.

Instead of telling him to get the fuck out of my house I yell, "Hey, everybody. Come down now, Cloud wants to tell us something."

Everyone but Race comes into the foyer. When everyone is looking at him he says, "I hate to break this to you girls, but somebody murdered Bunny at her house tonight."

Surprisingly, no one had any real reaction. In fact it was me who had to say something to fill the awkward silence in the room. "I'm sorry for your loss, Cloud." It's all I could muster.

"You sorry for my loss," he looks at the girls and then me. "Did you hear what I just said? Somebody murdered Bunny."

"We heard you, Cloud," Denim says running her fingers through her red curly hair. "But if truth be told, nobody fucked with Bunny like that. She was a troublemaker who made it her life's work to get into everyone else's business. Maybe somebody got tired of that and put her out of her misery. I'm just saying."

"You just saying," he repeats looking at everyone including me. "Ya'll act like I just told you the *Real Housewives of Atlanta* show just got cancelled." I chuckle, but he doesn't seem too pleased. "I'm telling you that Bunny was murdered. She was family."

Scarlett clears her throat and says, "Not for nothing, but I don't feel too good, Cloud. Let me go lay down before Sarge get's here." She catches the elevator upstairs.

Something about the way the smile spread across Scarlett's face tells me she was happy about the news.

After Scarlett left Denim says, "I'm gonna check on Jasmine, she still isn't feeling too well. Call me when your friend gets here, Bambi."

Suddenly I was alone with Cloud. "What the fuck is going on around here, Bambi?" He looks into my eyes. "Where are my cousins? And why are ya'll acting like it ain't a problem that Bunny's dead?"

"Kevin is not here yet, Cloud. Now I wish I could tell you something else. Maybe something that you want to hear about Bunny, but I can't do that. I didn't like Bunny, she was a no good bitch who stayed in a nigga's business. The devil came for her and now she's gone."

"When was the last time you seen her?" He says through clenched teeth.

"Look, I haven't seen that dead bitch since earlier when she came over my house with fake suitcases. I wasn't at her crib none today."

When I finally realize he struck me in the face, I am tasting my own blood and looking at his Christian Louboutin tennis instead of his face. I get up and look directly into his eyes. "I don't know what day and I can't tell you what time, but at some point in your life you're going to pay for putting your hands on me."

"I'm gonna be back here tomorrow sometime to talk to my cousin, if he's not here I'm gonna call the rest of my people to see if we can't get answers. Be ready for that shit."

"Do what you got to do," I open the front door. "Now get the fuck out of my house. You making it hot in here."

When he leaves I swallow a half a bottle of vodka and am feeling better immediately. I am about to get ready for Sarge to come over when Race catches the elevator upstairs from the basement. She has white powder all over her shirt, and face and she looks like she was baking a messy cake...from scratch.

"Everybody come down here," she yells into the house carrying a box in her hands.

"What is this about?" I ask looking her over. She seems overly excited and nervous at the same time.

I often worry about Race. She hangs downstairs a lot. And, although I know we are her family, I also know she has someone out there that she doesn't want us to know about. I hope they aren't taking advantage of her. I know it's not her mother or father, because she can't stand being around them. Still, I wonder who is it.

When all of us are finally standing in front of her she puts the box down on the kitchen counter. Then she pulls out a jiggly, rubber mask and hands it to me. "Put this on, Bambi."

The thing freaks me out and I hold it while it dangles in my hand. "You want to tell me what this is first?"

She walks up to me and puts it on the lower part of my face. It goes around my ears and hangs in place. At first it is cool but soon it warms to my skin. She digs into the box and pulls out some brown makeup the color of my skin, and mask. She smears it on my face and I'm so shocked I don't move. When she's done, she digs into the box and pulls out a dusty black hat. She stuffs my hair into it, and pulls it down over my head. When she's done, she steps back and smiles.

The first expression I see is Denim's. She covers her mouth and walks up to me, "Oh my God, Race!" Denim looks my face over, moving my head from left to right. "You are so good. How the...what...the..."

"What do I look like?" I ask.

Race grins and hands me a mirror from the box. Immediately I see what all the hoopla is about. I look just like a cute ass boy. She squared out my chin and strengthened my nose. The mask allows me to breathe and it feels so real I can't believe it.

"But, how were you able to know my measurements?" I ask looking at the mirror touching the mask. "I didn't come down to your shop."

Race giggles. "I can eyeball measurements," she responds. "Like the Kings could eyeball purp."

I look at the mask again and talk into it. "What's good, I'm Kevin Kennedy," I say into it. It's then that I notice the lips move but not as much as I want them too. The mask allows minimal movement.

"I don't know, Bambi," Scarlett says. "The lips don't look as real. I mean, if you don't talk much you good, but if you have to speak to them it could be a problem."

"She's right," Denim says. "Now that you speak more, it looks unofficial."

"Damn, this would've been cool too," I say.

Race looks disappointed. "I'm sorry, guys. I really wanted this to work out," she says.

"It will," I say looking at Race. "Girl you are a beast! I have to take back everything I said. You can transform mothafuckas with these masks." Her smile is so bright. "Race, did you make one of these for everybody?"

"Yes, they're downstairs." Her eyes enlarge and I can see she really wants to help.

"Good, because you all can wear them and I'll wear my hat low and man myself out," I say. "I'll be good."

Race seems pleased at first. And then she says, "I wanted to tell you guys, I don't think I can do this." *Not this shit again.* I think. "I figured what we can do is tell them that one of the kings is sick, and that he couldn't be there. Since the cocaine will be there, I don't see why they won't bite. They are about the white not nothing else...right?"

"Race, we went through this already. You have to go to the meeting tomorrow," I remind her. "They expecting four niggas. Not three bitches and a baby. You can't back out on us now, we need you." When there is a knock at the door I answer it. It's Sarge and a few of his men.

Everybody rolls their eyes but me. I move to give him a big hug but he pushes me back and moves for his weapon instead. At first I'm shocked until I remember why he did it. I'm wearing a face mask and a baseball cap. "It's me, Sarge." I remove my cap and my hair falls down.

"Oh shit," he looks me over and shakes his head. "Whoever did this did a good damn job. You fooled me for sure!"

I look at Race. "She's the best," I tell him. "Thanks for coming back over, Sarge." I can tell he is still a little uncomfortable about my boyish look and I love it. If I fooled Sarge it means we can fool The Russians if we play it cool.

"Anything for you," he touches my rubber nose with his rough finger. "I told you that."

When he looks at my sisters he looks at me, taps his chin and eyebrow twice. It's a secret message. I giggle. It means the enemies are near. He's talking about my sisters.

"I hate when ya'll do that secret language shit," Denim says. "Can we just get this over with? I'm tired and am not in the mood to be getting yelled at all day by Sarge."

"I'll try to be as quick as possible," Sarge responds. "How about all of you get dressed in your gear and meet me in the backyard."

"Do I have to?" Denim asks him.

"Yes, you definitely have to be there," Sarge yells at her. "Move your asses, now!" He yells like they are in the lineup in the army.

They amble up the stairs with major attitudes.

"When are you going to tell me what this is all about, Bambi?" He asks again. "If you have to dress like men, it must be serious. I'm already mad somebody shot you in the hand and, I don't think I can stand by and let something else happen to you again."

"Trust me when I say that this situation will be okay."

"And you need to trust me when I say I will take your secrets to my grave," Sarge responds. "Let me know what's going on. I can help you, Bambi."

"I can trust you, but I also love you," I tell him. "And I want to keep you as far away from this stuff as possible. I don't need you worrying. I just want you to help those girls man up. I know it's not a lot of time, but I don't have a choice right now."

"The others are at least listening, who I'm really worried about is Race," Sarge tells me. "She's very resistant, Bambi. She might not do well for whatever you need her for. You may want to leave her behind."

"I wish I could, but unfortunately I need her," I say in a low voice. I take the mask off and wipe my face with the edge of my shirt. "I don't understand why she can't just man the fuck up. This meeting is for everybody, not just us."

"Some people aren't built for combat, Bambi," he reminds me. "Some people are civilians. That's why soldiers like you and I are important. We protect. We serve. So, don't be so hard on her."

"For some reason I think she has it in her somewhere," I say.

"I doubt that," he responds.

I sigh. I want to tell him about The Russians so badly that I can hear myself giving him the play-by-play details. "Look now that they're gone and we aren't on the phone I want to tell you about that other thing. It didn't..."

Knock. Knock. Knock.

I walk past Sarge and answer the door. It's Cloud again. "What the fuck do you want?" I ask uninterested in being nice to him anymore. He raises the bandage that was once on my hand. I look at my gunshot wound. Where is my bandage? I shiver. I dropped it at Bunny's house. Fuck!

"Sarge, can you go handle business, I have to talk to Cloud alone," I say.

He pulls his ear. He's asking me am I sure. I rub my chin in response. He walks away.

"What's that about?" Cloud asks me looking at Sarge's back. "Is it some freaky sign language?"

"What do you want?" I'm trying to maintain control because I don't believe I was so careless that I could've left something so serious behind. I murdered Bunny and left DNA. So fucking stupid of me. I'm smarter than that. "As you can see I have company and am busy right now, Cloud."

"When I left here, and went back to Bunny's house, I noticed a forensic investigator was on his hands and knees looking for evidence. When I saw this stuck to the bottom of his boot, I knew whom it belonged to. You see when I was here earlier it was on your hand," he grabs my wrist and looks at my wound. "Now it isn't."

"How did you get it?"

"I had to fake accidently trip over this nigga's shoe while he was on his hands and knees and snatch it off. I almost got arrested because I wasn't supposed to be near the crime scene. So my only question to you is, why was this there?"

"I don't know," I shrug.

"So you telling me this is not your blood on this band aid?"

"No, it's not mine."

"So I guess you won't have any problem with me giving it to the police," he threatens.

He turns to walk away, and I grab him. Knowing words don't matter anymore, it's time to put in work. I kiss him sloppily in the mouth. When I see he responds I slide the band aid out of his hand, and lead him into my bedroom. I stuff it in my pocket. When the door is closed I push him up against the wall and drop to my knees. I remove his shoes and socks one by one. Then I unlatch his belt buckle and push down his pants. He's breathing so hard on my face my cheeks moisten.

"I love you, Bambi," he tells me in my ear. "I can't see life without you."

"I know, daddy," I say removing my shirt so that my breasts are bare. The only thing I'm wearing now is my fatigue pants and I soon take them off so that I'm standing naked. I hardly ever wear panties so he's in for a treat today.

He walks toward me and I say, "On your knees, nigga."

He drops to his knees so hard, I hear them thump. I walk backwards to the edge of my bed and spread my legs. Then I grab the top of my pussy, and pull up, so that my clit pokes out. "Lick me there, softly."

Before I know it his entire mouth is on my pussy. I haven't bathed today, which is unlike me, and I'm glad I didn't. I want him to have a dirty pussy since he wants it so badly. I need to see how far he'll go to be with me...to have me. It's obvious there are no limits because although he licks my button repeatedly, he can't stop sticking his tongue into my pussy and butt holes. I fart in his face and still he doesn't move.

When he isn't following instructions, I slap him in the face...hard. "I said lick my button, nigga. Make it wet too extra spit, I wanna feel how much you want this."

"I'm sorry," he says. The sensation is so good now I piss in his face and mouth. He allows me to wet him up, and when I'm done he says, "I see you a squirter."

What an ignorant ass nigga. That's not cum, that's piss. I don't say anything. I just let this nigga clean my pussy with his tongue. And, when I finally cum, I turn around on all fours and say, "Come get it while it's hot, baby."

When he rises I see that he is already rock hard. He pushes into my pussy and he's as stiff as a bat. I don't feel anything emotional with him. In fact I hate him, but I must do this to get him to keep our secret, at least until tomorrow. I don't want anything stopping me from going to that meeting, and getting that money. With twenty five million dollars after I split it with my

184

sisters, I can get lost and no one will find me...ever. Just one more day is worth giving up the juicy to a man I can't stand.

"Damn, baby," Cloud moans. "Oh, my God, oh my God...why is this pussy so tight? I never been in a pussy this tight before."

I want to tell him that it's because soldiers ripped my vagina out, and I had it reconstructed to be tighter. Instead I flex, back and wind my pussy onto his dick. When I glance at the clock it says 7:17pm. I want this over and done with. But when I look at the clock again, it's 7:57. Why is he taking so long?

I'm just about to push this dude off of me until he says, "I'm almost there, Bambi. I can't hold it anymore," he grabs my waist and pushes into me harder. "I was trying to wait for you to get yours but it's too good."

I knew he was holding back. "Don't worry about me, daddy. Just get this pussy."

When I feel him gush inside of me, I hop up, grab the band-aid in my pocket that I took from him, flush it down the toilet, and stand in front of him at the head of the bed. "Consider yourself paid in full. Now get the fuck out of my house, and I don't want to ever see you again, Cloud."

He laughs. "You are so smart aren't you? You think you can just flush something down the toilet and that be it? What makes you think that I gave you the right one, Bambi? How do you know it's not a replica? You moved too quickly and over-bet your hand, beautiful."

My heart is beating fast. He scoots off of the bed and gets dressed. He walks up to my naked body and says, "If Kevin doesn't come back you belong to me," he lifts my chin and kisses me sloppily in the mouth. I taste my own piss on his lips. "And, I need you to always remember that I have the ability to ruin your life."

# SATURDAY
# NOVEMBER 10<sup>TH</sup>
# 2012
# 7 00 PM

# BAMBI

e are standing in the living room. Dressed like men. I'm wearing Kevin's black jeans, and his oversized black leather bomber jacket. Nothing but my nose can be seen with the cap on.

Scarlett's wearing Camp's blue jeans and his black NorthFace coat. A red cap is pulled down over her eyes.

Denim is wearing Bradley's black jeans and his heavy burnt orange custom-made leather jacket, a black Orioles baseball cap is also over her head.

Race is wearing Ramirez's jeans, navy blue pea coat and a grey brood hat. Her stomach looks chunkier then it normally is, and I wonder why. Although Scarlett and Denim are wearing the half mask prosthetics that Race created to look more masculine, Race's entire face is covered with a mask. When she isn't speaking it looks so real, but the moment she opens her mouth, they will know it's a fake and that scares me. But, it was the only way that she would agree to go.

As I look at all of their stances they look real. Hard, and stiff just like men. Sarge did a good job with them...well...all accept Race.

"Race, you gotta take your polish off," I tell her noticing how her fingers are red. "You gonna get us late."

"I'm not taking my nail polish off," she says through her stiff face. "I'm just gonna keep them in my pockets."

"That's so dumb, Race," Denim says looking at her. Denim tugs the cap she's wearing. "If you forgot to keep them in your pocket just like you did now, you gonna do the same thing later on tonight. If you get us killed I'm gonna hurt you."

As we all considered what she just said, we couldn't help but laugh. It was the first laugh we had in a long time too. How was she going to kill her, if she gets us killed? It was too funny for words.

"You know what I mean," Denim says falling back into man mode.

"Okay enough of that, I need ya'll to walk to the back of the living room, and then walk back toward me. I need to see how you move."

Using their girly gait they walked toward the back of the living room. I hated that about them. If they stayed in character all the time, they wouldn't have to worry about falling out. Please, God just get us through this day.

When they were on the other side of the room, they finally walk toward me. Denim and Scarlett look so good walking it gives me chills. Their hands stuffed in their pockets, and stiff shoulders give them the thug appeal. As long as they don't have to speak, we're in the clear. But, Race on the other hand looks abnormal. Like she's Faggy Freddy from Virginia.

"Race, don't swing your upper body so much. Everything from the hips up should be stiff. Now do it again."

Denim and Scarlett take a seat, and Race walks back to the other side of the living room. She walks toward me again, and this time she looks like Faggy James from uptown. "Race, it's not working," I say frustrated with her. "You gotta be stiff! You floating too much in the upper body."

"I told you I don't wanna do this shit," she screams through her man face, before running up the stairs.

"Fuck," I yell hitting the wall. "She gonna get us killed!"

"Don't worry about it, things are going to work out," Scarlett says.

"Shut the fuck up," Denim tells her. "You always saying shit that don't make no fucking sense. If the four of us are not there, this plan is going to fail."

As they argue back and forth I remember how just three months ago, life for us was grand. We were married, had husbands, money, respect and love. Now we were falling apart and it didn't look like we would ever get things back together.

"I need for everybody to calm down," I say looking at the two of them. "Whatever beef you have with each other can be settled later. Right now I have to make this call."

I pick up the phone on the wall, take the number from my pocket for the cocaine delivery, and dial it. When the person answers I say, "Same."

He responds with, "Okay," and hangs up.

Thirty minutes later the front of the house lights up and we hear a large vehicle pull up in the driveway. When I look out of the window, a white truck with the sign FRUIT DELIVERY is parked outside. My heart rate increases. What are we doing? The person driving it hops into an awaiting silver car and pulls off our property.

I walk away from the window. "It's here," I say in a low voice. "Are ya'll ready?"

Scarlett and Denim look at me and shake their heads. Race is still upstairs. "Let me go get her." I take the elevator upstairs trying to think about what I was going to say to her in my mind. When I get into her room, she is on the phone and I stop before walking inside.

"Don't cry, I'm gonna do what I can to take care of you, baby," Race says in a low voice. "Okay, okay, I understand. Just let me come up with a plan." She pauses again. "Well how much money do you need for rent?"

As I ear hustle I realize that I'm stuck. Race is cheating. Or is she, since Ramirez is dead? Out of all of us I would've never thought that Race would carry on the extra-marital affair. Instead of being angry, I'm kind of proud of her. It makes me think she has an edge I didn't know was there. My only thing was, why was she taking care of a nigga? Shouldn't he be taking care of her?

"I love you too," Race continues. "Bye."

Here I am thinking I had to put in a big speech when it looks like the work was done for me already. Race was in need of some dough, so she had to come with us. "Race, the package is here," I say standing in her doorway. "You rolling with us or not?"

She jumps up off the bed. "Uh...I...don't know about this," she says.

Instead of begging her like before, I play on the newfound information I have. Judging by the conversation, she needs the money. "Race, I'm not going to beg you anymore, but if you want to give up twenty-five million dollars, that's on you. I want you to understand though, that if we pull this job off we not sharing it with you."

When I turn to walk away I wait on her footsteps to follow me. They don't come. I turn around and the light is still on in her room. Why didn't it work? I just heard her say she needed money. We stood to make enough to put us up for the rest of our lives. So what was the deal?

"Where is Race?" Scarlett asks me when I finally make it back to the living room. "She not coming?"

Denim rolls her eyes when Scarlett speaks.

"I really don't think so, ya'll," I say biting my lip. "We gonna have to go at it alone." Just the sound of my words makes my stomach spin.

"But I thought you said they were expecting four men. We need her," Scarlett continues.

I look up the stairs and at the elevator. Race still hasn't come down. "We got each other," I reply looking at them both. "For now that's going to have to be good enough."

We leave out of the house, and walk slowly to the truck. It's a large commercial white truck, but I'm use to driving vehicles this size from when I was in the army. I feel light headed. I get in the front and for some reason; Scarlett and Denim climb in the back. I think its weird until I see the front door of our house open. Race rushes out of the house. They must've been waiting on her to come, so they left a seat for her.

"Wait," Race yells running up to the truck. "I'm coming! I'm coming!"

I didn't know it until I saw her man-face, but before she came out I wasn't breathing. When she climbs into the truck I exhale. "You almost had us," I say. "Thank you so much for coming. We really need you."

"Don't thank me yet," she says under her facemask. "I may be the one who fucks this up for everybody."

"I doubt that," I say hugging her.

I pull out of our driveway and into traffic. My hands are shaking until Race places a soft hand over one of them. "Don't worry, we gonna be okay. I know it. I believe in you. That's why I'm here."

I feel confident now. I love the optimistic side of her.

"Can you please move your leg over," Denim yells at Scarlett in the backseat. *Aww shit, here these bitches go fighting.* "I don't even know why you touching me."

I continue to drive, and leave them to it.

"Denim, please stop," Scarlett begs. "I don't feel like arguing with you and shit. We got a lot to do tonight, and we need each other right now."

"Bitch, don't talk to me about shit. Like I said, when this is all said and done I'm writing you off for good. And, that's on everything. You lucky I don't bust you in the mouth right now, for what you did to Jasmine."

I remember that Scarlett is pregnant. For some reason she didn't tell the others, and it wasn't my place to let them know. So I look through the rearview mirror and say, "Denim, you not gonna hit nobody. What you gonna do is sit back there, and relax. Why you wanna act all crazy when we almost at our destination?"

"What is up with you, Bambi?" Denim says to me. "You seem obsessed with taking up for Scarlett suddenly. She's a grown woman. She don't need a protector. What are you fucking her or something?"

"And if she was, what difference would it make?" Race asks. "People kill me worrying about what other people do in the bedroom."

I look at Race and then back at Denim through the rearview mirror. "First off you know I'm not about that life. The only thing I'm pushing up on is dick, and don't ever insult my sexuality like that again. I don't even associate with mothafuckas who get down with other chicks. I barely talk to my mother."

Race sighs real loudly and I wonder why.

"Anyway, I'm not taking up for Scarlett," I continue. "I'm just tired of you arguing with her over something she may or may not have done. You don't have proof she hurt Jasmine on purpose. The girl said it was an accident so it was an accident."

"It's gonna come out that she hurt my baby one day, and when it does I'm gonna beat this white bitch's ass everyday for the rest of her life."

"Don't talk about the future, Denim," Scarlett responds. "Do the shit now!"

Why would Scarlett say that when she knows how Denim is? Through the rearview mirror I see Denim pull back her fist like the string on a crossbow, and slam it into Scarlett's mask and face. The next thing I see is Scarlett's wild arms hitting anything in reach. I used one of my hands to reach back and grab Denim, while trying to steer the truck with the other. The truck moves awkwardly from left to right, and I almost crash. Shit couldn't get any worse until I saw the red, blue and white lights of a police car spread across the back window.

Here I am driving a truck full of cocaine estimated at a street value of about a billion dollars, and these bitches are back here fighting. If we go to jail with this type of shit we going for the rest of our lives. Who's gonna take care of our children? Stupid!

"We are being pulled over," I say calmly. "Thanks a lot, bitches. And, I need everybody to get themselves together now."

Scarlett looks behind us at the cops and says, "Oh my, God. I can't get locked up! I can't get locked up!" She is more hysterical than average.

"None of us can get locked up, bitch!" Denim says. "We all in the truck with a stack of cocaine. They not just taking whites to jail. Niggas going too."

"But I got warrants," Scarlett clarifies. "Warrants for stuff I never told ya'll about. If they lock me up I'll never see any of you again."

I heard Scarlett, but my thoughts go elsewhere. Suddenly I can smell the scent of bananas, and apples behind me. I didn't notice it before. I'm not sure why, but it was the first time I realized that they actually packed the truck with fruit. I'm hopeful that we can get out of here now. If...we...are...cool.

I pull over and park. I quarterback the situation. "Anybody but Scarlett got papers on them?" Everyone shakes their heads no. "Good, now I need everybody but Scarlett to take off your facemasks and jackets," I tell them. "Try to look as feminine as possible." Like the picture on your driver's license.

"Why?" Denim asks me.

"Just do it," I say biting the inside of my lip again. "And, do it quicker."

I take off my coat, and hat to allow my hair to fall at my shoulders. I wait patiently. From the left side view mirror I can see a tall black cop approaching. It isn't until he is at my side that I see a serious glare on his face. This isn't going to be easy I know it.

He shines a flashlight into the truck. I don't look at my sisters to see how they react. I'm trying to be normal. "License and registration please," he asks me. He's no nonsense.

Oh shit. Is this truck even registered? I didn't stop to think about what we would need if we were pulled over. Now it's too late. I pop open the glove compartment and pray for a miracle. When it opens a folded sheet of paper with *Fruit Delivery* stamped on the side falls out. I search deeper into the compartment and locate the registration card. I dig in my pocket, hand him my license and the registration.

"Thank you," he says to me. "I'll be right back, ma'am," he says as he nods and walks away.

"What's going on?" Race asks. When I look over at her not only do I see she's still wearing the mask, but her hair is out and her neck is sweating. So she looks like a very strange man on dope.

"What the fuck, Race," I say looking out the side view mirror to make sure the cop isn't coming back. "Why didn't you take off the mask?"

"Oh shit," she pawns the mask, "I forgot. You want me to do it now?"

"No," I yell. "He already saw you like that. Just wipe the sweat off of your greasy ass neck." She quickly does it.

Damn this girl acts like she got shit for brains sometimes. I unfold the paper that fell out of the glove compartment. After reading it for a few seconds I smile. It appears that Mitch thought of everything already. So when the officer comes back, I feel half prepared.

"Where are you ladies, and gentlemen going tonight?"

"We have a fruit delivery for a hotel. Apparently there's some big Hawaiian themed party tomorrow and they need the fruit." I flash the papers at him showing the order from the hotel even though I know it's not required yet.

"What are the rest of your names?" he asks everyone else shining his light into the truck again.

"Race," she mumbles in a voice so low it's hardly audible.

"And you are?" He asks them in the back.

"I'm Denim, and this is my fiancé Turner," Denim turns Scarlett's face toward hers, and places a heavy kiss on her lips. To really add to the scene, she straddles Scarlett. I guess Scarlett decides to play along because she runs her hands up Denim's back and pulls her closer. They look like a man and a woman and the scene heats up quick.

When I look at the officer he looks stuck and embarrassed. But, more importantly, his dick is hard. "Well...I see," he clears his throat, "well let me let you people handle your business," he hands me the registration card, "you all have a good night."

When he leaves Denim wipes her mouth, plops back in her seat and crosses her arms over her breasts. She looks angrier now.

"That was smart as shit," I tell her. "You probably just saved Scarlett's life."

"Yeah, thank you so much, Denim," Scarlett responds. "I mean I know you mad at me, so you didn't have to do that."

"Shut up, bitch," Denim replies. "That move was for Bambi because we was fighting and almost fucked shit up. Like I said, when it's all said and done, you and me still got a problem. You better be ready for that day too!"

# BAMBI

When I pull the truck up to a warehouse, the lift gate opens automatically. I look back at my girls and say, "This is it, ya'll. The moment we've all been practicing for. I have faith in all of you that we can pull this off. We have to show and prove tonight. We make it out of this alive, we are millionaires for the rest of our lives."

"And if we don't?" Race asks.

"Then it's been nice knowing you all. And I love you very much," I tell them.

We hug each other, and I take a deep breath. I slowly roll the truck into the open warehouse. I park and hop out. My sisters follow my lead. As practiced they lean up against the truck and pose like men. They look strong and confident.

There are about ten men inside holding semi automatic weapons. Although me and my girls have something strapped to the inside of our right legs, we wouldn't be a match for this type of weaponry if something real kicked off. This means I need to outwit them with my mind instead.

Some men rush through our shipment and one checks the package, using a knife and his tongue.

"It's good," he yells out.

After five minutes, from another door to the right, came two white men walking in our direction. One has brown hair and he is holding something in a clear plastic cup. The other is taller, about five foot seven I guess, and he tugs his right ear. I wonder if that was some sign to take our drugs and kill us. Suddenly my plan seems stupid. I'm sweating, and I quickly wipe it off of my face, before they see it.

The taller one is applauding the entire way until he is standing in front of me. "We finally meet them, brother," he looks back at the shorter one. "The Kennedy Kings. Live, in person."

"Your product is legendary," the shorter one says with an accent pointing at me before taking a sip from his cup. "What you call it?"

"Virgin Pussy," I say in my deep voice. "Now are you ready to do business?"

"This one's straight to point," the taller one says. "I like that about you." He may have said he liked it but his eyes told me differently. "Anyway I am Arkadi Lenin, and this is my brother Iakov. And you are?"

"I'm Kevin Kennedy, and this is Camp, Bradley and Ramirez Kennedy." My sisters didn't move from position on the truck and I loved it. They looked official and unenthused by what was happening. Like this type of shit happens everyday. Even Race did a good job of faking it.

"Come, let's have dinner in office and chat," Arkadi says. "We have much to talk about."

"No thank you," I tell him. "We have your product, and in exchange we want our money. We're not here to take up too much more of your time."

"In my country, it is rude to bite hand of man who means to feed you," Iakov says sipping his drink again.

"And in my country it's rude to waste a nigga's time," I tell him looking directly into his eyes. "So it's a good thing that we are in my country." I pause. "You went through quite some trouble to meet us. Now I'm here and we have your delivery. If you don't want it I'll bounce and leave you to it. That's on you."

"Come, come...just one drink," Iakov says.

"I ate already," I say rubbing my belly. "I'm good over here. We all are."

"Let me make you better with good meal," Iakov says raising his cup.

"This nigga is tripping, let's bounce," I hear a deep voice call out behind me. The voice sounds all man, no woman, and I'm sure whoever used it on my team had practiced.

When I turn around I look at Denim and Scarlett, but they softly shake their heads no. Race is looking directly into my eyes letting me know it was her. I'm so proud of her that it takes everything in my power not to smile like the bad bitch that I really am.

"You heard my partner, either give us our money or this meeting is adjourned."

"You know," Iakov says sipping his drink again, "you are all some very pretty kings. I'd think you'd be more manly. More macho."

I'm scared. He's on to us. "So what are you, a lover of boys or something?" I ask. "We can hook you up with some if that's what you into. But, we real niggas over here."

Iakov wipes the smirk off of his face and moves toward me, but Arkadi stops him. "Let's not pass insults around," Arkadi says.

"Then lets pass money and cocaine instead," I reply.

Both Iakov and Arkadi study me. I'm not sure, but something tells me that they are weighing their options. Should they kill us or not. That is the question.

"Can you get more, when this is gone?" Arkadi asks me.

"If you got money, then you got a constant supplier," I tell him. "But if we do this again in the future, it must be done more efficiently. I hope you understand. Time is money and money is time. We got moves to make. Like I'm sure you do too. Now where is our paper?"

He snaps his fingers and someone pushes two crates in our direction. Arkadi pops off the lid and there's more money inside than I know what to do with. I'm trying to maintain my cool but now it's difficult. This is our blood money. What we're willing to die for.

"You're free to count it here if you like," he tells me.

198

I'm trying to get the fuck away from them. We'll take anything at this point. "We'll do that later, although I'm sure you
wouldn't want to ruin a good business relationship by cutting us
short," I respond.

"I like you, and can't wait to do more business with you in
future," Arkadi says.

"We'll see about that."

"Oh my, God, Bambi," Denim yells slapping my back
from the backseat. "Girl, you were so cool back there you got my
pussy wet, and shit! How the fuck did you pull that off?"

I laugh as I steer the truck. "You gotta be hard when you in
the military. Any sign of weakness can get you killed." The
thought of that time in my life makes me sad, and dampens the
mood. I wish I could put the war behind me. "But, fuck all that.
What's up with Race giving us the base," I nudge Race on the
arm. "Bitch, you ate that!" I tell her.

Her mask is off like everyone and she looks so innocent
and pretty again. Not the monster I just saw back at the warehouse.

"I was getting scared, Bambi," Race tells me running her
hand through her brown hair. "I thought he was about to play us
and the voice just popped out. I planned to use this if he didn't
give us our money though."

She raises her shirt and I am looking at a big prosthetic gut
that matches her skin tone. If I didn't know she was small to
begin with, I would believe it was her body. She lifted up the
fake stomach and inside of the prosthetic is a glock. My eyes pop
open.

"What the fuck?" I say to her. "How...how...I mean, do
you even know what to do with it?"

"Maybe," she laughs. "I probably could do a little something, something if I had too. But, I was going to kick it to you
and let you live with it."

As everyone laughs I think about the dream I had about us ruling the drug world. My sisters didn't want to hear it. They were too interested in getting out of the game and spending the twenty-five million dollar share. I want more now. And, I hate feeling bad because of it.

I was just about to ask them what they wanted to do now when I see a white man in a navy blue Honda Sedan following us. It was the same man I saw the day I fell asleep in my car. I wonder who he was, and if he is with The Russians or not.

"There's a bar over there, ya'll. Let's go grab a drink right quick," I say. "To celebrate."

"Are you crazy?" Denim asks. "We have a hundred million dollars in this truck. I don't know about you, but I want to get home. We almost died for that money.

"I know, but its packed under a bunch of fruit," I tell her. "It'll take I don't know how long to move it, if someone tried to steal it. We good. Let's chill for a minute."

"I don't know about this, Bambi," Denim says. "I really want to get back to Jasmine. Not to mention we're dressed like men."

I look out of my rearview mirror. The man in the car is still behind us. "Have just one drink with me," I tell them. "Please."

"I guess you not getting sober no more," Denim asks me.

Silence.

"Fuck it," Race says saving me. "After what Bambi pulled off, the least we can do is grab a drink with her. It'll be the last time we dress like men. Let's have fun with it."

With that I park the truck before they can dispute. We pile inside the bar, and I don't tell them about the man following us. I don't want them scared, because I want us to do this type of thing again in the future. I want more money. I want more power.

Once inside, while the girls are at the bar having a good time, I call Sarge. Fifteen minutes later he texts me to say he is outside. With that news, I grab my vodka shot off the bar, toss it back, slam it on the table and say, "Let's go ladies!"

"You trying to get us out just when we were starting to have fun," Denim says. "I'm feeling good as shit now, Bambi. Let's chill for awhile."

"Well I'm still trying to go home," Scarlett says. "It's been a long night and I got a lot to think about." She rubs her belly. She must be sick again.

"You would say some dumb shit like that," Denim tells Scarlett. "Always the party pooper."

"Well she's right, Denim. It's time to bounce," I say harsher.

When we walk outside and toward the truck, down the street I can see two green Hummers. I smile when I see Sarge wink at me from one of them. They are going to follow us safely until we get home. My nigga always has my back. The girls don't know about the danger looming in the air, and that's good. I don't want to scare them before I talk them into our new business venture. The sedan is also gone. Something tells me I haven't seen the last of the man in the sedan, or The Russians. That should be enough to scare me, but for some reason it doesn't.

# ONE MONTH LATER
# BAMBI

As I tape the last box in my bedroom, I look at how empty everything looks. Who would have thought that I would be leaving this house? The glamorous house I had come to love and know for so long. The house I built my life with Kevin in.

Although we are just moving now, I wanted to move a long time ago. I just don't feel safe here anymore. But, the girls wanted to find the perfect new home. It's funny how my sisters and me are loaded, but nobody wants to get separate houses. It means we are staying together. To tell you the truth I am glad, because everyday I leave this house I'm being followed. I want to know if the others are being followed too, but I don't want to spook them. I figure they would have told me by now if they were, at least if they knew they were.

Before being followed, I always imagined living in a mansion larger than the one we live in now. But I convinced them that we should buy more private land, and a home away from society. Because, then we could build on our land anytime we want, and build a fort around it. We settled on a large cottage-style home in Maryland. Although they call it a cottage, in actuality it was almost as big as this one. We had seven rooms, a full basement, a livable attic and the back of our home looked out onto a lake. It was cozy and it felt like a wonderful place to raise a family. Especially since Scarlett is expecting a new baby. She finally told the girls about the bundle of joy, and I think her and Denim are closer because of it.

After the deal with The Russians was done, we were able to focus on the fact that our husbands were gone. We cried most nights and, wished for death the other nights. I'm lonely all the time, and even started to welcome Cloud's daily consensual rape visits. Since Bunny's murder investigation was still open, he knew I had no idea if the real band-aid was still in his possession or not. So I gave him my body conditionally, and sometimes he didn't leave my bedroom. It was awful pretending to care for a man I didn't love in front of my sisters, but he enjoyed the pussy too much to care what they thought. Men are so vicious when they want to be.

I pick up the last box for my room and walk down the steps. It's so empty in our home now, that I can hear my footsteps echo throughout the house. When I move toward the door I focus on the three moving trucks out front. Although we paid for the movers to pack and relocate our entire house, the things in this box are precious and I wanted to deliver them to the new house myself.

They are the photos of my sons when they were born, pictures of Kevin and me on our wedding day, and the last bottle of vodka I bought. It was the same night we met with The Russians, and I decided to keep it as a souvenir of what I could do if I really tried. I didn't have one sip of liquor since that day. I'm sober again.

When I walk out of my house, and onto the porch, my mouth drops when I see my twins stepping out of a cab. Noah and Melo are facing me and I'm shivering. They look so regal, and so handsome that tears immediately flood my eyes and roll down my face. It's like I'm looking at Kevin times two.

I place the box down on the porch, and run up to them. But the moment I reach them their hard bodies act like walls. They don't embrace me. I look up into Noah's eyes first. He's closest to his father and seems the angriest. He's clutching a piece of paper in his hands, and I wonder what it is.

"Ma, where's dad?" He asks. "And, don't lie anymore and tell me he's away on business."

"Tell us the truth," Melo says in a softer voice. "Be decent, ma. Please."

I know I can't lie anymore. This is it. I knew this day would come but I wanted more time to tell the truth. "He's dead," I tell them grabbing their hands. Noah snatches away from me immediately, but Melo allows me to hold him a second longer.

Noah bites his bottom lip so hard, it bleeds. He does this whenever he is angry or worried about something. *Just like me.* "Did you kill him?" Noah asks me.

I hold my chest. "Noah, why would you think I would even be capable of something like that? I loved that man from the moment I looked into his eyes. He's my husband, and your father. I would never do anything like that to him or you two. He was murdered at the mass shooting at the casino. His name wasn't in the paper because they used fake names to travel." I'm speaking so loudly that Scarlett, Denim and Race come out of the house and stand beside me.

"Hey, babies," Denim says to Melo and Noah, "why are you here? What's going on?"

"Nothing, unless you consider the fact that dad is dead, and this bitch has lied to me everyday for the past month," Noah tells Denim.

Without a weapon he stabbed me in the heart. My son has never spoken to me like this. What has happened to him?

Denim steps in front of me and points a long finger in Noah's face. "I know you are upset, son. And, you have every right to be. But, if you ever disrespect your mother like that in front of me again I'm gonna forget we share a last name," she softly touches his face and points at him with the other hand. "Are we clear?"

Noah takes a deep breath and says, "Yes, ma'am." At that moment I know my son is still in his body somewhere, because he shows her *some* respect.

"Aunt Therese sent this to us the other day," Noah says holding the letter. "Aunt Bunny wrote this before she died. Aunt Bunny told Therese that if she died, that this letter needed to be sent to us at school. In this letter aunt Bunny said that if something were to happen to her, that you killed her. And, that you probably killed dad too."

I can't believe it. This bitch came back from the grave, and is trying to ruin my life. She wants my family even after death. Although I'm glad she is out of the picture, I know that if that letter gets in the hands of the police that I'm going to jail for the rest of my life. I need to take it from him, but how?

"Noah, I didn't kill anybody," I say softly. "I would never do what Bunny claimed in that letter." I reach for it.

"She has always hated your mother," Scarlett adds. "I wouldn't believe the letter if I were you son."

"Can I see it?" I ask him, so that I can plot to destroy it.

"No," he stuffs the letter into his back pocket. "Just stay away from me." He walks into the house leaving me outside.

Melo walks up to me, wraps his arms around me, and kisses me on the forehead. I fall into his embrace, and rest my head against his heart. It's beating loudly and I can't help but cry. He grips me tighter, and rocks me in his arms. It's like we're dancing to music only we can hear. He did this to me a lot when I was suffering from flashbacks in the war. It worked every time. Melo is so strong and so admirable.

"Ma, I don't know what's going on, but I'm home now, and you don't have to go through the problems alone. Noah will come around when he's ready, but if he doesn't I don't want you baring that cross. That's on him. Okay?"

I separate from him and look into his eyes. "Thank you so much, Melo. I'm sorry about your father. I wanted to tell you both but this is your last year in school and I didn't want you worrying because they never said your father's name in the shooting. It wasn't until we heard the alias that he used that we knew for sure." I lay my head on his chest again.

"What about his body?" He asks.

"We have to stay away from them now, Melo. You know what lifestyle your father led, and we can't be sure what they had on them."

He seems weakened by my response. "Look, how about you go to your room and take a shower. I'll cook us all a big meal. We'll spend some time together, before you go back to school and hopefully things will be better between me and your brother before you leave."

He separates from me again. "We not going back to school, ma."

"What? Why not?" I ask. "The best place for you to be is at school."

"She's right, Melo," Race says. "We just bought another house, and it's lovely. Go back and get your high school diploma, and when you come home, we can start all over right."

"Do it for your father, honey," Denim adds.

"Aunties, I respect all of you, and I know you know that. But, my father is dead, my mother is sick, and whether she knows it or not she needs me here. So I'm staying."

"I'm not sick, Melo," I tell him.

"Ma, you've been drinking again. Aunt Bunny told us that in the letter too." *I hate that bitch.* "I didn't believe it until I saw it in your eyes." He touches my face. "What kind of man would I be if I left my mother at a time like this? I'm not no sucker ass nigga, ma. I'm a man and a man takes care of his mother. So, I'm staying right here. Okay?"

"Melo, I wish I could change your mind."

"You would have to start by changing my heart first," he kisses me again. "But, that will never work because I love you too much." He hugs my sisters and walks into the house.

Turns out that moving day is cancelled. We had the beds brought back inside and sent everything else to the new house. The twins wanted to be here, and around their father's memories for a little while longer, and I decided to give them that honor. It was the least I could do since I lied to them about everything else.

I'm in my empty closet, and on the floor drinking vodka again. Turns out the last box didn't make it on the truck after all. I have pictures of my sons and Kevin spread out on the floor in front of me. I wonder how Noah would feel if he knew their precious father stepped out on me, fucked a slut and big Bunny, gave me crabs and had another child. Would he still be the greatest dad of all time?

I'm looking at a picture of the four of us that was taken during a trip to Hawaii. We are wearing yellow and red leis around our necks and we are happy. I miss times like this and would love to go back to the way things were. When we were a family, and happy, but I know it can never happen. Ever.

I take another swig when Scarlett walks into the closet. Her red hair is pulled back into a ponytail, and I can never get over how gorgeous she is. She sits on the couch in my closet and looks down at me.

"I love you," she says to me softly. "Very much."

I smile. Scarlett always knows what to say and do when I'm going through the hard times. I'm so happy that she's still around, and still in my life.

"I love you too," I tell her reaching out to touch her cold hand. "Very much." She sits on the floor with me and we hug before separating.

"I figure now is the best time to tell you something about my life," Scarlett says gently. "Its always best to hear someone else's horror story when you are dealing with one of your own. Consider this as my sincere gift to you."

"God bless you," I smile eager to get my mind off of my troubles.

She takes the bottle of vodka from me and swallows before I can dispute. She's pregnant and doesn't need to be drinking.

"I know it's bad for the baby, but I have to get my mind right," she says wiping her mouth. "Anyway, I was married before. He was a good husband, but I wasn't a good wife. We ended up having a daughter, and one night when I was angry, I hurt her bad. The day I met Camp I was due in court to answer for child abuse charges, and I never went. Which is why I have a warrant out for my arrest."

I'm stunned and confused. "You hurt her how?"

"I don't want to talk about that, Bambi. I really don't. I just wanted you to know my truth. And, I'm sorry but that's all I can say."

"But you're pregnant now," I say eying her small pouch-tummy. "How do you know you won't hurt that one too?"

"Because I won't," she says. "It's not in my heart any-more."

While I'm looking at her, I remember Jasmine. Denim always believed Scarlett hurt her, and now that she shared this with me, I wonder if it's not true. "Scarlett, please tell me you didn't—,"

"I didn't hurt Jasmine," she says. "It was an accident." She's quiet for a minute. "Bambi, I'm sharing this with you because it's time for honesty, but I hope you will keep this between me and you. If Denim finds out about my past she won't believe the thing with Jasmine was a mistake."

I had secrets too. Many of them, and I knew what it meant to keep them inside without sharing. But, Jasmine was my niece, and I didn't want anybody hurting her again.

"Scarlett, I'm going to keep your secret, but you must get help. You about to have a baby, and I need to make sure my niece is safe. Okay?"

"Okay," she smiles hugging me again. "Thank you, Bambi. And if there is ever anything you want to tell me, you can count on me to keep your secret too."

I believe her, but some things you have to take to your grave. And, I intend on doing just that.

# BAMBI

hen I wake up in my bed, I look up at the diamond mirror on the ceiling. I can't believe we were about to move and leave that mirror behind. By itself it's worth a half a million dollars.

When I get out of the bed, and my feet nestle into the carpet, I wonder why it's so quiet. I don't hear Jasmine's babbling, Scarlett's singing or Race's bumping around in the basement. When I remember that my sons are home, I wonder where they are too. I walk toward my bedroom door until my phone rings. I'm surprised its still on because I had my number transferred to the new house. I pick up the handset, yawn and say, "Hello."

"Mrs. Kennedy, how are you this lovely morning? Or should I call you Kevin Kennedy, since you did such a great job portraying him the last time we met."

The phone drops out of my hand and falls to the floor. I stare at it crazily. How did Arkadi get my number? I pick the phone up and say, "Hello?"

"Wow, I almost thought you weren't going to return. I'm glad to see that you came back. How are you this morning?"

"How did you get my number?" I ask trying to maintain authority in my voice. "And where is Avery?"

"It doesn't matter, but I would love to speak to your husband. Is he available? Or is he still dead?"

209

"I don't know what you're talking about, I...um...I never met you before. I...I mean...what do you want?" I'm losing control. I'm losing all cool.

"I want to see you again. We must talk in person about this relationship of ours. If it is going to work, we must spend more time together. Just you, and I."

"I'm not meeting with you," I say trying to regain control. "And I don't want you to ever call my house again! Do you hear me? Never call again!"

When I hang up I sit back, and look at the phone. I am praying that The Russians leave us alone. So we wouldn't be caught with millions of dollars, we buried our money on the land of our new house. What my sisters don't know was that I called Mitch earlier this week to buy more cocaine. The call didn't go too well, and he threatened my life for lying to him about Kevin being okay. About, Kevin being dead.

My plan was to take a portion of my money, buy more cocaine and make deliveries to the customers Kevin failed to make. But Mitch said since Kevin was gone he was out of the business and wouldn't sell anything to me. He said in this business loyalty rules, and that the Kings always kept his anonymity. He said people had been kidnapped and tortured to give up the drug connect. I said I knew about him now, and that I never said anything to anybody, not even the Russians. Mitch said what I know about him is a facade. He said I knew only what he wanted me to know, but that Kevin knows more. So without Mitch, meeting with The Russians at this time would be dumb. If I can't get the work, I don't need to meet the Russians again.

I walk around the house and just as I suspect, everyone is gone. I was going to tell them that it was time to move, and that I would not be taking no for an answer. When the doorbell rings, I answer it but no one is there. When I look down there is a small red box on my porch. I duck into the house, grab my gun and go back out. I'm shooting anything I don't recognize within one second.

I see nothing. After five minutes, I pick up the box and bring it in the house. It takes me another hour to open it because something tells me it is from The Russians. I place the box on the dining room table, open the lid and look inside. I pick up three soft brown things that are soaked in blood. When I realize they are three scalped faces, I drop them, and they fall at my feet. Although I've been around enough gore, I never saw it in this element. I'm at home and things like this aren't supposed to happen here. I'm supposed to be safe.

I walk back up to the box and pick up a picture inside. It's of Avery, his daughter and his wife. I get it now. It's a clear message. Crystal clear. I walk back into my bedroom and wait. Before long the phone rings. I know who it is so I take my time answering. "Hello."

"Now you see that we are serious, Mrs. Kennedy. If you want that to be the condition of your family, we will gladly oblige," Arkadi says.

"When we met with you, you knew who we were?" I ask as my hands shake.

"We found out earlier that day that Kevin and the Kings were killed. We weren't sure if the meeting would still go down, and was surprised when we saw all the things you ladies went through just to meet with us. Although you were not men, you were very convincing. You did an outstanding job."

"That's why your brother called us pretty kings."

He laughs and I hate his creepy voice. "I slapped my brother later for that mistake. Unfortunately he can't keep secrets as good as I can," he pauses. "Well, enough with the pleasantries, I want to meet with you again, Bambi. Without the man clothes that is."

"Look, I can't get any more work," I tell him. "My supplier has cut me off so meeting you will be in vain. You gonna have to find somebody else."

"Why find someone else when I have you? Your brand is highly sought after." He pauses. "And if you even think about leaving, let me give you the new address to your home. It's 1456 Feather Lane." My heart rate increases. "Your new house is quite lovely, but it won't save you from me or my organization if I want to touch you."

"So you were responsible for that white man following me all those times?"

"Of course, and I know more about you than you think. I will call you in two days with the details of our meeting. By the way, we saw your sons and they're very handsome young men. It would be a shame to kill them before they even had a chance to make you proud."

# BAMBI

I t's darker tonight than it usually is outside, and I feel something evil coming on. As I watch my sons climb into my mother's car and pull off, tears roll down my face. I didn't want them to go away so soon, but I knew they couldn't stay here either. Although I knew The Russians weren't lying when they said they knew everything about my family, I would rather them come at me then my children. On my request Denim sent Jasmine to be with her mother Sarah, although she fussed about it the entire time.

When they leave I walk back into the living room with my sisters. They are sitting on the sofa waiting for what I have to tell them. "There's a problem."

"What do you mean?" Denim asks as she stands and approaches me. "Are you worried about the boys or something?" She scratches her red curly hair. "If you are don't worry about it, Noah will get over his thing with you. It'll just take some time...his father just died."

"No, this isn't about the twins," I tell them. "It's about the Russians."

"What do you mean?" Race asks sitting next to Scarlett on the sofa. "They got their product, and we have our money. So we should be good to go our separate ways. Right?"

"They knew we weren't Kevin and them when we held the meeting," I say. "But, they still wanted the coke and was hoping that Mitch would make the drop off. We fucked them up when we brought the work and showed up instead as men. Now they want to meet with me again."

"But we can't get more coke," Denim says. "What we did was a one time thing. You know that."

"They don't care that the arrangement was temporary," I try to explain. "Since we were able to get our hands on that much cocaine, they assumed we could get more. What they really want is Mitch, and they're using us to try to get to him."

"Bambi, you have to get us out of this shit," Race says. "All I want to do is move on and start a life. I can't be involved in any of this shit."

While I am looking at Race's lips, I notice a sudden flurry of sparkles behind Scarlett's head. When her eyes popped open, and red blood traces down her left arm, I know immediately what's happening. What I thought was sparkles was actually shattered glass coming from the living room's window. Someone is shooting from the outside, into our home. Since we didn't hear a sound, they must be using silencers.

"Get on the floor!" I yell. "Somebody is shooting!"

I try not to focus on Scarlett's bloodied body. Please God don't let her be dead. I can't think about her right now. I need my mind right. If the Russians are trying to kill us I don't understand why. As far as I know we have an understanding. I was waiting on their call so we could schedule a meeting. So why do this to my family?

Scarlett's limp body falls off of the sofa and to the floor. Denim tumbles to the carpet and crawls toward Scarlett. When Denim has Scarlett's body, she drags her out of the line of fire and into the basement.

With Scarlet safe, I unleash the hammer from my waist and rush to the window. Before I could let off one shot, I notice someone out of the corner of my eyes busting off too. Race is by the window blasting shot after shot. I can't believe how confident she is holding the .45. It's like she owns it.

With her help, I fire out of the window next to the door. Another bullet comes crashing into the window next to where I am, but it misses me. When I feel a stream of cold air, I see the door open and Race rushing outside. The blasts from her gun are persistent and I wonder how many bullets she has left.

I follow her outside and see all of our cars in the driveway have flat tires and shattered windows. They don't want us to get away. This is an assassination attempt. When I see a man approach her from the left, I fire into his head and throat. The sound of Race's clicking gun tells me she's out of bullets. "Go reload, Race! I got this."

Instead of going back into the house, she drops the gun and releases another from the back of her jeans. Her and I both manage to kill three more men together to protect our home. We fire at anybody trying to do us harm. I wish I knew who these people were.

When I see a black Yukon pull up in our driveway, I'm about to fire into the windows until someone says, "Get your family and let's go! About five niggas are on the way to kill anything breathing in that mansion. We don't have a lot of time."

"Who the fuck are you?" I ask still aimed in his direction.

"Cloud sent me. I'm one of his friends," he looks behind him. "Are you coming or what?"

"How do I know it's not a set up?" Race asks.

"Because with all this time I could've shot you already," he looks behind him again. "Now unless ya'll want to get out of here yourself, come the fuck on! You got two minutes."

I thought about losing my friend Tatiana in the war, and realized I couldn't lose another person I loved. Since our transportation is ruined, and we didn't have another way out I say, "Race, get into his truck. I'm going to get Denim and Scarlett."

I rush into the house, and run down into the basement. The moment I reach the bottom step, I slip on Scarlett's red blood. When I look at my clothes, her blood is everywhere on me, and I can't help but think about the baby she's carrying. I hope the child is alive. I get up off of the floor.

"Denim, help me get Scarlett up the stairs," I yell. "We gotta get out of here now. Some niggas are on their way to finish us off."

Together we pull Scarlett up the stairs and hoist her into his truck. Scarlett's head rests in Denim's lap and her eyes are barely open. The driver peels out of the driveway and we enter the path of three cars full of killers. Race rolls the window down, fires out of the truck and kills the driver in the first car. The other two cars crash into the back of him causing a major explosion.

Our driver manages to get us off of our property before any more damage can be done. We are on the road for a minute until Denim looks down at Scarlett and says, "She's going to die!" Denim looks at me. "She's losing too much blood. I gotta get her to the hospital." When we reach a light, God must've been on Scarlett's side because a cop car is next to us. Denim opens the door and hops out.

"What the fuck are you doing?" The driver asks trying to look normal in the truck although a cop is next to him. "We got fire arms in here!"

"Saving my friend's life," Denim says pulling Scarlett out into the street. "Ya'll go ahead."

"I'm going with you," I say moving to get out.

"No! You got too much blood on you," she looks behind her probably to make sure the killers aren't back on our trail. "I don't want them thinking you did this. Just get out of here!" She slams the door and hits the truck with her hand. "Go now!"

When the driver pulls off, from the back window I see the police officers helping Scarlett out of the street.

As I think about everything, my head spins. What is happening to us? Who wants us dead? And, more importantly why?

After twenty minutes we end up in the Frederick Douglas housing project in Southeast Washington DC, nicknamed Emerald City. The driver parks the truck, opens Race's door and says, "Come with me."

We follow him into a building and down some stairs. We approach a door and I look behind me. Although I have one bullet in my gun, I plan to use it wisely if something kicks off.

Our driver gets in front of us, removes a key from his pocket and opens the door. He goes in first, and Race second followed by me. The moment the door is closed behind us, Race is kicked in her face with a Nike boot, and knocked out. I'm about to use my bullet wisely when I'm struck in the face with a man size blow. I'm out cold.

When I come to, I'm on the floor, leaning against a wall next to Race. Our wrists are tied behind our backs and the driver is sitting in a chair with three men behind him.

"Are you okay?" I ask Race. She doesn't respond. She seems stuck or mad at me.

"I hope they didn't hit you too hard," the driver says to me looking at the tall man to his left. "I told the nigga that you were a lady, and he didn't have to hit you that hard. After all, once we took your guns you were harmless." I examine him without him knowing. I'm looking for weaknesses. Something I learned in the military. He's shorter than he appeared in the truck, not very attractive and wearing a bulky cell phone on his hip.

"Cut the shit," I say. "What do you want with us?"

"You are as smart as you are beautiful," he says. "Because of it, I'll respect your question. First let me introduce who—"

"Nigga, I'm not interested in who the fuck you are," I tell him. "I'm a trained killer. And before long your name won't matter because John Doe will be used to describe your body."

All three of them laugh at me. I remain as serious as I was when I started.

"How do you plan on doing that? I'm the one holding all of the cards not you."

"Are you sure?" I ask. "Because if you were holding all the cards, you wouldn't be holding me and my friend hostage. It's obvious that I have something you want. So you need me, not the other way around."

He nods. "Very smart," he replies telling me something I already know. "My name is Donatello, and I understand that since Kevin has been gone that you and the other bitches have inherited a rack of coke or money. Which one is it?"

"Who told you that?"

"The late great Bunny," he replies.

I look at Race and we both shake our heads. "Bunny lied to you, and that's why I took care of the bitch. That close casket funeral...that was my handy work." When I feel Race staring at me I remember that she and my other sisters did not know I was involved with Bunny's murder before now. But, I don't have time to explain to her why I killed Bunny. Our lives are on the line. "I don't have anything you asking for, so all that shit you staged at my house was for nothing."

He put both of his hands up in the air. "No, mama, I'm gonna keep shit real with you, the shoot out at your crib was not us. The Kennedy Kings didn't deliver packages and niggas are after them. You beautiful ladies just got caught up in the mix. I happened to be at a poker game, heard about the hit and wanted to put my bid in before they killed ya'll. Them niggas wanted blood, I want the work or the money. So technically I saved your lives. For now anyway."

"And like I said, we don't have shit," I persist hoping that if they tortured us, that Race could hold her own. "Let us not forget that my friend Denim saw your face."

"Lots of niggas saw my face who I robbed. That's why I'm one of the most wanted niggas alive," he laughs. "Now you have some money or the weight somewhere. I know, because before Bunny was murdered, we placed an order."

"Like I said, you got the wrong information, son."

"I'm gonna make shit difficult for you," Donatello says. "Real difficult, are you sure you want to do that?"

"I am if you are," I say.

"We gonna see about that."

# BAMBI

I feel like I've been held hostage for three days, but it may be longer. Donatello hasn't returned since the first day. Instead of putting us in pain, I think he is choosing the abandonment route. That shit don't work with me. I prefer to be left alone.

It is dark in the room we are in and I can hear Race's shallow breathing. My throat is so dry my tongue keeps sticking to the roof of my mouth.

"Why did you kill Bunny?" Race asks me in a heavy voice.

I can't see her face, but I tell her the entire story.

"I'm glad she's dead," Race tells me when I'm done. "Although I'm not looking forward to seeing her in the afterlife."

I think about Bunny's monster face and say, "Me either." I think about Kevin and the life we led before this moment. I would love to see him again. I gotta know why he broke my heart. "Do you regret any of it? Marrying into the Kennedy family? The money? The cars? The boat rides and crazy parties?"

She sighs. "I don't regret anything, Bambi. Before becoming a Kennedy, my life was drab. I was weak, and needed to work on myself, but I didn't know where to start. Ramirez gave me a little excitement but I was still living through him. I relied on him to be my protector, and when he died it felt good to finally do it for myself. I lived more in the last few months than I have my entire life. No regrets over here," she continues.

I think about how she was handling the gun. "How were you able to fire like that? So effortlessly?"

"A good friend of mine told me that you have to stand up for something." I laugh because I told her that. "So I practiced at the gun range," she giggles. "When I hold a gun in my hands, I feel alive, Bambi. It's like the gun is an extension of who I really am. I just wish I would've realized it before this moment." She sighs again. "I don't want to die, Bambi. Not like this." Race pauses. "What do you think they are going to do to us?"

I sigh. "Right now they are fucking with our minds. They figure not having food and water will make us tell them whatever they want to know. If it comes to torture, and you can't hold out, I'll understand if you tell them where our money is."

"I'll hold out for as long as I can," Race responds.

When a door opens allowing a blast of light to spill inside, I see Donatello's smug face. Big mistake. He's alone and he has two bags filled with McDonald's food in his hand. I don't think I've ever smelled anything so delicious in all my life. My stomach feels like it has hands and is trying to reach out of my gut, and snatch the bag from his grasp.

He turns the light on, and looks at us. "I bought you some food," he steps closer to me, and next to the wooden chair. "You both can have all you can eat, if you tell me what I want to know. Where is the money or the work?"

"Fuck you, nigga," I say mad he's playing mental games with us.

He laughs. "What about you?" He asks Race. "You feel as sure as she does? Or do you want something to eat and drink?"

Race turns her head to the right and remains silent. She swallows loudly so I know she wants the drink.

"I like your steez," he tells me. "Both of you." He steps closer to me. And, the moment he does, I clip his ankle with my foot. His body falls down and he bangs his head on the edge of the chair a few feet in front of me. He passes out. I ease my foot under his underarm, and using all my might, drag his limp body toward me. His head is between my legs now, and he's finally coming too. But, it's too late because I press my thighs around the muscles of his neck and squeeze.

He's clawing at my arms, and face, but I've done this type of shit plenty of times before. I feel a tingly sensation course through the veins in my pussy. It feels as good as it would if I was getting my pussy ate out. I'm in ecstasy as I moan out my orgasm. He can't fight for his life anymore. I look down at him, the sweat from my forehead falls onto his face and dampens his eyelashes. I don't let him go, until the vessels in his eyes are red and bleeding.

When I'm sure he's dead, I breathe heavily over him. In that minute he and I are alone until Race says, "What the fuck was that?" She looks scared of me.

"A murder," I tell her. I focus back on his limp body. He has a pocketknife on his hip next to the bulky phone on his waist. I push his body sideways and kick the phone and the knife repeatedly. The knife falls on the floor followed by the cell. I bring my leg up to my chest and drag the knife toward my hip with my foot. I push the knife to the back where my hands are, and manage to slide it up the wall. I flip the button to eject the blade and cut the rope.

When I'm free, I cut Race out too. I try to move to the phone to make a call but Race grips me and says, "Thank you for saving my life. I owe you." Tatiana told me that before, and I hope Race wouldn't live to regret it also.

I hug her back, but rush to the phone. I call the one person I can count on in times like this. He never lets me down.

When Race and I walk out of the building, I exhale. We are eating Big Mac's and drinking soda. It's the best thing I've ever tasted. Although it's chilly, the sun fights for position and it's warmth brushes against my face. I can truly say that I never felt this type of freedom before, not even when I was discharged from the army.

When I squint and walk out of the apartment complex and onto the street I see four Hummer's. Sarge's truck is in the front.

PRETTY KINGS BY T. STYLES

He's standing outside of it. He salutes me and I salute him back. My smile couldn't be brighter.

"Sarge is over there," I tell Race sipping my soda. "I know how much you love your boo," I joke.

"I never thought I'd be so happy to see him again," Race says as she throws the Big Mac paper on the ground. "When you know how much I fucking hate him. I'm gonna kiss the shit out of his ass."

"You should love him now," I remind her as we continue to walk toward him. "He's the one who gave you your swag to meet The Russians."

"I do love that nigga."

I'm smiling wider until...I see something. I drop everything in my hands.

"Bambi, what's wrong?" Race asks me. I don't answer. "Bambi, what's up you're scaring me."

When we make it to Sarge's truck I say, "Take her home."

I give him signs that he alone understands. His eyes widen, and he looks around. "Bambi, I'm not leaving you out here by yourself. Don't play me."

"If you love me you will. So the question is do you love me or not," I ask firmly. When he doesn't respond to me I repeat, "Do...you...love...me?"

Silence stands between us. After some time, he touches Race on the back and says, "Get in." He looks around again, but he doesn't see what I do. If he did it would be over, and a war would take place right there. "I need you to protect my family."

"I got it," he says.

I smile, touch him softly on the cheek and wait for them all to pull off. When they are away, I walk down the block. When I reach the navy blue Honda Sedan, I open the back passenger door and slide inside. The white man who usually follows me looks at my face in the rearview mirror.

He laughs and says, "How did you know I was here?"

I look out of the window at nothing in particular. "I smelled you." I look at him in the mirror. "Now take me to them. I'm ready to get this shit over with."

# BAMBI

Since I'm tied up for the second time this week, I'm starting to think I'm bad luck. I'm completely naked, gagged and sitting in a wooden chair. In front of me are Iakov and Arkadi, The Russians. Unlike Donatello, as their hostage, I have been treated horrifically. I've been struck in the face with their fists, poles, and even belt buckles. In the end they wanted one thing, Mitch McKenzie's name and whereabouts. They wanted my drug connect, and I will never give it to them.

"I've found out a lot about you," Arkadi says standing in front of me. My dried blood is all over his hair, and clothes. "You are very resourceful and resilient."

"She's also very beautiful," Iakov adds. My blood stains the plastic cup in his hand, but he doesn't care. These are natural born killers. "Well, for black bitch anyway."

I don't respond. I learned a long time ago that the best way to get at someone is to give them extreme silence. Although every portion of my flesh is inflamed and bruised, I still keep my soundlessness.

"We went to both of your homes the other day," Arkadi continues, "new and old one. We also visited your mother's house and your father's residence where he stays when he's in town. We did all that only to discover that everyone you loved has vanished."

Hearing this causes me to grin. I told Sarge to protect my family and that's exactly what he did. That's why I love that man.

"I'm glad you think this is funny," Arkadi says. "But, it won't stop us from making time with you memorable. So, are you going to give us connect's name and address, or do I have to put you in more excruciating pain?"

Iakov laughs and pours himself another cup of vodka. He walks up to me. "Come on, Bambi, tell us what we want to know. Let us return you to family, and love ones. Don't be martyr all for some chorn who supplies cocaine. It's not worth it."

*You don't even know what you're talking about.* I think. *The man in charge of my product has skin as white as snow.*

"Why be hero?" Arkadi asks. "He wouldn't do it for you."

I maintain my silence, raise my head and look to my left. Just knowing what they want and keeping it from them is enough to make me go harder than ever. I'm thinking about Kevin, and how he use to love me. I think about my twins, Melo and Noah, and how handsome they looked when they came home. I think about my sisters. I think about my life, and all of the things I wanted to share with them. I'll never get to see the women my twins choose to marry. I'll never get to hold my grandchildren, and I'll never get to tell them how sorry I am for lying to them about their father's death. I'm not ready to die, but for the game, I will if I have too.

My thoughts continue to float until I see a flash to my left. Arkadi is holding a knife and the shine from it blings. He walks up to me and rubs the blade along the right side of my face. He slices me horizontally once. He slices me twice. He slices me three times. He slices me four times. The pain causes my eyes to water. I want to cry out, but inhaling the metal scent of my own blood makes me angrier. Fuck the Russians! I've seen worse. I've experienced worse.

"What is name of your connect?" Arkadi asks me again.

I maintain my silence and can feel my tears rolling down my face. Although I'm thinking about a lot of things, snitching is not one of them. I keep my gaze toward the west, and avoid eye contact with him at all times. My flesh is open on my face and I can only imagine how I look. Monstrous.

"I have to give you credit," Arkadi says pointing the blood soaked blade at me. "You're stronger than I imagined. Then again, any woman who mastermind her husband's death would be."

I look at him for the first time.

"Oh yes, we are aware," Iakov says sipping his vodka again. "Although we just learned of it the other day, we are aware all the same."

My bottom lip trembles. I want to tell him that he's a fucking liar, and maybe spit in his face, but I don't.

"You are very good at what you do. There's no need to hide anything from us. We know everything," Arkadi continues.

When he makes his last statement, what happened a few months ago comes flooding back to my mind.

# TWO MONTHS EARLIER

*The sky was dark as Bambi pushed her Rolls Royce down the street. Mary J. Blige's voice relaxed her mind as she thought about her perfect life. Kevin had proven time after time that there wasn't a thing Bambi could do to get him to leave her. Her loud outbursts, waking up in cold sweats and crying uncontrollably, did not cause Kevin to stray.*

*Bambi was on her way home to celebrate her seventeenth wedding anniversary with Kevin. In the seat of her car was a beautiful black and gold wrapped box, with a red ribbon on the top. Inside of it was an 18kt gold Rolex Daytona watch with diamonds in the face and bezel.*

*She was just about to get off the highway when she spotted Kevin's Bentley going past her at a rapid speed. He was on the phone and appeared to be arguing with someone on the other line. Bambi wondered where he was going and decided to follow him. When he took an exit, she took the same one. Something about how he looked felt off.*

When he pulled into Sunny Meadows Apartments, and parked, Bambi did too. Bambi observed her surroundings and tried to determine where they were. She didn't know anybody in the neighborhood and she wondered whom Kevin knew there.

When Kevin parked, and knocked on a door, she watched him go into an apartment. Since it was a floor level apartment, Bambi parked, and eased out of her car. Her Louboutin boots clicked toward the window of the apartment. She looked behind her to see if anyone was watching. When they weren't she peeked through the window. From the slits of the blinds she could see a woman and a little boy on a couch inside.

Kevin reached in his pocket, and handed the woman some money. The girl counted the money and yelled at him. From outside Bambi could hear him say, "Don't talk like that around my son! Watch your fucking mouth!"

Bambi looked at the little boy, and felt light. Although Bambi didn't know it at this point, the little boy and the woman would be the same people who approached her at the doctor's when she got her medicine, after being shot.

Bambi stumbled back, and ran toward her car. On her way she bumped into a short dude and another guy. They were the woman in the apartment brother's. The shorter one smirked at her and said, "If that's your car over there, you must be Mrs. Kevin Kennedy."

Bambi ignored him and rushed to her car. She was so distraught she wouldn't recognize his face when later he would shoot her in the hand in a hospital.

Bambi jumped in her car, and drove away from the scene. She was crying, driving angrily and frantic. Her husband...the love of her life had a baby outside of her marriage. She couldn't believe it. When her phone rang and she saw Cloud's number, she answered.

"Why didn't you tell me, Cloud?" Bambi cried to him while driving down the street. "Why didn't you let me know that my husband was unfaithful?"

"Bambi, I can't get in the middle of that," Cloud said. "That's your husband and he never loved that bitch. It was a *one-night stand. He fucked her the one time ya'll had a fight. He regrets the shit to this day...trust me."*

*"But you knew this and didn't say anything," she sobbed. "I won't ever talk to you again," Bambi pledged. "When you see me, you're dead to me."*

*"Don't say that shit," Cloud said. "Don't turn your back on me when I know you know how I feel about you."*

*"Don't...ever...say...anything...to...me...again," she repeated.*

*"What do I have to do?" He asked. "What I gotta do to keep you in my life, Bambi? Say the word and I will do anything." Cloud never fucked Bambi, but he loved her like he had.*

*"I want you to hurt him," she said. "I want you to make Kevin pay for what he did to me."*

*Silence.*

*"Bambi, I can't do that," he said. "He's my cousin."*

*"Well you can't do nothing for me then." She hung up on him, and called the one man she could always count on. Sarge. "Sarge, I need you to do something for me."*

*"Anything," he said.*

*"Kevin hit me," she lied. "And I want the nigga dead."*

*She could hear his teeth chattering from the phone. He was ensued with anger. "Tell me where to catch this nigga when he is away from you, and off guard. On my mother it will be done."*

*Bambi told him all about the trip to LA. She told him about his favorite gambling spots, and she told him to aim for the head. Sarge promised to handle the business and he was there waiting to attack. But, plans got changed when some crazed employee with a grudge on his shoulders came in and shot up the casino. Because of it, Sarge was unable to go through with the plan.*

*The Russians found out about everything...but Bambi couldn't be sure how.*

I look at The Russians. "Although we couldn't bug your car, we bugged your friend's. Your friend Cloud has quite a mouthpiece on him," Arkadi says. "He told someone on phone that Kevin was going to LA, and how you asked him to hurt your husband after finding out he cheated on you. We have tapes of that conversation. Since Kevin is not alive, we figure you were successful in your attempt."

I'm laughing inside. *They don't know shit.* A disgruntled employee killed Kevin, not me. Yes I wanted the mothafucka dead. Yes I wanted him dealt with, but it doesn't mean I didn't love him. He fucked up everything we built when he stepped out on me, and had a baby with that slut. In the end he got exactly what he deserved. Murdered.

"Bambi, who is your connect?" he asks me again wiping the blade down my breasts and my belly.

I maintain my silence and it's killing them.

"In my country at one time there was a secret sect called Skoptsy," Arkadi says to me. "And in sect, castration was done on men, and mastectomies on women to keep in line with teach-ings on forbidden lust." He runs the blade over my nipples and for the first time I shiver. "It was considered wrong to lust after anything and anyone if you were a member of sect." He turns my chin, and looks into my eyes. "And you lust after many things, your husband's cousin, money and even power. Don't you, Bambi?"

I'm as strong as ever until he pushes my thighs apart and eases the blade across my clit. It betrays me and hardens under the touch of the blade. I know now what they are about to do. Instead of cutting off my breasts, they are going to remove my clit, making me half a woman.

I am a woman. A strong woman. I could live without breasts knowing that I could replace them in an instant. I can even live without my natural long hair. But, I could never walk the earth, without being able to satisfy the feeling of being aroused by a man.

When Iakov splashes the vodka into the gashes of my sliced face and it burns, I know it's time to speak. I swallow and say, "I can provide you with the purest cocaine in the world," I look back and forth at them. "The type of product that's as pure as a baby's pussy." I pause. "In turn you can offer this product to your clients or step on it five times and it will still be the best. I'm able to do that for you," I assure them. "But if you do what your eyes tell me you want to," I swallow, "and, castrate me...even if you released me I would kill myself." I look into their eyes harder. "But no matter what you do to me, I will never...ever...give you the connect. That product belongs to my family and me. Respect that and I can make you both rich men. Buck the system and you can kill me now. It doesn't make me any difference anymore. I'm ready to die."

# EPILOGUE

*S*ix months passed and the summer was relentless. Money, drugs, and mayhem flooded the DC streets and the Pretty Kings controlled it all. Just as Bambi's dream predicted they were the reining kings of the drug industry. Under ruthless Bambi's watch, and with The Russians in her pocket, they doubled the amount of money they were making. Men and women threw themselves at the women just to be a part of their world.

Bambi was in her old house folding clothes on her bed. When she walked to the mirror, her scarred face reminded her of the monster she'd become. Although the Pretty Kings had a new home, and stayed in it every so often, they decided to maintain Bunny's mansion too. Besides, her twins liked it there, and agreed to go to college if they were allowed to stay.

Race had become a totally different person. Her sex appeal was on blast at all times, and she finally knew who she was. She kept a gun in one hand and Carey's ass in the other. By all accounts, she was muscle to the Pretty Kings Empire. But it was Sarge and his platoon mates who molded her, and shifted her way of thinking. Men and women were scared of her. Sarge decided to work for Bambi to protect her properly, and it was nothing he wouldn't do for the woman he secretly loved.

Just recently Bambi dispatched Race to put in work. Two of their employees stepped out of line and Race put them and their families out of their misery. She was ruthless. On the outside Race was good, but inside she was still unhappy. She was in love *with Carey and couldn't share it with her sisters. Sure Carey was taken care of better than she ever was when Ramirez was alive. And, yes Race spent three nights out of the week in Carey's bed. But, not being able to realize their relationship fully made Race feel like a liar.*

*Although originally mad at her family, Denim bought a new house for her mother. She didn't want to, but she also allowed Grainger to move in it. But, Denim made it clear that if Grainger didn't do her job, by taking care of Sarah, she would throw her jealous ass out on the streets.*

*Unlike one of her sisters, Denim couldn't date just yet. Her heart still belonged to Bradley, and she was good with forever being in love with him, and him alone. Besides she was all about Jasmine, the drug empire and her money. Anything else was for everybody else.*

*Scarlett's eight-month old pregnant belly didn't stop her from meeting another man. Although she couldn't be sure if he was with her for her money or her heart, she welcomed the company. Ngozi was African and his chocolate skin was darker than Camp's. He was also more violent. But he accepted her for who she was, and even admired the bullet wound that ran along the side of her neck. Which, she got when enemies fired into the house.*

*At first Scarlett welcomed being slapped and kicked around, but when he tried to beat the baby out of her belly, she knew she had a problem on her hands. It got so bad that she even threatened to tell the Pretty Kings about the abuse. Until he said he would leave the house, wait to catch her alone and slice the white baby out of her body and sell it in the black market. She contemplated telling Denim, since they got closer after the meeting with the Russians, but she was truly afraid of her new boyfriend.*

*Ngozi moved himself into the house, used her money like it was his, and fucked her every which way but lose. Ngozi's sex was the stuff of legends, and that was what roped her originally. But, a storm was coming her way, and she could feel it.*

*The sun was shining brightly when Bambi moved toward the window to look out of it. She was thinking about her life, and what was to come. When she saw a white box van pull up into the driveway, her eyes widened, and she went into attack mode. Bambi reached for her .45. But, just like the soldier that Race was now, she was already outside with an AK-47 aimed at the vehicle, and ready to protect the family.*

*Not feeling like waiting on the elevator, Bambi rushed downstairs and outside of the house. Now both Scarlett with her pregnant belly, and Denim were also outside pointing their weapons at the vehicle. But, when the door of the van slid open, and out popped Ramirez, Camp and Bradley, followed by Kevin, the girls were in a state of shock.*

*They all dropped their guns and rushed to the men to embrace them. They were alive. They were actually alive. Bambi on the other hand, wasn't so excited. What could their return mean for everything she rebuilt? Suddenly she felt lightheaded, and couldn't stand on her feet. And, when Kevin looked into Bambi's eyes with pure anger, she passed out cold.*

# PRETTY KINGS 2

## SCARLETT'S
## FEVER

THE CARTEL PUBLICATIONS

"We Reign Supreme"

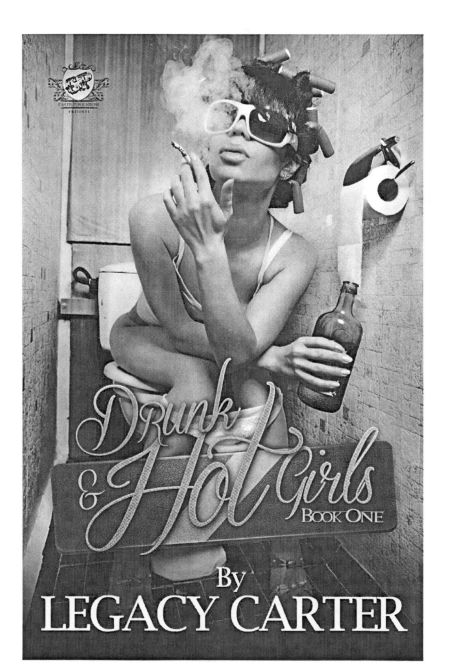

**Drunk & Hot Girls**

Book One

By

**LEGACY CARTER**

CARTEL PUBLICATIONS
PRESENTS

**The Cartel Collection**
**Established in January 2008**
**We're growing stronger by the month!!!**
www.thecartelpublications.com

Cartel Publications Order Form
Inmates ONLY get novels for $10.00 per book!

| _Titles_ | | _Fee_ |
|---|---|---|
| Shyt List | _____ | $15.00 |
| Shyt List 2 | _____ | $15.00 |
| Pitbulls In A Skirt | _____ | $15.00 |
| Pitbulls In A Skirt 2 | _____ | $15.00 |
| Pitbulls In A Skirt 3 | _____ | $15.00 |
| Victoria's Secret | _____ | $15.00 |
| Poison | _____ | $15.00 |
| Poison 2 | _____ | $15.00 |
| Hell Razor Honeys | _____ | $15.00 |
| Hell Razor Honeys 2 | _____ | $15.00 |
| A Hustler's Son 2 | _____ | $15.00 |
| Black And Ugly As Ever | _____ | $15.00 |
| Year of The Crack Mom | _____ | $15.00 |
| The Face That Launched a Thousand Bullets | | |
| | _____ | $15.00 |
| The Unusual Suspects | _____ | $15.00 |
| Miss Wayne & The Queens of DC | | |
| | _____ | $15.00 |
| Year of The Crack Mom | _____ | $15.00 |
| Familia Divided | _____ | $15.00 |
| Shyt List III | _____ | $15.00 |
| Shyt List IV | _____ | $15.00 |
| Raunchy | _____ | $15.00 |
| Raunchy 2 | _____ | $15.00 |
| Raunchy 3 | _____ | $15.00 |
| Reversed | _____ | $15.00 |
| Quita's Dayscare Center | _____ | $15.00 |
| Quita's Dayscare Center 2 | _____ | $15.00 |
| Shyt List V | _____ | $15.00 |
| Deadheads | _____ | $15.00 |
| Pretty Kings | _____ | $15.00 |

*Please add* $4.00 *per book for shipping and handling.*
The Cartel Publications * P.O. Box 486 * Owings Mills * MD * 21117

Name: _____

Address:_____

City/State:_____

Contact # & Email:_____

*Please allow 5-7 business days for delivery. The Cartel is not*
*responsible for prison orders rejected.*

CPSIA information can be obtained
at www.ICGtesting.com
Printed in the USA
LVOW08s1823021216

515532LV00001B/111/P